Indian Territory

MATT BRAUN

St. Martin's Paperbacks

This is a work of fiction. All of the characters, organizations, and events portrayed in this novel are either products of the author's imagination or are used fictitiously.

INDIAN TERRITORY

Copyright © 1985 by Matt Braun.

For information address St. Martin's Press, 175 Fifth Avenue, New York, NY 10010.

ISBN: 978-0-312-97093-2

Our books may be purchased in bulk for promotional, educational, or business use. Please contact your local bookseller or the Macmillan Corporate and Premium Sales Department at 1-800-221-7945, ext. 5442, or by e-mail at MacmillanSpecialMarkets@macmillan.com.

Printed in the United States of America

Pinnacle edition / August 1985
St. Martin's Paperbacks edition / September 1999

St. Martin's Paperbacks are published by St. Martin's Press, 175 Fifth Avenue, New York, NY 10010.

10   9   8   7   6   5   4   3   2

COURTROOM SHOOTOUT

"Marshall Irvin," he intoned, "I order you to remove yourself and those men from my court. If you refuse—"

A strangled scream echoed off the walls. Bud Wilson leaped past Irvin, his Remington six-gun extended at arm's length. The pistol roared and Proctor staggered backward into the defense table. In the next instant gunfire erupted throughout the courtroom.

Ryan acted on reflex alone. He saw the Light Horse sergeant's carbine aimed directly at him. Ryan's arm moved in a blurred motion. The Colt appeared in his hand and spat a sheet of flame. The slug impacted beneath the sergeant's breastbone and jerked him sideways. . . .

A hail of lead whistled across the room as the Light Horse Police exchanged shots with Wilson and the Cherokees. The ranks of both sides were winnowed as though chopped down by a giant scythe. Three of the Cherokees were hurled backward. Another dropped, and finally Wilson staggered . . .

Through a haze of gunsmoke, Ryan sensed all around him the carnage of a bloodbath. He was vaguely aware that he'd been wounded himself . . .

NOVELS BY MATT BRAUN

WYATT EARP
BLACK FOX
OUTLAW KINGDOM
LORDS OF THE LAND
CIMARRON JORDAN
BLOODY HAND
NOBLE OUTLAW
TEXAS EMPIRE
THE SAVAGE LAND
RIO HONDO
THE GAMBLERS
DOC HOLLIDAY
YOU KNOW MY NAME
THE BRANNOCKS
THE LAST STAND
RIO GRANDE
GENTLEMAN ROGUE
THE KINCAIDS
EL PASO
INDIAN TERRITORY
BLOODSPORT
SHADOW KILLERS
BUCK COLTER
KINCH RILEY
DEATHWALK
HICKOK & CODY
THE WILD ONES
HANGMAN'S CREEK
JURY OF SIX
THE SPOILERS
THE OVERLORDS

To Leslie, Nicole, and Darren

CHAPTER ONE

The town took shape like a wintry mirage. On a wooded creek bank Ryan reined his gelding to a halt. He sat studying the distant buildings.

A light February snowfall covered the plains. Located in the southeastern quadrant of Kansas, the town stood framed against an overcast sky. It was called Parsons, the latest in a line of railheads advancing across the prairie. As yet, it appeared on no map.

Somewhat bemused, Ryan slowly inspected the layout. Only last spring he'd ridden through here on his way to Abilene. From Fort Smith, where he served as a deputy U.S. Marshal, it was a five-day trip by horseback. At the time there had been nothing along Labette Creek except a vast expanse of prairie grassland. But now, bundled in a mackinaw against the cold, he saw a bustling little metropolis. He was impressed and all the more curious about the man who had summoned him.

Parsons was the offspring of the railroad. Chartered several years ago, the Missouri, Kansas and Texas had begun operations in Junction City. The company name, too cumbersome for everyday use, had been shortened by natives to the

"Katy." Last year, the summer of 1870, the line had laid track to the border of Indian Territory. Then, some miles above the border, the Katy turned eastward and began laying track toward Sedalia, Missouri. The juncture, situated on a fertile prairie, was only a stone's throw from Labette Creek. Here, seemingly overnight, Parsons sprang from the earth.

Windswept and sprawling, the town was a beehive of activity. Along the main thoroughfare was a collection of stores and businesses, clapboard buildings wedged side by side. Immense piles of trade goods, offloaded at the Katy depot, were stacked in snow-crowned mounds. Beyond the main street board shanties and canvas tents were rapidly being replaced by newly built houses. The population was approaching two thousand, and the inhabitants seemed charged with the galvanic energy peculiar to boom towns. Parsons had assumed a look of permanence.

Gathering the reins, Ryan kneed his gelding forward into the creek. A short distance beyond the opposite bank, he skirted the train depot and the rail yards. The main street was jammed with wagons and a noonday throng crowded the boardwalks. As he rode past, he noted that everyone, even the farmers, seemed in a hurry. Farther uptown he spotted the Belmont House Hotel directly across the street from a bank. At the hitch rack he stepped down from the saddle, then loosened the cinch. He left the gelding tied out front.

Inside the hotel he took a moment to shrug off his mackinaw. The lobby was furnished with a horsehair-and-leather sofa and several easy chairs. The room clerk behind the desk was painfully frail, with a pursed smile and round moist eyes. He nodded as Ryan crossed the lobby.

"Good afternoon, sir."

"Afternoon," Ryan replied. "I'm looking for Colonel Robert Stevens."

"Oh, yes sir! Colonel Stevens is in room 201. Just take the stairs and turn left."

The clerk's snap-to-attention reaction amused Ryan. But it was hardly more than he'd expected. Colonel Robert Stevens was, after all, managing director of the Katy railroad.

Upstairs he turned left and proceeded along the hallway. He idly wondered if Stevens' rank was from wartime service or simply an honorary title. On second thought, he decided it wasn't worth asking. He rapped on the door.

The man who opened it was attired in a broadcloth coat, with matching vest and trousers. He was of medium height, with brown hair receding into a widow's peak and nut-brown eyes. Something about him gave an impression of raw vitality, an air of enormous confidence. He smiled cordially.

"May I help you?"

"Colonel Stevens?"

"Yes."

"I'm John Ryan."

"Well, do come in, Mr. Ryan. I'm delighted to see you."

Stevens thrust out his hand. Ryan pumped his arm a couple of times and moved through the door. The room was a combination bedchamber and parlor overlooking the town's main street. A brass bed along with a dresser and washstand were positioned off to one side. Nearer the windows were a small desk and two overstuffed armchairs.

"Allow me to take your coat."

Stevens hooked his hat and mackinaw on a hall tree. Then, leading the way, he motioned Ryan to one of the chairs. After seating himself, his eyes flicked over Ryan in rapid assessment. He noted the leather vest and and boots, and his gaze touched briefly on the Colt .44 strapped to Ryan's hip. He settled back, crossed his legs.

"You come highly recommended, Mr. Ryan. Oliver's letter was nothing short of a testimonial."

The reference was to Oliver Logan, U.S. Marshal for Western Arkansas and Indian Territory. Ryan shrugged off the compliment. "Oliver tells me you're old friends."

"Indeed we are," Stevens acknowledged. "We met some years ago in Washington. That was before his appointment west, of course."

"And before you got involved with the railroad."

"Exactly." Stevens was silent a moment. "I understand you've resigned as a deputy marshal. May I ask why?"

"Oliver must have explained it in his letter."

"I would prefer to hear it from you."

"Why not?" Ryan said equably. "Last month the President appointed Joseph Story as judge of the Western District Court. Story is a crook and an incompetent, and I won't work for either. It's just that simple."

"What do you mean by 'crook'?"

"Well, for one thing, he's appointed his cronies as chief prosecutor and court clerk. For another, the word's out that payoffs will buy leniency in criminal cases. I don't hold with corruption, so I quit."

"Why doesn't Oliver resign?"

"I guess he's too old to start over."

"And you're not?"

"Judge for yourself."

Stevens had already rendered judgment. He knew that Ryan had served with distinction in the Union Army. Following the war, he'd drifted westward, working at a variety of jobs. Then, at the age of twenty-eight, he had been hired by Oliver Logan. That was four years past, and by all accounts he had found his true vocation as a lawman. He had been assigned to Indian Territory the entire time and lived to tell the tale. He'd also killed nine outlaws in wilderness shootouts.

And now, scrutinizing him closely, Stevens understood why he came recommended so highly. He was whipcord lean, lithe yet broad through the shoulders, perhaps a shade less than six feet tall. His manner was deliberate and steady, somehow assured beyond his years. But it was his eyes, curiously pale and very direct, that set him apart. The effect of his gaze was striking, as though he looked at nothing and saw everything. His weathered features and sandy hair in no way dispelled the impression.

"Tell me," Stevens said at length, "how much do you know about the railroad business?"

"Not a whole lot."

"You're aware we intend to build through Indian Territory?"

"So I've heard."

Ryan actually knew a great deal about the Katy. Through Oliver Logan, he'd learned that Stevens was an influential man with influential friends. The Department of the Interior had ruled that the first railroad to lay track to the Kansas state line would secure the exclusive right to enter Indian Territory from the north. Last summer, in a dead heat with other companies, Katy construction crews won the race to the border. As an added prize the Katy was awarded 1,300,000 acres in federal land grants along its Kansas right-of-way. Only two days later Congress passed a bill opening government lands in southern Kansas to settlement.

The Katy reaped a sudden windfall. Homesteaders and immigrants were pouring into Kansas, more than sixty thousand settling there in 1870. The virgin soil, along with a favorable climate and abundant streams, made it appear the promised land. In the months that followed, the Katy easily disposed of its federal grant. The price was ten dollars an acre, generating cash revenues in the millions of dollars. Quite clearly, Colonel Robert Stevens had friends in Washington.

Still, the largest prize of all was on the horizon. By federal grant the Katy would be awarded five alternate sections of land per mile on each side of its railway through Indian Territory. The purpose of the grant was to provide sufficient incentive for a company to spend the millions involved in construction costs. And in the case of Indian Territory, the incentive was very great indeed. The Katy grant, similar to that awarded for the first transcontinental line, would be ten square miles for each mile of road constructed. In total, the prize would represent 3,064,390 acres.

"I'm curious," Ryan said quietly. "How do the Indians feel about it? Won't a railroad through there open the Nations to settlement?"

"The price of progress," Stevens remarked. "Indian Territory is the key to a railway system throughout the entire Southwest. Here, let me show you."

Twisting about, he took a rolled map from the desktop.

Then he leaned forward and unfurled it between them. His finger stabbed at the map.

"The shortest route to Texas is through the nations of the Five Civilized Tribes. A straight line between the Kansas border and Colbert's Ferry on the Red River."

"And after that?" Ryan asked.

"An empire!" Stevens said expansively. "We already have a grant to extend our road from Indian Territory through Texas to the Rio Grande. We'll eventually link Old Mexico and the Far West to the eastern markets. Just think of it!"

"Sounds like you've been burning the midnight oil."

"We have indeed. But what we're after now is to win the race to the Texas border. Then we'll connect with our Missouri division and establish an outlet to St. Louis and the East."

"What do you mean by a 'race'? I thought you had right-of-way through the Nations."

"Only the north-south route," Stevens advised him. "The Atlantic and Pacific has east-west right-of-way, and they're building from Missouri right now. We have to shut them off from the western markets by extending track to the Red River."

Ryan's expression revealed nothing. Yet he understood that Stevens was talking about establishing a monopoly of trade with Texas and the Far West. After a moment he shifted in his chair.

"How does all that involve me, Colonel? Your letter to Oliver wasn't too clear about what you have in mind."

"Have you ever seen a camp at end-of-track? Where we establish our supply depot until the next leg of the road is built?"

"Not that I recall."

"Well, it gets rough, very rough. There's always lots of money at end-of-track. Usually a settlement of some sort springs up as well. So it attracts whiskey peddlers and gamblers and prostitutes. What some people call the sporting crowd."

"I'm familiar with them," Ryan noted.

"You're also familiar with Indian Territory. Which in itself adds considerably to our problems. So I'd like to offer you the job of special agent."

Ryan looked at him without expression. "What exactly does a special agent do?"

"Keep the peace," Stevens answered. "Hold down violence and make the sporting crowd toe the mark. Enforce the law."

"Whose law?" Ryan rocked his hand, fingers splayed. "In the Nations, there's Indian law and there's white man's law."

The problem he alluded to was essentially one of bureaucratic bungling. Of all the legal tangles created by federal government, law enforcement in Indian Territory was perhaps the most bizarre. White men, whatever their crime, were subject to arrest only by federal marshals. On the other hand, federal marshals could not arrest an Indian unless it involved an offense committed against a white. Light Horse Police, who enforced tribal law, were unable to arrest whites regardless of circumstances. The situation oftentimes became confusing and dangerous.

"To be quite frank," Stevens said, "I'm not worried about Indians."

"You should be," Ryan observed. "There are still some savages in the Five Civilized Tribes. They just don't like *tibos*—white men."

"Perhaps so. But my main concern is with the sporting crowd, or perhaps I should say with the safety of my construction crew."

A moment elapsed while the two men stared at one another. Then Ryan spread his hands. "What legal authority would I have?"

"I'll arrange to have you appointed a deputy sheriff here in Kansas. That should suffice until we reach the Texas border."

"Sounds pretty thin."

Stevens smiled. "Any badge is better than no badge at all."

"How much does the job pay?"

"Five hundred a month plus a bonus when we cross the Red River."

Ryan whistled softly. "That's a lot of money."

"You'll earn it."

An instant of weighing and calculation slipped past. Finally, with a tight grin Ryan nodded. "Colonel, I guess you've just hired yourself a special agent."

"Excellent! I'm delighted to have you on board, John."

There was a rumbling knock at the door. Then it opened and the entryway seemed momentarily blocked of light. The man who entered was tall and burly, with massive shoulders and a cannonball head. His hair was wiry and red, and his ruddy features were complemented by bushy ginger eyebrows and a ginger mustache. He lumbered across the room.

Stevens rose, motioning to Ryan. "John, I'd like you to meet Tom Scullin, our construction superintendent. Tom, this is John Ryan, our new special agent."

Scullin stuck out a gnarled, stubby-fingered hand. "Pleased to meet you. By your getup, I take it you're not from the old country?"

"A ways back." Ryan quickly extracted his hand from the big man's crushing grip. "My folks came over in '39."

"Aren't you the lucky devil. Most of my boys are fresh off the boat, and there's a fact."

"Your boys?"

"Our construction crew," Stevens interjected. "Tom has dubbed them the Irish Brigade."

"So now," Scullin went on bluffly, "you're to be our guardian down among the red heathens. Have you had experience at it, then?"

"Some."

"Some!" Stevens echoed. "John's too modest by far. For the past four years, he's served as a deputy U.S. Marshal. And all of it spent in Indian Territory."

"You don't say." Scullin wagged his head appreciatively. "Well, John Ryan, I'd think you'll do very nicely. Very nicely indeed."

Stevens resumed his seat. "Enough of your blarney, Tom. Why aren't you on your way to end-of-track?"

"Would you have me leave without sayin' good-bye? The construction train's loaded and we'll pull out within the hour."

"Which brings us back to the question you keep avoiding. Our plans for Indian Territory are delayed until we have a direct link to Missouri. So I ask again—how soon will you reach Sedalia?"

"By the Jesus!" Scullin said in a booming voice. "A mile a day, and there's my word on it. You'll have your connection in thirty days, no more."

"Good. I'm pleased to hear it. And I'll hold you to your word, Tom."

"You'll have no need! Trust an Irishman to deliver every time."

Scullin winked at Ryan and walked toward the door. When he was gone, Stevens laughed and shook his head. "It's like pulling teeth to get a commitment. But Tom hasn't failed me yet. He always delivers."

Ryan appeared thoughtful. "I heard him mention thirty days. Are you planning on me starting then or now?"

"Consider yourself on the payroll as of today, John."

"You mean to let me loaf for a month?"

"Hardly. We leave for Indian Territory tomorrow morning."

"Any particular part?"

"The Cherokee Nation. You can act as my guide."

"You've never been there?"

"No, never."

Ryan smiled. "You're in for a shock, and then some."

CHAPTER TWO

Ryan and Stevens rode out of town shortly after sunrise. They were trailed by a packhorse loaded with victuals and camp gear. Where they were headed accommodations for travelers were virtually unknown.

Their route southward was along the Texas Road. Originally blazed by traders, the trail began on the Red River and meandered northward through the nations of the Five Civilized Tribes. At the Kansas border, it made a dogleg northeast and terminated at old Fort Scott.

Only a few years ago the Texas Road had been a major trade route. Herds of longhorn cattle were driven to midwestern railheads and quickly shipped on the hoof to eastern markets. Then in 1867 the Kansas Pacific Railroad laid track to Abilene. Located in central Kansas, Abilene cut time and distance to the Texas border. Cattlemen quickly switched to the Chisholm Trail, which bisected Indian Territory some miles west of the Nations. Abilene boomed and longhorn herds along the Texas Road became a thing of the past.

As Ryan and Stevens rode south, they steadily moved backward in time. Where the railroads ended, the borderlands of the frontier began. Squatters were homesteading the Cherokee Strip, which extended along the border and acted as a buffer between Kansas and Indian Territory. But settlements were often a day apart, connected by flinty backcountry trails. Some freight wagons, drawn by mule or oxen, still plied the Texas Road. An occasional stagecoach hauling passengers between Dallas and Kansas City clattered past, but Ryan and Stevens pretty much had the road to themselves. White men seldom ventured on horseback into Indian Territory.

Upon crossing into the Cherokee Nation, Stevens became quietly attentive. He scanned the terrain with a railroader's eye, measuring grade and topography. Kansas was composed largely of windswept plains and offered no particular obstacle to laying track. But the Nations were a land of rolling hills, and farther south, certain parts were distinctly mountainous. The rainfall was also heavier, and dense woodlands covered much of the terrain. Spongy bottomland along the Neosho River was choked with canebrakes and vast thickets of blackjack. Mulling it over, Stevens concluded that Indian Territory presented a formidable challenge. Both the people and the land were decidedly inhospitable.

Yet for all its drawbacks, the Nations were unquestionably a wildlife paradise. While the buffalo herds had migrated westward, there was still an abundance of game. Great flocks of turkey swarmed over the woodlands; at dusk the timber along the creeks was loaded with roosting birds. Deer were plentiful, and grouse and plover, pound for pound the most toothsome eating imaginable, were everywhere. Fat, lazy fish crowded the streams and river shallows, eager to take a hook baited with grasshopper or worm. It was truly a land where no man need go hungry.

Every night Ryan pitched camp along the riverbank. Stevens was strictly a tyro outdoorsman, more hindrance than help. But Ryan was amused rather than critical and gladly undertook most of the chores. After staking out their horses, he would walk off into the woods with his shotgun. He would return shortly with a young turkey or a bag of grouse and kindle a fire. By sundown a spit loaded with wildfowl would be roasting to a golden brown. A quick trip to the river produced catfish or trout, which were soon simmering in a skillet. With the coffeepot bubbling, there was nothing to do but wait and savor the rainbow of aromas.

On their second night out Ryan took a seat before the fire. Stevens, who was lounging nearby, watched silently as he swabbed out his shotgun. The weapon intrigued Stevens, for it wasn't a run-of-the-mill scattergun. An expensive double-barrel Greener, it had mule-ear hammers with a single trigger, and the barrels had been trimmed to half their normal length. Until now Stevens had restrained himself from prying. Tonight his curiosity got the best of him.

"Tell me, John," he asked in a casual tone, "why do you carry a shotgun? I thought everyone out here preferred a rifle or a saddle carbine."

"Most folks do." Ryan paused, peering through the barrels from the open breech. In the firelight the twin bores looked big as mine shafts. "Lawmen generally stick to a scattergun, though. I reckon I just got in the habit."

"What makes a shotgun preferable?"

"Well"—Ryan glanced up at him—"when you shoot a man, you want two things to happen. You want him to go down, and you don't want him to get up. That's what ends fights."

"I see. But don't those short barrels put you at a disadvantage? You're awfully limited on range."

"You'd be surprised. I've never yet tangled with a man at any considerable distance. Seems like it always happens fast and too close for comfort."

Stevens was tempted to ask still more questions. Like most easterners he'd never before encountered an authentic mankiller. Ryan's sidearm, which was a Colt Army .44 converted to metallic cartridges, was no less intriguing than the shotgun. But the railroader sensed that Ryan would indulge his curiosity only so far. He wisely changed the subject.

"How much farther to Boudinot's?"

"Couple of days. Maybe a little less."

"You're not altogether keen on the idea, are you?"

"I'm not being paid for my advice."

"I'd still like to hear your reason. What do you have against Boudinot?"

"Let's just say I don't trust turncoats. Anyone who sells out his own people won't think twice about doing it to a *tibo*."

"I disagree. Boudinot is widely respected in Washington. And I might add he's one of the few Indians who is."

Ryan shrugged. "I think you just made my point."

Ostensibly the purpose of Stevens' trip was diplomacy. He planned to conduct negotiations with William Ross, principal chief of the Cherokee Nation. But he had also arranged a secret meeting with Elias Boudinot. Some months ago in Washington, they had concluded a business deal known only to themselves. He meant to assure himself of Boudinot's support before calling on Ross.

The delicacy of the situation was compounded by tribal politics. William Ross and Elias Boudinot were avowed enemies, leaders of rival factions. A dedicated Unionist before the Civil War, Ross had nonetheless approved the Cherokees' alliance with the Confederacy. Circumstances, and the proximity of Confederate troops, left the Cherokee Nation no alternative. Ross, who considered it a white man's war, sought only to preserve his people.

Elias Boudinot, on the other hand, was something of an opportunist. Casting his lot with the South, he had served in the Confederate Army throughout the war. Afterward he'd been instrumental in forming the Southern Party, which stood in opposition to Ross' Union Party. In 1865, following the cessation of hostilities, federal commissioners were appointed to negotiate treaties with the Five Civilized Tribes. As spokesman for the Southern Party, Boudinot had actively courted the favor of the commissioners. He had also formed alliances with railroad companies lobbying to acquire right-of-way through the Nations.

The upshot of the negotiation was a victory for Boudinot. The treaty proclaimed a general amnesty and restored to the Cherokees their confiscated property. But it also required them to grant future right-of-way to railroad companies, as well as providing for the erection of military posts within the Nation. Still, it had represented something of a Pyrrhic victory. In the aftermath neither Boudinot nor the Southern Party had been able to gain control of the tribal government. These days Boudinot spent a good deal of his time hobnobbing with Washington politicos.

All of which dovetailed neatly with Stevens' own goals. Watching Ryan clean his shotgun, he decided to press the issue. "Why do you consider Boudinot a turncoat?"

"For one thing, he wants to do away with tribal ownership of the land. Parcel it out to individuals in lots of a hundred sixty acres. For another, he believes the Nations should be placed under a territorial governor appointed by Washington. None of that would work to the benefit of the Cherokees."

"I didn't realize you were an advocate of Indian rights."

"I'm not," Ryan informed him. "I just don't like turncoats—red, white, or polka dot."

"Well, I still think you're wrong about Boudinot. He wouldn't dare pull a fast one on me."

"It's your railroad."

Ryan loaded the shotgun with double-ought buckshot. He snapped the breech closed and laid the Greener across his saddle. Then he took the spit off the fire and began dissecting grouse with his knife. He glanced up at Stevens with a wry smile.

"What's your pleasure, Colonel? White meat or dark?"

On the fourth day they sighted Fort Gibson. There, deep in the heart of the Cherokee Nation, the road veered off to the southwest. At the Arkansas River crossing they turned southeasterly onto a rutted wagon trail. Toward sundown they passed through the settlement of Webbers Falls.

Their destination was the farm of Stand Watie. A leader in the Southern Party, Watie was also the uncle of Elias Boudinot. Yet unlike his nephew, he chose to use his Indian name. Boudinot's father, some years before his death, had adopted a white man's name. For the most pragmatic of reasons the son elected to follow his father's example. As Elias

Boudinot he found a warmer reception among Washington power brokers.

Stand Watie, while not so flamboyant as his nephew, was nonetheless a man of considerable prestige. During the Civil War, Watie had risen to the rank of brigadier general in the Confederate Army. It was a military honor accorded no other Indian and stemmed from his command of the Second Regiment Cherokee Mounted Rifles. After Lee's surrender at Appomattox, he had continued to lead his cavalry on guerrilla raids for almost three months. By holding out, he'd earned a singular distinction in the prolonged and bloody conflict. He was the last Confederate general to surrender his sword.

Watie's farm had been purposely selected for tonight's clandestine meeting. The area around Webbers Falls was an enclave of Southern Party members, all former Confederates. The chance was therefore slight that there would be any loose talk about two white men visiting the farm. Stand Watie still commanded the loyalty of his wartime comrades, and a certain military code prevailed even now. No one who valued his life would risk being branded a traitor.

Stevens and Ryan rode into the farmyard shortly after nightfall. The front door opened and a shaft of lamplight spilled across the porch. Stand Watie stepped outside, waiting for them to dismount. He was tall and portly, with a ramrod-stiff bearing that belied his age. His greeting was civil, though somewhat restrained.

Inside they were ushered into the parlor. Boudinot strode forward, clasping Stevens' hand with a show of warmth. He was a full head shorter than his uncle, somewhat stocky in build, and attired in a dark, conservative suit. When they were introduced, Ryan noticed that his hand was damp with sweat. Boudinot invited them to be seated, commenting that the women and children had retired for the night. Their discussion would not be interrupted.

Stevens came straight to the point. "Day after tomorrow I'm scheduled to meet with William Ross. I thought it worthwhile that we review our agreement beforehand."

Boudinot frowned. "I understood we were in accord when we met in Washington."

"We were, and I trust we still are. However, since then a new element has entered the picture."

"What might that be?"

Extracting a cigar from inside his coat, Stevens struck a match. He lit up in a wreath of smoke. "I've decided to propose a bond issue. It's an accepted procedure whenever a railroad builds through an area. The purpose, of course, is to help defray construction costs."

"With one slight difference. White communities want a railroad and they're willing to raise a bond issue to ensure they aren't bypassed. The Cherokees, by and large, have been opposed to the project from its inception. A bond issue would simply stiffen their opposition."

Stevens rather enjoyed jousting with Boudinot. He thought of the other man as an educated redskin and took amusement at his fancy manner of speech. Fixing Boudinot with a look, he puffed importantly on his cigar.

"Elias, the matter isn't open to debate. I prefer to have the Cherokee Nation committed by way of hard cash. And I expect your Southern Party to support it in the tribal council."

Boudinot and his uncle exchanged a quick glance. Stand Watie's features were unreadable, and there was a moment of oppressive silence. Then Boudinot threw up his hands. "Very well. You are assured of our support."

"Good," Stevens said easily. "Now on to other matters. Are you familiar with White Oak Creek?"

"Yes, of course," Boudinot replied. "It flows into Neosho maybe thirty miles below the border."

Stevens nodded. "I have information that the A&P survey line will run through there. I suggest you plan your town site for that general area."

For the next hour or so Stevens and the two men huddled around a map of the Cherokee Nation. Ryan sat quietly off to one side, solely an observer. Their discussion centered on an elaborate scheme to force the Atlantic and Pacific to detour around White Oak Creek. The purpose, insofar as Ryan gathered, was to delay construction of the rival railway. While it was unstated, Ryan discerned still another element in the conspiracy. Boudinot and Watie, in payment for their support, would be allowed to organize a major town site. The Katy would guarantee its success by establishing a terminal on the location.

To Ryan there was a certain irony about their secretive intrigue. Some thirty-five years ago Boudinot's father had been involved in a similar conspiracy. The elder Boudinot, along with others, had signed a secret treaty which ceded the tribe's ancestral southeastern lands to the federal government. Yet ancient Cherokee law exacted the death penalty for unauthorized land cessions by members of the tribe. Following removal of the Cherokees to Indian Territory, there had been a settling of accounts. The elder Boudinot and his co-conspirators were executed in unceremonious fashion. All in all, Ryan thought it was perhaps a case of like father, like son. It seemed there was a trace of conspiracy in the Boudinot blood.

When the meeting ended, there was another round of handshakes. Stevens appeared pleased with himself, nodding and smiling all the while. Stand Watie walked them to the door, his nephew trailing a pace behind. Outside the three men paused for a last word as Ryan moved toward the hitch rack. Halting beside his horse, he stooped down and tightened the cinch. As he straightened up, he saw Stevens wave and turn away from the house. Boudinot and Watie were framed in a streamer of lamplight from the doorway.

The night suddenly erupted in gunfire. Almost in unison the sharp crack of two rifles sounded across the yard. Stand Watie cursed, grabbing his left arm, and tumbled off the porch. Stevens flung himself to the ground, scrambling toward the hitch rack. With surprising agility, Boudinot dove headlong through the doorway. He kicked the door shut as he rolled into the house.

All thought suspended, Ryan reverted to sheer instinct. He pulled his shotgun from the saddle scabbard, stepped around his horse, and thumbed both hammers to full-cock. The buttstock was seated against his shoulder as the rifles cracked again, showering Stand Watie with dirt. Silhouetted against the fiery muzzle flashes, Ryan saw two men materialize from the dark not thirty yards away. He aimed high, triggering both barrels with a double tap of his finger. The scattergun exploded with a thunderous roar.

Buckshot sizzled across the yard in a deadly hailstorm. One of the men reeled sideways in a strange haywire dance. He lost his footing and went down in a tangle of arms and legs. The other man buckled from the impact and dropped his rifle. He slumped forward without a sound. Tossing the shotgun aside, Ryan drew his Colt and slowly walked forward. He circled the men, watching them closely under the faint starlight, alert to any movement. At last, one at a time he rolled them over with the toe of his boot. They were both dead, chopped to pieces by buckshot.

Ryan struck a match and inspected the bodies. In the flare of light he saw that they were both Indian, and doubtless Cherokee. As he turned away, Stand Watie crawled to his feet, clutching a nasty arm wound. The door opened a crack and Boudinot cautiously peered outside. Approaching the house, it occurred to Ryan that all the shots had been fired at the two kinsmen. There seemed little question that someone was aware of the conspiracy and had invoked ancient tribal law. The dead assassins merely underscored the point.

Elias Boudinot and Stand Watie were marked for death.

CHAPTER THREE

—————⚬⚬ʌⱱⱱ⚬⚬—————

Tahlequah was the capital of the Cherokee Nation. Set among gently rolling hills, it lay some eighty miles south of the Kansas border. To many, it was considered the hub of progress in Indian Territory.

It was midmorning as Ryan and Stevens rode just south of Tahlequah. For the last hour they had passed magnificent baronial homes with colonnaded porches anchored by towering Grecian columns. The setting was one of antebellum plantations transplanted from a more gracious era. The lavish estates were outnumbered by log cabins and unpretentious frame houses, but it was obvious that wealthy Cherokees lived on a scale befitting their position. Some were farmers, and others, clearly, were gentleman farmers.

Stevens, much as Ryan had predicted, was somewhat awed. The tales he'd heard about the Five Civilized Tribes were far exceeded by reality. While he knew that the Cherokees maintained plantations before the war and were slave owners as large as any in the South, he was dumbstruck by the extent of their progress along the white man's road. He expected to find advanced savages a step above the nomadic Plains Tribes, who had evolved into tillers of the soil after being pacified by the federal government. Instead he found a people who cultivated the land with something approaching reverence. Theirs was a thriving agrarian society that rivaled even the most prosperous midwestern farm community.

William Ross lived five miles south of Tahlequah. Like many prominent Cherokees, he and his family operated a sprawling plantation prior to the Civil War. His home, which was reminiscent of Old South mansions, was a two-story structure with tall columns and a wide veranda. The house commanded a sweeping view of the countryside, and split-rail fences bordered its mile-and-a-half-long driveway. Outlying the main grounds was an orchard with over a thousand apple trees.

Upon sighting the house, Stevens began revising his strategy for dealing with Ross. He reminded himself that William Ross was the most influential man in Indian Territory. A graduate of Princeton University, he'd been groomed from youth to assume leadership of the Cherokees. Before he had taken over, his uncle, John Ross, had been principal chief of the tribe for more than forty years. Since 1866, he had, if anything, surpassed the stature of his late uncle. Above all others, he'd been elected president of the Intertribal Council, which was working a coalition of the Five Civilized Tribes. And judging by his baronial home, he was something more than a blanket Indian with a fancy education. Stevens thought to himself that diplomacy rather than demands might better suit the moment.

A stable boy took their horses as William Ross greeted them on the veranda. He was a dignified man, with strong, angular features and piercing eyes. His bearing was straight and square-shouldered, a posture of austere self-assurance. He wore a frock coat with dark trousers and a somber black cravat. He welcomed them with something less than warmth.

The inside of the house was, if anything, even more imposing than the grounds. The ceilings were high and the staircase facing the entrance rose like an aerial corridor. Large wall mirrors flanked either side of the hallway, and double French doors opened on to a room appointed with ornately carved furniture and an immense piano. Opposite was an informal parlor, and beyond that, a tall-windowed study. The study was quite masculine, paneled in dark wood with leather wing chairs set before a broad mahogany desk. The bookcases occupying one wall were lined with history tomes and works of literature.

Ross indulged in small talk for only a short while. The meeting had been arranged by letter, at Stevens' request, and there was a certain protocol to be observed. But after his visitors were seated, Ross quickly dispensed with preliminaries. He ignored Ryan, whom he took to be an aide of some sort. His full concentration focused instead on Stevens.

"Your letter was somewhat vague, Mr. Stevens. May I inquire the exact nature of your business?"

"Of course," Stevens said pleasantly. "First, I wanted to personally advise you that the Katy will begin construction quite shortly. We plan to start laying track the first week of March."

"So, our respite ends."

"I beg your pardon?"

"The Cherokee Nation, Mr. Stevens, does not want your railroad. We look on it as an invasion of our tribal lands—nothing less."

"But unavoidable, Chief Ross. And I might mention, sanctioned by the treaty of 1866."

"A regrettable fact, but nonetheless at odds with the interests of my people."

"Progress won't be denied," Stevens intoned. "However, there's no reason your people should suffer in the process. With your assistance, they might profit very handsomely instead."

Ross eyed him keenly. "Are you selling or buying, Mr. Stevens?"

"Oh, I'm buying! And paying hard cash, I might add. The Katy is in a position to pump upwards of a million dollars into your economy. Sound interesting?"

Stevens went on to explain the proposition. Railroad ties were laid at a rate of 2,600 to the mile, and the Katy had some

250 miles to traverse to the Texas border. Simple arithmetic indicated that nearly 700,000 ties would be needed, and Stevens was willing to pay the generous sum of a dollar a tie. He thought the contract would best be administered by the tribal governments.

Ross was a skilled negotiator. He deferred judgment on the ties and shrewdly waited to hear the next proposal. Somewhat nonplussed, Stevens raised the matter of trailing longhorn herds to railhead. By long-standing practice, each of the Five Civilized Tribes had always charged a per-head tax for the privilege of trailing through Indian Territory. The Cherokees, whose land abutted Kansas, charged the most, seventy-five cents per cow. Stevens outlined his plan to resurrect trailing along the Texas Road while the Katy was building south. But to stimulate trade, he wanted the Cherokees to set the example by reducing their tax to twenty-five cents. Everyone, Indians and railroad alike, would benefit.

Once again Ross deferred any decision. Outfoxed, Stevens was forced to move on to the next topic. He reluctantly broached the matter of a bond issue. Though it was unstated, he clearly wanted the Cherokees to set a precedent for their Indian neighbors to the south. He reviewed the benefits to the tribe, which would include more backcountry depots and a major terminus located in Tahlequah. His suggestion was that an equitable bond issue would be something on the order of $500,000.

"I think not," Ross said with a querulous squint. "In Kansas you could bludgeon communities into paying such extortion. The Cherokees are under no duress to meet your demands."

Stevens gave him a dull stare. "How would you like it if the Katy bypassed Tahlequah altogether?"

"Very much," Ross said crisply. "In fact, I urge you to bypass the entire Cherokee Nation. We would be much happier if there were no stopovers at all."

Stevens took a deep breath, let it out slowly. "Would you at least put the question to the tribal council?"

Ross' tone was clipped, incisive. "The bond issue is a dead issue, Mr. Stevens. You need pursue it no farther."

Their eyes locked. Stevens boiled inwardly, but he knew he was beaten. After a long silence, he spread his hands in a bland gesture. "What about the other proposals?"

"Would you and Mr. Ryan care to join me for noontime?"

"Well, yes, thank you. We would enjoy that very much."

"Fine." Ross stood. "I'll just send for Major Tappin. He's our tribal treasurer, as well as commander of the Light Horse Police. I'd like him present when we resume negotiations."

Ross walked quickly from the study. When the door closed, Stevens turned and looked at Ryan. His voice was tinged with exasperation.

"Any idea what he has up his sleeve?"

"Tell me," Ryan said, deadpan. "Have you ever been between a rock and a hard place?"

"I'm not familiar with the expression."

"It's a form of the old squeeze play. I think you're about to get educated—by the redskins."

The negotiations were suspended for lunch. Shortly before the noon hour they were joined by Major David Tappin. He was swarthy, somewhat darker than the usual Cherokee, with marblelike eyes and sleek, glistening hair. His manner was one of ill-disguised mistrust, guarded contempt.

Ryan was on speaking terms with Major Tappin. Previously, as a deputy marshal he'd had occasion to work with the Light Horse Police. He knew that Tappin, whose principal responsibilities were tax collection and law enforcement, wielded considerable power within the Cherokee Nation. Some said he was second only to William Ross, and no man to have for an enemy. Ryan never doubted it for a minute.

Still, lunch was not altogether an ordeal. At the table they were joined by Ross' daughter, Elizabeth. She was an exquisite young woman, with dusky golden skin and dark raven hair. Her eyes were extraordinary, emphasizing her high cheekbones and delicate features. She relieved much of the tension around the table by simply being there. Her presence precluded any discussion of business.

After lunch there was yet another surprise. Ross suggested that his daughter would be happy to show Ryan around Tahlequah. The offer was made in such a way that it would have been impolitic to refuse. Stevens looked chagrined, for it was apparent that Ross and Tappin wanted him to themselves. Ryan, on the other hand, wasn't the least bit offended. He thought the girl a welcome, and very attractive, alternative.

A horse and carriage were waiting outside. Ryan helped Elizabeth into the seat, then took the reins from a stable hand. The sky was a perfect cloudless blue, and a warm sun offset the chilly air. The unseasonably pleasant day somehow eased a potentially awkward situation. After getting acquainted, Elizabeth deftly turned the conversation to her people. She was proud of her heritage and quite well-versed in the origins of the Cherokee Nation. On the way into town, she told him things known to only a few white men.

In old tribal language, she noted, the word for Cherokee was *Tsalagi*. The ancient emblem of bravery was the color red, and bravery was believed by her people to originate from the east where the sun rose. So in essence *Tsalagi* meant "Red Fire Men" or "Brave Men." While most Cherokees had been converted to the Christian faith, tribal lore had not disappeared entirely from everyday life. Even today, the people still thought of themselves as the *Tsalagi*. The Cherokees' ancestral homeland was once in the Southeast. What was known now, Elizabeth observed, as Tennessee, Alabama, and Georgia. In 1830, under pressure from white frontiersmen, Congress passed the Indian Removal Bill. A legalized form of larceny, the legislation granted western lands to the Five Civilized Tribes in exchange for their ancestral birthright. Over the next several years, a total of 18,000 Cherokees were herded westward over what became known as the Trail of Tears. Of that number, more than 4,000 men, women, and children perished before reaching Indian Territory. The Cherokees still honored their memory by resisting all things white.

In Tahlequah Ryan continued to act the rapt listener. Though he was familiar with the inner workings of tribal government, he gladly allowed Elizabeth to go on with her guided tour. Their first stop was the capitol building, which dominated the town square. All governmental offices as well as the council chambers were housed in the two-story brick structure. The building was only slightly less stately than the capitol in Kansas, and there was an air of bustling efficiency about the place. Ryan was once again impressed by the fact that the men who governed here wore swallowtail coats and conducted themselves like seasoned diplomats. It occurred to him that they were far more dignified than their counterparts in Washington.

The Cherokee Nation, Elizabeth explained, was virtually an independent republic. White men were not allowed to own property except through intermarriage, and unlike western Plains Tribes, the Cherokees accepted no annuities or financial assistance from Washington. For practical reasons their form of government was patterned on that of the white man. A tribal chief acted as head of state, and the tribal council, similar in structure to Congress, was comprised of two houses. Issues were closely drawn, and the two political parties, the Union and the Southern, were bitterly hostile toward one another. Seldom was an accord reached until the pressure of events forced a compromise.

On another note Elizabeth commented that Tahlequah was recognized as a symbol of progress throughout Indian Territory. While they drove around the square, she pointed out the supreme court building, a sturdy brick hotel, and several prosperous business establishments. Her voice took on an added note of pride when they passed the offices of the *Cherokee Advocate*. The newspaper was printed in both English and Cherokee, the two languages side by side. She went on to relate that the Cherokees, of all the Indians in America, were the only ones with an alphabet. Their language could therefore be written, books and newspapers printed. No other tribe was able to preserve its culture so completely in the ancient tongue.

By now Ryan was aware of her in the way of a man seated beside a bonfire. There was an air about her, something in her carriage and poise that he found captivating. Then, too, there was an aura of innocence mixed with sensuality. The silk of her teal-blue gown and the hat perched atop her head merely enhanced the image. Her figure was breathtaking, with a stemlike waist, rounded hips, and firm, youthful breasts. Her voice, which was proper, was at the same time warm and somehow intimate. He'd known many women, but none with such verve and sultry beauty. The combination was irresistible.

Upon leaving town he finally got her to talk about herself. Elizabeth told him she had attended the Cherokee female seminary and afterward gone East to a finishing school. She'd returned only last year, shortly before her mother died. Since then, she had acted as hostess for her father's many social functions. She made no mention of suitors or plans for marriage.

Elizabeth was no less intrigued by Ryan. She knew of his reputation as a marshal, and like most Cherokees, she had little sympathy with the white man's law. Yet when he looked at her, she was aware of an elemental force such as she'd never experienced. She felt strangely drawn to him, and she sensed she could trust him. Still, she pushed the impulse aside, kept herself under tight control. Her father had ordered her to question John Ryan. To find out, subtly, why he'd gone to work for the Katy.

"And you?" she inquired innocently. "Fair's fair, after all. Tell me something of yourself."

"What would you like to know?"

"Well, let's start with where you're from."

"Fort Smith, most recently. Until last week I was a deputy U.S. Marshal."

"Last week!" she repeated. "You mean you've just joined the railroad?"

"To be precise, six days ago."

"Imagine that. And what is it you do, your position?"

"Troubleshooter," Ryan said with a slow smile. "I keep the peace for the railroad."

"Are you talking about trouble with Indians?"

"No, ma'am. I'm talking about gamblers and whiskey peddlers, the construction crew. They'll give me all the trouble I can handle."

"Then you weren't retained because Mr. Stevens expects problems with the Cherokees?"

"Not unless I was hired under false pretenses. And if that's the case, Stevens will have to get himself another man."

Surprise washed over her face. "Why do you say that?"

"I've always thought the Cherokees do a pretty good job of policing themselves. So far as I'm concerned, it ought to stay that way."

"I wish more people shared your views."

She threw him a quick, enigmatic glance. Then her eyes suddenly shone and she smiled. Ryan had the impression that he'd just been subjected to some sort of test and passed. He laughed without quite knowing why.

Some while later, he parted with Elizabeth on the veranda of the Ross home. A moment after she went through the door, Stevens stepped outside. His features were set in a scowl of barely contained rage. As the stable hand brought their horses around, Ryan decided it would be wiser not to ask. But then on the way into town, Stevens let it out in a rush of anger.

The price of railroad ties had been doubled over what he'd offered. The Cherokees wanted two dollars each and there was no choice but to go along. As William Ross had pointed out, all the trees belonged to them!

Ryan tactfully smothered a laugh. He thought Stevens understood little about Indians and even less about the Cherokees. The Red River suddenly seemed a million miles away.

They rode in silence toward Tahlequah.

CHAPTER FOUR

The sky was like dull pewter. Heavy clouds hung ominously overhead and the Texas Road stretched northward toward the border. A flock of crows took wing from a stand of timber along the river.

Stevens' mood was abstracted. Tahlequah was two days behind them, and he'd maintained a thoughtful silence since departing the Cherokee capital. Ryan sensed that the railroader was nursing wounded pride, but he welcomed the respite, for he was absorbed in thoughts of his own. His mind, as though playing tricks on him, conjured fleeting images of Elizabeth Ross. Not surprisingly, he liked what he saw.

Late that afternoon they crossed into Kansas where the river made a sharp dogleg to the northwest. Some miles ahead lay the frontier settlement of Chetopa. While sparsely populated, no more than an outpost along the Texas Road, it was the first sign of approaching civilization. Of still greater consequence, the Katy tracks ran through Chetopa on the way to the border. A thin ribbon of steel extended magically onward to the horizon.

Upon sighting the rails, Stevens seemed somehow revitalized. His glum mood evaporated as they crossed the border, and he sat straighter in the saddle. He motioned toward the broad expanse of prairie.

"All this was once Osage land."

"I know," Ryan said, wondering what prompted the remark. "Whiskey smugglers used to run wagons from here into the Nations."

Stevens nodded absently. "The damnable Cherokees would do well to heed the lesson. Otherwise they might go the way of the Osage."

The statement required no elaboration. The Osage had once been one of the most powerful tribes on the western plains. Warlike, they terrorized every tribe within striking distance, including those resettled in Indian Territory. Then during the Civil War, the Confederacy pressed the Osage into service against the Union. As a result of this unfortunate alliance, the Osage were compelled to cede vast amounts of land to the federal government following the war. Only last year, after one-sided negotiations with Washington, the Osage were forcibly removed to a reservation in Indian Territory. Their ancestral lands, encompassing some eight million acres, were then opened to settlement by an act of Congress. The Osage were now reduced to subsisting on government handouts.

"There's a difference," Ryan said at length. "The Osage tried to hang on to the old ways. The Cherokees tend to bend with the wind. They're red, but they know how to think white."

"Do they, indeed?" Stevens grunted. "You certainly wouldn't know it from their attitude. And unless they change quickly, they'll find out how the game is really played."

"What game?"

"The only game that counts—politics!"

"I don't follow you."

Stevens was silent a moment. Then he gestured with his cigar across the prairie. "Last summer all this—the Osage lands—went on the auction block to settlers. You recall that?"

"Yeah."

Stevens gave him a crafty look. "A month before the public

announcement, I bought a fifty-thousand-acre tract north of Chetopa. The price was seventy-one cents an acre."

Ryan stared at him. "Got it sort of cheap, didn't you?"

"I got it cheap and sold it dear. So you see, it pays to have friends with political clout."

"Like the Secretary of the Interior?"

"Please," Stevens said lightly. "I never divulge a source. But suffice it to say I do have some rather well-placed connections."

"And you think those connections will help you with the Cherokees?"

"John, there are no ironclad guarantees in politics. But when the time is right . . ."

Stevens' voice trailed off. He grinned and wedged the cigar into the corner of his mouth. Ryan was left to draw his own conclusion, and it took no great effort. He thought Stevens was telling the truth, probably understating it to some degree. The Cherokees were in for rough sledding.

An hour or so later they spotted Chetopa. The settlement was a crude collection of buildings, seemingly scattered at random beside the railroad tracks. As they rode nearer, Stevens glanced around at Ryan, and the railroader jerked his head toward the ramshackle buildings.

"We're being met in Chetopa."

"How do you know?"

"I arranged it before we left Parsons. George Walker, our chief surveyor, should be waiting there now."

"What's he going to survey?"

"The Cherokee Nation," Stevens said, "I delayed until now in the hope we would have William Ross' cooperation. We don't, but that's neither here nor there. We'll proceed with our plans anyway."

"I gather you didn't mention it to Ross?"

Stevens merely nodded. "I want you to act as guide for Walker and his survey crew. Your knowledge of the country will speed things along."

"Guide," Ryan asked, "or bodyguard?"

"I see no reason to anticipate trouble."

"Maybe, maybe not. But you ought to understand something. I didn't sign on to be the Katy's hired gun against Cherokees."

"As I recall, you dispatched those two at Stand Watie's place without any great qualms."

"They started it," Ryan said flatly. "When somebody opens fire in my direction, I've got this peculiar habit. I shoot back."

"I ask nothing more," Stevens countered. "Just protect Walker and his men, bring them back alive. I daresay you won't find it any problem at all."

"And if I do?"

"Handle it however you see fit. I trust your judgment implicitly in such matters."

Ryan lapsed into silence. He felt he'd been snookered, for it was obvious that Stevens had purposely delayed mentioning the assignment. But it was a reasonable request, and one that fell within the bounds of his job. Short of quitting, he saw no practical way to refuse. He decided to go along.

"When do we leave?"

Stevens smiled. "Tomorrow morning should be soon enough."

Later after supper, Stevens called a meeting. While there was no depot in Chetopa, construction crews had built a supply shack near the tracks. There beneath a lantern, he huddled with Ryan and Walker around a map of Indian Territory. He traced a line southward from the Kansas border.

"George, your survey line should generally follow the Neosho River. From what I've seen, it's fairly decent topography."

"How are the grades?"

"Not as steep as I'd expected."

"Anything special I should look out for?"

"Only the rivers and streams. We may encounter a problem with eroding banks. So select your approaches very carefully."

Walker was short and squat, thick through with muscle. His face was moonlike and he was bald except for tufts of hair curled over his ears. He knuckled back his hat, staring at the map.

"There's the original line we marked. Straight south from the border, then angle off toward Tahlequah and Fort Gibson. Any changes since we talked last?"

"Just one." Stevens indicated a spot north of Tahlequah. "Survey a line from there due southwest to the Three Forks area."

Walker looked astounded. "You plan to bypass Tahlequah and Fort Gibson?"

"Let's call it a contingency plan."

Stevens stood there a moment longer. Then his gaze slowly moved from the map and fixed on Ryan. The corners of his mouth lifted in a sardonic smile.

"The contingency being our reception by the Cherokees."

The survey party resembled a small caravan. Apart from George Walker, there were two assistant surveyors in the crew. Their gear and equipment required three packhorses, with the tripod-mounted surveyor's level lashed tight onto the gentlest animal.

Four men and seven horses quickly attracted attention, and Ryan knew from the outset that secrecy would be impossible. There was simply no way to hide so many white men on a trek through the Cherokee Nation. Nor was it possible to disguise their purpose with the surveyors constantly plotting a north-south line.

Their first day out Ryan spotted a lone Indian observing their activities from a distance. The rider, who was mounted on a black-and-white pinto, trailed them until they pitched camp. There seemed little doubt that word of their presence would reach Tahlequah by morning. Ryan kept his suspicions to himself, for there was nothing to be gained in bothering the other men. But his vigil became more watchful, constantly alert.

Ryan found the surveyors better trail companions than Stevens. They were accustomed to sleeping on bedrolls, with no complaints about hard ground or chilly nights. Even

better, one of Walker's men was a master cook over an outdoor
fire. With the abundance of game, Ryan easily supplied several tasty choices for the evening meal. Everyone pitched in
with the camp chores, and by the end of the first day they'd
fallen into an easygoing routine. They were comfortable with
one another in the way of men who thrived on wilderness
travel.

After supper Ryan took the first watch. To protect against
horse thieves, a guard would be posted throughout the night.
Before dawn each man would take his turn. The two assis-
tants quickly crawled into their bedrolls. Walker, who had
drawn the dawn watch, joined Ryan at the fire. Hands to the
flames, he was silent for a time, as though lost in thought.

"You expect trouble, don't you?" he asked.

Ryan sat cross-legged, the shotgun cradled over his knees.
He studied the question a moment. "What makes you say
that?"

"You're a little on edge. Waiting for something to happen."

"Never hurts to be careful."

"I get the feeling there's more to it than that. Is there something Stevens didn't tell me?"

"Let's just say we're not welcome here. The Colonel and
William Ross didn't exactly see eye to eye on things."

"Small wonder," Walker said with a low chuff of mirth.
"Stevens is used to getting his own way—especially with Indians."

"What's the story on the Atlantic and Pacific?" Ryan
asked. "The Colonel seems to think they could still bollix his
plans."

"No doubt of that. The head of the A&P is a fellow named
Andrew Peirce. He plays rough, very rough."

"How so?"

"Well, for one thing, Peirce and his backers are trying to
get control of the Missouri Pacific line. If they do, then we'll
have lost our connection to St. Louis. They'll just close the
door."

"And that would block the Katy from the eastern markets."

"Exactly," Walker affirmed. "The Missouri Pacific would

join with the A&P to create a direct route from the southwest. To put it mildly, we'd be left out in the cold."

"So Stevens has to beat the A&P through Indian Territory. Otherwise he loses all the marbles."

Walker nodded. "That's why he needs cooperation from the Cherokees. A construction delay of any type could turn into a disaster."

"Well, George, just between you and me, he's no diplomat."

"What do you mean?"

"I mean he doesn't understand Indians. They get stiff-necked and stubborn when a white man treats them like inferiors. And that goes double for the Cherokees."

"Is that why you think we'll have trouble?"

"Hard to say if we will or we won't. I wouldn't give odds either way."

Ten days later they halted on the southern boundary of the Cherokee Nation. They were four miles below Fort Gibson, on the banks of the mighty Arkansas. Across the river lay the Creek Nation.

Ryan led the survey crew north from the river. As Stevens had directed, he retraced their route to Fort Gibson and they proceeded along the Texas Road. Not far north of the military post, three mounted Indians approached them, riding south. The riders were light-skinned, apparently Cherokee half-breeds, and one was mounted on a black-and-white pinto. All three had carbines laid across their saddles.

Ryan watched them closely. His scrutiny centered on the one who rode the pinto. No great believer in coincidence, he was convinced he'd seen the horse before. A gut hunch told him the pinto's rider was the man who had shadowed the survey party their first day out. The man was still on their trail and no longer alone. As they passed in the road, Ryan stared hard at the man on the pinto. The rider glanced at him, then looked quickly away. In that instant Ryan knew his instincts hadn't failed him. He'd seen a peculiar glitter, something cold and deadly, in the Cherokee's eyes.

A mile up the road, Ryan reined his horse aside. He

motioned Walker and the surveyors on, ordering them to ask no questions. Twisting around, Walker saw him dismount and lead his horse into the woods. Some moments later he reappeared with the shotgun cradled across the crook of his arm. He took up a position behind a tree at the side of the road.

Still looking back, Walker's eyes suddenly narrowed. He saw the three Indians ride into view perhaps a half mile to the rear. As the survey party rounded a bend in the road, he lost sight of the riders. His last impression was of Ryan pressed against the base of the tree, waiting. He wondered why the Indians were following them; he wondered what Ryan intended to do.

The crack of a rifle shot sounded in the distance. No more than a beat behind came the dull roar of a shotgun blast, followed instantly by another. A deafening silence followed. Walker reined about, halting his men in the middle of the road. He was torn between staying put and going back when he heard the thud of hoofbeats. A lone rider appeared around the bend in the road.

Ryan took his place at the head of the column. He said nothing, ignoring their stares. His features were set in a grim scowl, eyes pale and stony. No one asked any questions.

CHAPTER FIVE

A week later the survey party rode into Parsons. George Walker and his crew went straight to their hotel rooms. With suppertime approaching, they were looking for a hot bath and a civilized meal. Walker seemed in no hurry to deliver his survey report.

At the hotel Ryan was informed that Robert Stevens had moved into a private railroad car. He stabled his horse and walked down to the Katy supply depot. Dusk fell as he crossed the main tracks and approached the private car, which had been shunted onto a nearby siding.

Ryan was in a foul mood. For the past week he'd done little but dwell on the shooting incident. Since accepting the job of special agent, he had killed four men. Which was almost half the number he had buried during *four years* as a marshal. At that rate, the number might jump to a score or more before the Katy traversed Indian Territory. He had no intention of allowing that to happen.

Unlike some lawmen Ryan was not a killer by nature. He believed certain men were fated to be killed, and he thought that others, by the viciousness of their crimes, deserved the ultimate penalty. Yet he was an advocate of reason and law over the rule of the gun. He preferred to bring lawbreakers, even murderers, to justice before the courts. A legal hanging, in his opinion, was by far the greater deterrent to outlaws. So he killed only as a last resort.

Tonight he intended to voice that very thought. All the way from the Cherokee Nation, he'd been preoccupied by the latest shootout. While he had pulled the trigger, he in no way faulted himself. He had fired only after being fired upon; in that sense, the killings were unavoidable. The fault, in his mind, fell instead on Robert Stevens. The latter's motives were murky, and he couldn't put his finger on the exact cause of the bloodletting. But something about the whole assignment stunk.

Mounting the steps, he climbed to the rear platform of the car. Through the door window, he saw Stevens seated in an armchair, smoking a cigar. A manservant lighted the last of the overhead lamps, then disappeared into the kitchen up forward. Ryan knocked on the door, three hard raps. Stevens turned, looking somewhat irritated, and rose from his chair. A moment later he opened the door.

"Well—John! Where did you come from?"

"Just rode in," Ryan replied.

"Excellent! I've been expecting you for the last day or so. Please, come inside."

Stevens ushered him through the door. Entering along a narrow companionway, Ryan noted that the bedroom door was closed. Moving into the main room, he saw that it was lavishly appointed. To the rear was a parlor area, with paneled walls and ornately carved furniture. Toward the front was a dining area with a candlelit table, fine linen, and an array of bone-white china. Ryan saw that two place settings were arranged on the table.

Still smiling, Stevens motioned him to an armchair. Ryan sat down, dropping his hat on a nearby table. The luxurious surroundings made him all the more aware that he was covered with grime and trail dust. It occurred to him that the Katy's general manager lived in the style befitting a man of wealth and influence. Stevens took a chair opposite him.

"Where's George?"

"Up at the hotel," Ryan observed. "He said he'd write up his report tonight."

"Then I'm doubly glad you dropped by. I'm anxious to hear how things went."

"If you're talking about the survey, it went fine. Walker and his boys got it done just the way you wanted."

"And the new route," Stevens inquired, "bypassing Tahlequah and Fort Gibson? Any problem with that?"

"No," Ryan said tightly. "No problem with that."

Stevens arched one eyebrow in question. "From your tone, I take it something went wrong."

"Wrong as it could go. I had to kill two men."

"Damn!" Stevens muttered. "Who were they?"

"Cherokee breeds."

"Why did you kill them?"

"No choice," Ryan said in a low voice. "They trailed us all the way down to Fort Gibson. Whether or not they meant to do us harm is anybody's guess. I never got a chance to ask."

"What happened?"

"I traced them just north of the fort. Before I could ask their business, one of them took a shot at me. I killed him and another one who tried to make a fight."

"Are you saying there were more than two?"

"Yeah," Ryan acknowledged. "The third one took off and never looked back. I let him go."

"Were George and his men involved?"

"Not directly. I'd sent them on ahead."

"How about the Army? Did you notify anyone at the post?"

"No."

"And the Cherokees? Did you report it to anyone in Tahlequah?"

Ryan shook his head. "I figured the wisest thing was to let well enough alone. No telling who sent them."

"Sent them?" Stevens repeated, frowning heavily.

"Well, they damn sure weren't robbers. Not the way they trailed us for ten days."

"You think they were spies?"

"Or worse."

"Oh, come now! Aren't you exaggerating slightly? Why would anyone want to kill our surveyors?"

"You tell me."

"How would I know?"

"You must've known there was a risk."

"I knew nothing of the kind."

Ryan searched his eyes. "Then why'd you send me off to bodyguard George and his boys?"

Stevens met his stare. "Are you accusing me of something?"

"Not yet. I'm just asking you a simple question."

"You asked me the same question before you left. And I'll tell you now what I told you then. Walker needed a guide."

"You're a liar," Ryan said bluntly.

There was a long pause as the two men examined one another. Then Stevens rose and moved to a window at the side of the car. He stood there for several moments, a cigar clenched between his teeth, staring out at the darkening sky. Finally he turned back, his features set in a somber expression.

"All right," he conceded, "I wasn't altogether frank with you. I suspected something might happen."

"Why?"

"Well, after all, an attempt was made on the lives of Boudinot and Stand Watie."

"That's tribal business, between the Cherokees."

"Yes, but quite obviously someone ordered it."

Ryan gave him a narrow look. "What's that got to do with the survey crew?"

"I can only hazard a guess. It seems rather apparent that the someone—whoever he is—doesn't want a railroad built."

"So the place to stop it was before it got started—the surveyors."

"That seems a reasonable explanation."

"Only one man could issue that kind of order."

"I agree."

"And you think William Ross sent three breeds out to kill us?"

"How could I think otherwise? Particularly when I'd informed him only days before that we plan to start construction next month. The timing of it squares too neatly to be coincidence."

Ryan pulled at his earlobe, thoughtful. "Ross doesn't strike me as an assassin. It's not his style."

"Indeed?" Stevens countered. "Nothing happens in the Cherokee Nation without Ross' tacit permission. You should know that better than I."

"Maybe so. But my instinct tells me different. And I'm generally not wrong."

"I suggest we stick to deductive reasoning. I wouldn't care to wager my life on instinct."

"You wagered my life, not to mention the surveyors'. Even after you'd already *deducted* all this."

Stevens admired the tip of his cigar. "You have a point. I've no real excuse except to say that there was no alternative. Without a survey line, we can't lay track."

"What about the truth? You could've told me what you suspected."

"To be quite honest, I couldn't take a chance on losing you. I was concerned you might quit rather than lead the survey party."

"I don't scare that easy."

"No, I daresay you don't. The way you challenged those half-breeds proves that."

"There's something else I don't do."

"Oh?"

"I refuse to work for a man who won't level with me."

"Suppose we write it off as an error in judgment?"

"You lied to me," Ryan said in a measured tone. "Do it again and we're all through—then and there."

"I understand."

"Fair enough."

Ryan stood and collected his hat. As he turned to leave, the bedroom door opened. A compelling, attractive woman in her late twenties moved into the parlor area. She was blond and tawny, rather statuesque, with inquisitive, bold eyes and a vivacious smile. Stevens stretched out his hand and drew her forward.

"John, I'd like you to meet Sally Palmer. Sally, this is the fellow I was telling you about, John Ryan."

"Oh, yes," Sally said in a throaty voice. "You're Bob's special agent."

Ryan nodded. "Pleasure to meet you, Miss Palmer."

"Please, just call me Sally. Everyone does."

Ryan thought it an understatement. Up close, there was something common, almost bawdy, about the girl. She wore a velvet gown, her rounded shoulders were bare, and rather too much of her cleavage was exposed. He found it amusing that Stevens, who was a married man, had himself a camp follower. Sally Palmer, to all appearances, was not too far removed from the oldest profession.

She looked at his dusty trail clothes. A wise smile brushed the corner of her mouth. "Bob said you've been to Indian Territory. How was life among the savages?"

"About like usual."

"You've been there before, then?"

"Off and on." Ryan took a step back. "You'll have to excuse me. It's been a long trip and an even longer day. Colonel, I'll see you in the morning."

Nodding to Stevens, he turned and walked from the car. Outside, through the window he saw Stevens seat the girl at the dining table. The manservant materialized from the kitchen and began pouring wine. Ryan chuckled softly to himself.

Stevens clearly intended to live the good life while building his railroad.

Ryan took his time next morning. He figured he'd earned a respite, however brief. Nor was he in any great rush to resume talks with Stevens.

Shortly before nine, he walked in the direction of the rail yards. His mind almost reluctantly turned to Stevens. He wasn't entirely satisfied with their conversation of last night. He considered it a toss-up as to whether or not Stevens would level with him in the future. The railroader was clearly unaccustomed to taking others into his confidence.

Even more worrisome was the matter of William Ross. Ryan still wasn't convinced by Stevens' argument. He found it difficult to believe that a man of Ross' stature would stoop to conspiracy and assassination. The fact that Ryan was attracted to Elizabeth Ross did nothing to color his opinion. He simply felt that her father was an honorable man, above resorting to murder. His gut hunch told him that the answer lay somewhere else.

All that left a very large question mark. If not William Ross, then who? Someone had engineered a rather elaborate scheme, involving secrecy and cold-blooded murder. Whoever was responsible clearly had many dedicated men under his command. Four Cherokees had already lost their lives; that number in itself indicated a conspiracy of some scope. Obviously then, the leader had to be someone of importance within the Cherokee Nation. But the *who*, at least for now, remained a mystery.

On one point there was no doubt. In less than a month Ryan had killed four members of the conspiracy. So the leader of the group had, in all likelihood, added Ryan's name to the death list. Wherever he traveled in Indian Territory, he would now be a marked man. He reminded himself not to get careless.

At Stevens' private car, he knocked on the door. Footsteps sounded from within, then the door opened. The manservant greeted him with a polite nod.

"Good morning, Mr. Ryan."

"Morning. I'd like to see Colonel Stevens."

"Sorry, sir, he's out."

"Any idea where he went?"

"I believe you'll find him at the surveyor's office."

"Much obliged."

As Ryan turned to leave, Sally Palmer suddenly appeared

in the companionway leading to the main room. She was attired in a gauzy peignoir worn over a nightgown.

"Well, hello there!" she called. "Come on in."

"No, thanks," Ryan said. "I'm looking for the Colonel."

"I expect him back in a few minutes. Hang around. I'll give you a cup of coffee."

"Don't go to any bother. I'll just—"

"No bother!" She waved to the manservant. "Henry, get Mr. Ryan a cup of java."

"Yes, ma'am."

Henry disappeared into the kitchen. Ryan allowed himself to be led into the main room. Following Sally, he noted that her peignoir was quite sheer and very revealing. The fabric, like curves in melted ivory, clung to her long, lissome legs and voluptuous figure. She took a seat across from him at the dining table.

"So tell me. How's it feel to be back among civilized people?"

"All right," Ryan said without inflection. "Not that I've got anything against the Cherokees. For the most part, they're pretty decent."

"Do tell?" She gave him a glance full of curiosity. "Bob told me you barely escaped with your scalp. He said those surveyors owe you their lives."

Ryan looked uncomfortable. "That's stretching it quite a ways."

"Oh, c'mon! Don't be modest."

Henry emerged from the kitchen. He set a cup and saucer in front of Ryan, then poured from a steaming coffeepot. Finished, his gaze shifted to Sally.

"If that's all, ma'am, I have errands in town."

"Sure, Henry, you run along. I'll hold down the fort."

Henry departed with a perfunctory nod. As the door closed, Ryan took a sip of his coffee. He was aware that Sally was looking him over with more than casual interest. She had enormous hazel eyes that seemed to dance with secret laughter. She smiled warmly.

"Bob tells me you were a deputy marshal."

"Yeah, I was."

"Maybe we have mutual acquaintances."

"Where from?"

"Abilene," she responded. "I got to know Tom Smith before he was killed. Everybody liked him lots."

"Doesn't surprise me. He was a damn fine lawman."

"Have you heard the latest? The town fathers are all set to offer Wild Bill Hickok the marshal's job. Isn't that a riot?"

"It's liable to be a riot and a half. I understand there's no love lost between Hickok and the Texas drovers."

"He won't last long in a cowtown, then. Texans are there in swarms the whole summer."

Ryan studied her over the rim of his cup. "Way you talk you must have left Abilene just recently."

"You might say that." She returned his look without guile. "I met Bob there last summer. We kept in touch and he finally made me a proposition. As you see, I accepted."

"Nice work," Ryan remarked dryly, "if you can get it."

"Well, he's sweet to me and it beats working in a parlor house."

"Yeah, I suppose it would."

She gave him a puckish smile. "You weren't fooled, were you? I saw it in the way you looked at me last night."

Ryan grinned. "I've seen the inside of a few parlor houses in my time."

"See there, I knew it! We're birds of a feather."

Sally suddenly stood. Her look was at once sensuous and humorous, somehow bold. She moved around the table with catlike grace and stopped beside his chair. Her voice was sultry.

"Do you like me, John?"

"Why?"

"Because I like you. And I'm not exactly a one-man girl."

"Stevens would be sorry to hear it."

"What he doesn't know won't hurt him."

She laughed and cupped his face in her hands. The scent of her perfume and the warmth of her body seemed to envelop him. She bent lower and kissed him fully on the mouth. Her lips were moist and inviting, and her tongue performed an artful mating dance. Ryan sat perfectly still, not responding. At last, pulling back slightly, she stared down at him with earthy wisdom.

"Don't worry. Henry won't be back for at least an hour."

"What about Stevens?"

"I lied!" She laughed gaily. "He told me he'd be gone all day."

Ryan moved her hands from his shoulders. He stood, collecting his hat off the table, and moved out of reach. She gave him a puzzled frown.

"What's wrong?"

"No sale," he said evenly. "But don't take it personal. I never mess around with the bossman's lady."

"Foolish man. You don't know what you're missing."

"I've got a pretty fair idea."

"C'mon, be a sport—take a chance!"

"Guess I'm not much of a gamblin' man."

A vixen look touched her eyes. "It's a long way through Indian Territory. And nothing but squaws till we cross the Red River."

Ryan shrugged. "I reckon it's my loss."

"Well, there's always another time. You'll be around and I'm not going anywhere." She paused, lowered one eyelid in a slow wink. "The offer's always open."

"I'll keep it in mind."

"Oh, I know you will . . . especially at night."

Her musical laughter followed him out the door.

CHAPTER SIX

On March 7 the Katy entered Indian Territory. It was a Monday morning, and there was still a nip of frost in the air. The spot chosen to cross the border was known as Russell Creek Valley.

Colonel Robert Stevens and Tom Scullin stood at the end-of-track. Their eyes were directed southward, and for a moment neither of them spoke. Behind them some fifty cars loaded with construction supplies stretched northward. The Irish Brigade, Scullin's construction crew, were gathered a short distance away. At last Stevens looked around, and stuck out his hand.

"Tom, let's build a railroad."

Scullin pumped his arm. With a nutcracker grin, the construction boss turned to the Irish Brigade. He raised a mighty forearm and pointed them toward the Cherokee Nation.

"Awright, me boyos! Lay track!"

The Irish Brigade, some two hundred strong, belted out a lusty cheer. The sun, edging over the horizon in an orange ball of fire, lighted the valley as they surged forward. A mile of roadbed had already been graded in preparation for the first day's track laying. At Scullin's command a mule-drawn wagon pulled up beside the grade and men began offloading rough-hewn ties. Not far behind, the iron men dumped a load of rails.

Stevens watched them in silence for a short while. He was aware that Scullin preferred he not linger at end-of-track. The construction boss was something of a benign tyrant, driving the Irish Brigade with equal doses of curses and encouragement. He boasted that he could whip any man on the payroll, and he stood willing to prove it at the slightest provocation. But he preferred to work his men in his own way, without anyone looking over his shoulder.

Still, there was something special about today. Stevens risked overstaying his welcome for a final word with the massive Irishman. When he could delay no longer, he finally motioned southward.

"How long to reach Big Cabin Creek?"

"God's blood!" Scullin huffed. "You've asked me that no less than a hundred times."

"Then one more time won't matter, will it?"

"I'll tell you what I've been tellin' you. Thirty miles in thirty days, God willing. I cannot do better."

Big Cabin Creek was Stevens' initial objective on the drive south. It lay thirty miles beyond the border, where the military road from Fort Gibson split off from the Texas Road and angled northeast. Stevens was determined to reach the fork of the trail no later than early April. Otherwise there would be no railroad in place when the spring cattle drives trailed north out of Texas. He was counting days and a fortune in freight charges won or lost.

"Thirty days," he mused out loud. "That would put us across Big Cabin Creek on April sixth."

"Aye," Scullin agreed. "Unless there's heavy spring rains, or God forbid, a flood. We've a bridge to construct before we'll be crossing the creek."

"Yes, but our engineers always precede the tracklaying crew by at least a day. Surely we won't be delayed more than a day or so completing the bridge?"

"Maybe. Maybe not. As I said, it depends on the rain."

"All right, let's assume the worst. We'll suppose it rains the second Flood. I could always build stockyards *this* side of the creek."

Scullin looked at him, puzzled. "Why would you do a foolish thing like that?"

"Simple economics," Stevens said quickly. "You've never understood that there's more to building a railroad than just laying track."

"It's the cattle drives you're talkin' about?"

"Indeed it is! No less than a hundred thousand beeves will be trailed out of Texas this summer. And right now Abilene is the closest railhead."

"Which means the Kansas Pacific would profit handsomely."

"Profits," Stevens added, "that would defray a large percentage of our construction costs. But only if we lure the cattle trade away from Abilene."

"So you've no choice but to establish a railhead, and soon."

"No choice whatever."

"But you've still not answered my question. Why build stockyards this side of the creek? Would a few more days make so much difference?"

"A few days might turn into weeks, even a month. Spring floods are unpredictable."

Scullin shook his head. "Aren't you being a bit pessimistic?"

"I prefer to plan for contingencies. I'd call it realism, not pessimism."

"I say it makes no sense. The stockyards belong on the south side of the creek, not the north."

"No, Tom," Stevens corrected him. "The stockyards belong wherever they can be built in early April. Only then can I send agents into Texas with word of a new railhead. And closer than Abilene by two weeks trailing time!"

"Why not wait until we're farther south? A railhead on the Arkansas would cut the time in half."

"I want the cattle trade now—not later."

"Have you heard it said, a man's reach should never exceed his grasp?"

"What's your point?"

Scullin lifted his hands in a shrug. "Perhaps you're overreaching yourself, Colonel. You want everything, and you want it fast. Some would say too fast."

"And what would you say, Tom?"

"Well, to quote some wise man, Rome wasn't built in a day."

Stevens laughed. "I'll settle for thirty days to Big Cabin Creek. A deal?"

"By the Jesus," Scullin muttered. "Will that get you out of my hair and back on your fancy car?"

"Yes, gladly."

"Then it's a deal."

"I knew you wouldn't let me down, Tom."

"Go on with you! I've work to do."

Still chuckling, Scullin turned to leave. He stopped suddenly and Stevens' eyes followed the direction of his gaze. A short distance uptrack Ryan reined his horse past a work crew. His hat was tugged low against the morning sun and his shotgun was balanced across the saddle. He looked armed for bear, and his features did nothing to dispel the impression. As he approached, he nodded to them.

"Morning, Colonel. Tom."

The two men returned his greeting. Without stopping, he rode past them, eyes fixed on the distance. They watched as he continued on to a point beyond the graders. There, halting his horse on a low rise, he sat staring off into Indian Territory. After a moment Scullin whistled between his teeth.

"I've not asked," he said to Stevens, "for it was your own business. But now my curiosity has the best of me."

"About what?"

"About John Ryan. What was your reason for hiring him?"

Stevens gave him a sideways glance. "We needed a special agent, and Ryan was the best man available."

"All the same, I understood his job was to maintain order at end-of-track."

"And so it is."

"Then suppose you tell me"—Scullin paused, nodding to the solitary figure on horseback—"why has he killed four men, and scarcely a month on the payroll?"

"Four Indians," Stevens noted. "There is a difference."

"Indian or white, the question still holds."

"Ryan did what needed doing. It's as simple as that."

Scullin was silent a moment, considering. "There's a rumor around that someone intends to stop us from building a railroad. Any truth to it?"

"Tom, I never deal in conjecture. After all, why borrow trouble?"

"You've not said yes or no."

"Well, anything's possible. At the moment we're considered intruders by the Cherokees, but there's nothing to worry about."

Scullin motioned toward the construction crew. "Those boys are loyal to me because I look out for 'em. I'd like to keep it that way. You're sayin' my boys are in no danger?"

"I'm saying you need not concern yourself. John Ryan will attend to any . . . problems."

Stevens grinned and slapped Scullin across the shoulder. Turning away, he walked off alongside the construction train. Some distance uptrack an unloaded supply train stood waiting with his private car coupled to the rear. He strode toward it with a purposeful air.

Scullin stared after him only a moment. Then his gaze swung back to Ryan and the uncased shotgun. His brow furrowed in a dark scowl.

Off to the southwest, a treeline marked the path of Russell Creek. Like a sentinel, one hand resting on the shotgun, Ryan studied the trees. He had the prickly feeling he was being watched.

After several minutes, he looked away. There was no movement in the trees, nothing that appeared out of the ordinary. Still, something told him there was more to the feeling than imagination. For the moment, though, he decided to play a waiting game. He turned his attention to the track-laying operation.

The lead element was the grading crew. With picks and shovels and mule-drawn scrapers, they transformed rough earth into a level roadbed. Behind them another crew laid the ties and leveled each one with the roadbed surface. Next in line were the iron men, five men to each five-hundred-pound rail. After they dropped the iron in place, the spikers moved up and quickly anchored parallel rails to the crossties. Ten spikes to the rail, three blows to each spike kept the air ringing with the metallic whang of sledgehammers.

Farther back the screwer crew finished spiking rails and screwed down fishplates to secure the rail joints. Following them were the gandy dancers, who levered up ties by wedging a shovel blade beneath the tie and bouncing up and down on the shovel handle. The filler gang moved in then and finished bedding the loosened ties with stone ballast. The last crew in the operation was the track liners. Their job was to check the alignment of the rails and inspect ballast underneath the ties. The final step was a close once-over by the tracklaying boss.

Uptrack from the work gangs was the construction train. Every mile of track laid required forty carloads of supplies, plus food and water for the men and animals. So the construction train, for all intents and purposes, was a self-contained town on wheels. Hauled by one locomotive and pushed by another, the train was a ponderous collection of freight cars and flatbeds, several three-decker rolling bunkhouses and one entire boxcar devoted to the mess kitchen. Scullin's quarters were in one end of a car near the front of the train. The opposite end was his office, complete with desks and a telegrapher-clerk.

Observing the operation, Ryan was struck by the efficiency of it all. On the surface it looked like a madhouse flung into chaos. But upon closer examination it became apparent that there was a synchronized chain of events not unlike a finely balanced clock. The parts, operating with seeming independence, ultimately meshed together and brought about a frenzy of construction. It was clear to him, watching them now, that Scullin and the Irish Brigade had earned their reputation. No one built a better railroad or built it faster.

Ryan's attention was suddenly drawn back to the treeline. He saw four Indians ride out of the heavily wooded grove and halt beside the creek. Their horses began swizzling water, but he wasn't fooled. They'd been there all the while, secreted in the trees. Despite appearances, the Indians weren't simply watering their mounts. They wanted him to know the railroad was being watched.

Tom Scullin, who had also seen the riders, walked forward. He stopped beside Ryan, gazing for a moment at the four Indians. Then, reining their horses about, the men rode south along the creek bank. When they were some distance away, Scullin finally looked around.

"Cherokees?" he inquired.

"Nobody else."

"Have they some mischief in mind?"

"Yeah," Ryan laughed. "I'd say that's a safe bet."

"What is it they might try?"

"Blow up the tracks. Set fire to the supply cars or wreck equipment. Hard to say where it would start—or end."

"You being the special agent, what do you suggest?"

"We ought to post guards, especially a night watch. You pick the men and I'll assign them to shifts. Sundown to sunrise."

"I'll see to it," Scullin agreed. "Of course, my boys aren't gunmen. They're more experienced with their fists or pick handles."

Ryan smiled. "Want me to give them a few pointers?"

"I'd think you're the one to do it."

There was an awkward pause. Scullin held his gaze a moment, then looked down at the ground. "Do you mind if I ask you a personal question?"

"Go ahead."

"Understand, I'm not judgin' you. It's just—"

"Curiosity."

"Of sorts, yes." Scullin glanced up, cleared his throat. "The Colonel tells me you did what needed doing. I'm talking about the four men you killed."

"So what's your question?"

"Was the Colonel tellin' me the truth?"

"You think he'd lie?"

"I'm askin' you."

"No." Ryan looked at him without expression. "You're asking me if Stevens hired himself a professional killer, aren't you?"

"Since you put it that way, I suppose I am."

"I'm going to make an exception in your case."

"Exception?"

"Normally, any man who asked me that would pay a stiff price."

Scullin tensed, somehow standing taller. A muscle pulsed in his jaw and his great hands knotted into fists. Then, looking closer, he saw no animosity in Ryan's face. What he saw instead was sardonic amusement, a hint of laughter. His hands slowly unknotted.

"What makes me the exception?"

Ryan shifted in the saddle. He seemed to weigh his words before he spoke. "It's a long haul to the Red River. I've got a feeling we'll both need a friend before we get there."

"Because the Colonel never lets the right hand know what the left hand's doing—is that it?"

"Close enough," Ryan said. "Where I'm concerned, I think he knew he'd get a fight of some kind from the Cherokees."

"So he purposely went out to hire himself a gunhand."

"That's about the size of it."

Scullin looked at him questioningly. "Why do you stay on, then?"

"In a way Stevens was right." Ryan motioned off into the distance. "Somebody out there means to stop the Katy—no matter who gets killed."

"And I take it you mean to stop this somebody?"

"Last time out," Ryan said stonily, "his men tried to kill me. That tends to make it personal."

"Well spoken," Scullin rumbled. "So tell me now, would you care to join me for supper tonight? I might even offer you a drink."

"I'd like that, Tom. Thanks."

"One thing, though."

"Yeah?"

"Would you not bring your shotgun? I promise you'll find no red heathens at my table."

Scullin walked off with a booming laugh. Ryan stared after him a moment, chuckling softly. Then his eyes shifted to the treeline, and all humor melted from his face. The prickly sensation returned and with it his unease.

He still felt watched.

CHAPTER SEVEN

Sam Irvin showed up unexpectedly. The Katy was some six miles into the Cherokee Nation, having spanned Russell Creek with a timbered bridge. The track-laying crew had so far delivered on Scullin's promise of a mile a day.

A deputy marshal, Irvin worked out of Fort Smith. He'd worn a badge most of his adult life, serving as a federal lawman for the last five years. He was on the sundown side of thirty, with a bulge around his beltline and flecks of gray in his hair. Yet no one, least of all the men he hunted, was fooled by his fatherly appearance. When crossed, he was a dangerous man.

Ryan and Irvin were old friends. Over the years they had teamed up on several assignments in Indian Territory. On occasion each had saved the life of the other, which engendered a very special sort of kinship. In a gunfight Ryan knew of no one else he'd rather have as a partner. Many men were what he tended to categorize as toughnuts: they thrived on rough-and-tumble fisticuffs and eagerly invited trouble. But a man like Sam Irvin was another breed entirely. When words failed, he never resorted to fists or a contest of physical strength. He pulled a gun.

Irvin rode into camp late Sunday afternoon. The construction crew was quitting for the day, having just completed the sixth mile of track. Ryan, as he'd done every day, had stationed himself some distance ahead of the graders. He grinned upon spotting Irvin, genuinely pleased to see an old comrade. Still mounted, they shook hands warmly.

"Long time no see," Ryan greeted him. "How the hell you been?"

"Fair to middlin'," Irvin allowed. "No need to ask about you. Any fool could see you're in hog heaven."

"Yeah, sure," Ryan laughed. "All I've got to do is wet-nurse a whole railroad through the Nations. It's a cushy life."

"Beats chasin' a bunch of hard-ass badmen."

"I take it you're on the hunt."

Irvin nodded. "Ed Garrett was killed four days ago."

"Where?"

"Creek Nation," Irvin said. "Outside of Okmulgee."

"How'd it happen?"

"Ever hear of a robber named Jack Spainyard?"

"I recall the wanted circulars."

"Well, him and a couple of other hardcases went on a spree. Started out, they robbed a Texican horse buyer just north of Okmulgee."

"And Ed Garrett went after them?"

"Caught 'em too," Irvin said dourly. "Only he must've got a mite careless. They killed him."

"Damn shame," Ryan said, tight-lipped. "Ed was a better peace officer than most."

"It gets worse. Spainyard and his gang hightailed it into Cherokee country. They took a farmer and his family hostage and holed up night before last."

Ryan waited, knowing there was more.

"Then the bastards," Irvin went on, "raped the farmer's wife. All three of them took turns—all night."

Irvin avoided his eyes as though embarrassed by the words. Like many lawmen, he was hardened to murder and the ways of cold-blooded killers. Yet he was acutely uncomfortable with the thought of a woman being violated, forced to perform indecent acts. Ryan finally broke the silence.

"Was the woman Cherokee?"

"Yeah," Irvin affirmed. "But Garrett's murder takes precedence. So Oliver Logan ordered me to bring 'em in—or kill 'em."

"By yourself?" Ryan asked, surprised. "Seems like Oliver would have sent along some help."

"We're damned shorthanded, John. Since Judge Story took over, he's fired about half the deputies. Told everybody the money had to be appropriated to 'court costs.' Which means it'll wind up in his own pockets."

"Jesus Christ," Ryan muttered. "That'll double every marshal's workload."

"Doubles the territory we've gotta cover too."

Irvin's statement underscored an already critical problem. Law enforcement in Indian Territory was a grueling business, conducted under the strangest circumstances ever faced by men who wore a badge. With the advance of civilization, a new pattern of lawlessness began to emerge on the plains. The era of the lone bandit gradually faded into obscurity, evolving into something far worse. Outlaws began to run in packs.

Local peace officers found themselves unable to cope with the vast distances involved. Gangs made lightning strikes into Kansas and Missouri and Texas, terrorizing the settlements, and then retreated into Indian Territory. These wild forays, particularly bank holdups and train robberies, were planned and executed with the precision of military campaigns. In time, due to the limitations of state jurisdiction, the war became a grisly contest between the gangs and the federal marshals. But it was hide-and-seek with a unique advantage falling to the outlaws.

Once in the Nations the gangs found virtual immunity from the law. And by any yardstick, they enjoyed the oddest sanctuary in the history of crime. While each of the Five Civilized Tribes maintained Light Horse Police, their authority extended only to Indian citizens. However heinous the offense, white men were exempt from all prosecution except that of a federal court. It was the marshals who had to pursue and capture every wanted white man. The Nations quickly became infested with fugitives from justice. Curiously enough, the problem was compounded by the Indians themselves.

All too often the red men connived with the outlaws, offering them asylum. Few in the Nations had any respect for white man's law, and the marshals were looked upon as intruders. So the job of ferreting out and capturing lawbreakers became a herculean task. Adding yet another obstacle, even the terrain itself favored the outlaws. A man could lose himself in the mountains or along wooded river bottoms and live outdoors for extended periods of time in relative comfort. Tracking badmen into the Nations was a dirty, dangerous business. It was no job for the faint of heart.

Judge William Story merely intensified the problem. With his reduction in the number of federal marshals, the outlaws' advantage suddenly became a deadly edge. The favorable terrain and a general atmosphere of sanctuary were now improved by too few lawmen chasing too many desperadoes. The Nations swarmed with killers and robbers and dozens of small gangs like the one led by Jack Spainyard. Outnumbered and outgunned, marshals were forced to ride alone into Indian Territory. Sam Irvin clearly was faced with the specter of his own death. That was the thought Ryan expressed now.

"Aren't you playing into a cold deck?"

Irvin smiled. "Oliver Logan figured it the same way. He told me to drop by here and ask you to lend a hand."

"Lend a hand! Hell, I'm a civilian now."

"I got the authority to deputize you."

"What about my job here? The Cherokees are on the warpath, and no bones about it, I can't just walk out."

"John, I need your help," Irvin said solemnly. "We go back a long ways or I wouldn't ask. Course, you don't owe me nothin'. . . ."

"Don't soft-soap me," Ryan cut him short. "You know damn well you meant to put me on the spot."

"A man does what he has to."

Ryan pondered it a moment. "How long you figure it'd take?"

"Couple of days. No more'n three at the outside."

"Any idea where Spainyard and his bunch are holed up?"

"Nope," Irvin admitted. "But I thought our first stop ought to be Tahlequah. Major Tappin might've heard something."

"While we're there, why not ask him for the loan of a few Light Horse? You said the farmer and his wife are Cherokee."

"Maybe," Irvin said doubtfully. "I just don't want any argument about jurisdiction. Spainyard killed a federal marshal, and that makes him ours—not Tappin's."

"By 'ours' I assume you mean you and me."

Irvin grinned. "You as much as said you'd come along."

"Yeah, but it'll take some powerful explaining to Tom Scullin. He's the Katy construction boss."

Irvin motioned toward the tracklaying gangs, who were trooping back to the supply train. "All the men look full-growed to me. You'd think they could wet-nurse themselves for a couple of nights."

"If they can't," Ryan noted, "I'm liable to be an unemployed special agent."

Irvin eyed him with a crafty look. Shaking his head, Ryan reined about and gigged his horse. They rode off in search of Scullin.

Late the next afternoon Ryan and Irvin entered the Cherokee capitol building. Upstairs they were ushered into Major David Tappin's rather monkish office. The furnishings consisted of a desk and chair and a lone file cabinet. The tribal treasurer apparently believed in the brisk conduct of business.

Forced to stand, Ryan and Irvin planted themselves in front of the desk. Tappin finished signing a letter and carefully returned the pen to the inkwell. Then he sat back in his chair, hands flat on the desk, and stared at them. His mouth was razored in a polite smile.

"Gentlemen," he said civilly. "What brings you to Tahlequah?"

"Jack Spainyard," Irvin told him.

"Of course," Tappin said matter-of-factly. "I understand he killed one of your marshals."

"After which," Irvin said, "him and his men raped a Cherokee woman. We have reason to believe he's holed up somewheres hereabouts."

"Indeed?"

"We thought maybe your Light Horse might know where—just exactly."

Tappin sat perfectly still for a moment. Then his gaze shifted to Ryan. "Have you resigned from the railroad, Mr. Ryan?"

"No," Ryan said. "I've been deputized on a temporary basis."

"Too bad," Tappin remarked. "Your work with the Katy seems a little beneath you. Some people might even call it a gun for hire."

Ryan ignored the barb. "We're not here to talk about the railroad. We're looking for Jack Spainyard."

"And welcome to him!" Tappin said shortly. "We're already overrun with your outlaws and gunmen."

"Glad to hear it," Irvin interjected. "You won't argue about jurisdiction then?"

"No, not this time. Take him back to Fort Smith and hang him."

"In that case let's go back to my first question. Any ideas as to his whereabouts?"

Tappin spun around in his chair. He opened the top drawer on the file cabinet and riffled through a folder. Extracting a sheet of paper, he consulted it briefly and closed the drawer. Then he turned back to them.

"Spainyard and his men were reported camped on Blackgum Creek."

"How long ago?"

"Day before yesterday."

"And you made no effort to notify Fort Smith?"

Tappin smiled. "You seem to forget, Marshal, we

Cherokees are a very backward people. We haven't the benefit of the telegraph."

"Would it make any difference if you did?"

"Perhaps," Tappin said equably. "Perhaps not."

"Well, thanks for your time anyway."

"You're entirely welcome."

"One more thing," Ryan said, almost as an afterthought. "We were wondering if you could spare a couple of Light Horse. It would improve the odds some."

"Spainyard is your responsibility. I couldn't jeopardize my own men, not under the circumstances."

"You've got a funny way of looking at things, Tappin."

"Do I?" Tappin said pleasantly. "Well, no matter. I understand you thrive on long odds."

"What's that supposed to mean?"

"A passing comment," Tappin said, nodding to Irvin. "Good day, Marshal. Always a pleasure to see you."

Outside, Ryan led the way along the corridor. He was quietly seething, but he said nothing as they went down the stairs. Finally, as they emerged from the front door, Irvin chuckled and shook his head.

"You know something, John? I don't think that son of a bitch likes you."

"He especially doesn't like who I work for."

"What was all that about you thrivin' on long odds?"

"Hard to say, Sam. Tappin talks in riddles about half the time."

Yet it was no riddle to Ryan. He'd understood perfectly what the remark meant. Tappin was talking about the four dead Cherokees, the ones he'd killed.

As of today, he'd been put on warning.

Dawn tinged the skyline. Blackgum Creek, flowing swiftly from winter melt-off, wound through a tangle of hills and wooded undergrowth. Nothing stirred where the stream made a sharp dogleg and gurgled off in a southeasterly direction. A deafening stillness hung over the land.

Ryan and Irvin were crouched behind trees on the slope of a hill. Below them, just past the bend in the stream, there was a small clearing where three horses were tied along the treeline. Around a smoldering campfire, the outlines of three men in bedrolls were dimly visible. In the dusky light, a tendril of smoke drifted skyward.

The lawmen had approached from the northwest shortly before dawn. They had hidden their horses in a stand of trees some distance upstream and slowly and with great caution had catfooted through the woods. Upon spotting the clearing, they had crouched down. Now, their eyes fixed on the sleeping figures, they spoke in whispers.

Irvin, who was armed with a Winchester carbine, nodded toward the clearing. His lips barely moved. "What d'you think?"

"Looks good," Ryan said. "I doubt they'll roll out before sunrise. So there's no need to rush it."

"You figure we ought to separate?"

Ryan understood that the older man was offering a suggestion. He studied the terrain a moment, estimating time and distance. On the opposite side of the creek, the woods were thick and brushy, skirting the shoreline. He judged the stream itself to be eight feet wide, studded in spots with large stones. The ground underfoot was still damp with dew, and therefore quiet.

"I'll cross over," he said softly. "You cover me till I'm on the other side. Then I'll work through those trees and come up directly opposite the camp. We'll have them in a crossfire."

Irvin nodded. It was the very plan he'd had in mind himself. Once Ryan was in position, there would be no need to delay further. His own field of fire already enabled him to cover the clearing from woods to creek bank. He glanced at the younger man.

"Don't take no chances."

"It's your show." Ryan shrugged. "How do you want them—dead or alive?"

"I'll give 'em one chance to surrender."

"And if they don't?"

"Kill 'em," Irvin said flatly. "Save the trouble of hangin' them anyway."

"Whatever suits. I'll wait for you to make the first play."

Ryan climbed to his feet. Angling downslope, taking it one step at a time, he drifted toward the dogleg. There, like a wraith, he moved clear of the treeline and forded the creek, hopping from boulder to boulder. On the far side he quickly took cover in the brushy undergrowth. Quiet as wood smoke, he slipped through the shadowed timberland. Within ten minutes he was positioned immediately opposite the campsite. He waited behind the broad trunk of an oak tree.

Jack Spainyard suddenly awoke. Reacting to a faint noise or some instinct, he went from deep sleep to a state of instant alertness. He sat up in his bedroll and looked around the clearing. Then his gaze shifted to the woods.

Ryan froze. On the opposite side of the creek, Irvin went still as a stone monument. Hardly breathing, they held themselves motionless as Spainyard scanned the trees. For a long moment they were like partially hidden hunters who had inadvertently spooked their quarry. They waited in the deepening silence.

Finally Spainyard crawled out of his bedroll and stood. As he stepped from the blankets, he pulled a pistol from his waistband and peered warily into the trees. His eyes flicked to the tethered horses, then moved back to the woods. His look was at once guarded and puzzled, and he hesitated only briefly. He rapped out a sharp command to the other two men.

"Lem! Chuck! Haul your ass outa there. Let's go!"

Irvin reacted instantly. As the two outlaws scrambled from their bedrolls, he threw the carbine to his shoulder. He centered the sights on Jack Spainyard's chest.

"Hands up!" he yelled. "Do it, goddammit! Now!"

Spainyard snapped off a hurried shot. He fired in the general direction of the voice, already moving toward the woods as he pulled the trigger. Irvin levered three quick shots from the carbine. The slugs pocked crimson dots on Spainyard's shirtfront and he lurched sideways in a grotesque reeling dance. He went down, arms and legs akimbo, firing another shot as he fell. He dropped to the ground in a lifeless ball.

At the first shot the other two men sprang to their feet. Guns drawn, they seemed intent only on escape. One of them backed across the stream, firing wildly at the muzzle flash of Irvin's carbine. As he turned to the creek bank, Ryan stepped around the tree and triggered one barrel of his scattergun. The fist-sized load caught the outlaw in the brisket, splattering bone and gore. Legs pumping crazily, he stumbled backward into the creek. He hit the water with a loud splash.

The sound of the shotgun stopped the second man. Sprinting toward the horses, he halted in midstride and turned to fight. His pistol leveled as he spotted Ryan across the creek, and he fired. The slug shaved bark off the trunk beside Ryan's head and whistled harmlessly into the woods. Ryan let go with the shotgun, and in the same instant Irvin touched off another round from the carbine. Struck by a load of buckshot, the outlaw clutched his stomach as a carbine slug plowed through his rib cage. Like a puppet with his strings gone haywire, he collapsed to the earth.

A stillness descended on the clearing. Irvin started downslope, and Ryan waded across the creek. They met beside the campfire and stood for a moment staring down at Spainyard's body. The ground was puddled with blood, and the stench of bowels loosed in death filled the air. Irvin wrinkled his nose, slowly wagged his head. His voice was somehow rueful.

"Dumb bastards never seem to learn."

"What the hell," Ryan told him. "It beats hanging."

"Yeah, I reckon it does."

Irvin walked off to inspect the other two bodies. Ryan broke open his shotgun, extracted the spent shells, and reloaded. He started upstream to collect their horses.

The stench of Jack Spainyard followed him. His pace quickened, but he knew he'd never walk fast enough. It was a smell no man ever outran.

CHAPTER EIGHT

The delegates began arriving on a sunny March afternoon. Their attendance at yet another Intertribal Council gathering marked a worsening situation. The Katy was now twelve miles into Indian Territory.

The meeting had been called in Muskogee, capital of the Creek Nation. Not quite ten miles from Fort Gibson, the town was located south of the Arkansas River. It was situated roughly in the center of Indian Territory, and therefore accessible to all the delegates. The Five Civilized Tribes, as well as several smaller tribes, were represented.

Hastily convened, the purpose of the meeting was to devise a united strategy. Ancient tribal animosities led inevitably to squabbling and a breakdown in solidarity. But a mood of compromise prevailed as wagons and groups of horsemen made their way into town. Today the council would discuss encroachment by the railroad and various land-grab schemes. And it would address as well an even greater threat—the federal government. Finding some means of staving off the devious tactics of white politicians was a matter of critical urgency.

Nearly two hundred delegates gathered in the local meeting

hall. While allied, they represented separate peoples and divergent interests. Yet beneath all the jealousy and bickering, they were nonetheless brothers in blood. There was a businesslike air about them, the somber dignity of those faced with mutual peril. They met to consider the onrush of white domination.

John Ryan was the only *tibo* present. He rode into Muskogee shortly after the noon hour and dismounted outside the meeting hall. Officially, he was there as the emissary of Colonel Robert Stevens and the Katy railroad. While he could not address the council as a whole, he'd been ordered to work behind the scenes. His ostensible goal was to present the railroad's position in the most favorable light.

For all that, Ryan was still very uncomfortable. Stevens, though he never actually stated it, clearly expected him to spy on the proceedings. The council members crowding into the hall resented that their actions would be scrutinized by an uninvited white man. The looks they gave Ryan were laced with hostility. He felt like the worst sort of interloper simply because he was a *tibo*, and as far as the Indians were concerned, an enemy.

Yet the truth was something altogether different. Ryan was sympathetic to the Indians' cause and their long list of grievances. His years as a marshal had taught him that the Nations were another world, one that mystified most white men. And he understood that men were generally compelled to destroy what they failed to understand. So human nature, abetted by railroad barons and power-hungry politicians, represented a formidable threat to the Five Civilized Tribes, which were now confronted with the specter of their own dissolution.

At root was the fact that so many people coveted Indian lands. Choice homesteads had already been claimed by a flood of immigrants and settlers. The clamor to open all public lands to settlement had intensified as the westward migration gained strength. With the scarcity of good farmland, one of the primary targets of this movement was the Unassigned Lands. Ceded by the Creeks and Seminoles as a home for tribes yet to be resettled, the Unassigned Lands embraced some two million acres of well-watered, fertile plains. White settlers were also eyeing the Cherokee Outlet.

Spawned by federal bureaucracy, the Cherokee Outlet was one of the government's more bizarre creations. Earlier in the century, when the Cherokees were resettled in Indian Territory, they were granted seven million acres bordering southern Kansas. At the same time they were also granted a westward corridor, providing a gateway to the distant buffalo ranges. Comprising more than six million acres, roughly 150 miles in length, it was designated as the Cherokee Outlet. The legal status of this strip was confounding from its inception.

While the Cherokees held title to the Outlet, they were forbidden to dispose of it in any manner. Their lands to the east were sufficient for the entire tribe, and as a result they seldom ventured into their western grant. The upshot was a huge land mass that had remained unoccupied for the past thirty years. All that changed when the Chisholm Trail was blazed through Indian Territory. Texas cattlemen discovered a lush stretch of graze watered by the Canadian and Cimarron rivers. The Outlet made a perfect holding ground for longhorns, where cows were fattened out before the final drive to railhead at Abilene. For the last two trailing seasons, vast herds were halted a week or longer in the Outlet.

Word of this grassy paradise spread and quickly drew the attention of homesteaders. In short order, a public outcry arose over both the Unassigned Lands and the Outlet. The settlers were backed by several influential factions, all of which had a vested interest in the western expansion. Politicians and merchant princes and railroads, all looking to feather their own nests, rallied to the cause. Alone in their opposition to settlement were the Five Civilized Tribes. Their dealings with the government over several generations formed a chain of broken pledges and unfulfilled treaties. They saw settlement as a device for the enrichment of white farmers and greedy politicians.

In Washington those same politicians were holding out a wide array of enticements. Efforts were under way to convince the Five Civilized Tribes that their best interests would

be served by abolishing tribal government. They were told
that full citizenship within the Republic would afford them
equality before the law, voting rights, freedom of speech and
worship, and improved schooling. Still, based on their experience with *tibos'* promises, they had good reason to doubt
the faith of the government. So all of them—Cherokee,
Creek, Choctaw, Chickasaw, and Seminole—were unwilling
to exchange independence for the dubious privilege of citizenship. Indian leaders, as well as the lowliest tribesman, preferred the old ways to the white man's road.

For all their resistance, however, the Indians were weighed
down by a sense of fatalism. Educated men such as William
Ross knew that their people were in the process of slow but
certain absorption into the white culture. Once the railroad
was extended to Texas, pressure would mount for the settlement of Indian Territory. The Five Civilized Tribes numbered
less than fifty thousand people, and much of their land lay
untilled. The movement to gain control of those millions of
acres would ultimately put the tribes in an untenable position.
So their leaders sought to forestall the inevitable by devising
some bolder delaying action. The Intertribal Council would
meet today to consider that very question.

Inside the council hall, Ryan paused at the rear of the
room. There was no sanction against whites attending, but he
was under no illusions. The men crowding through the door
eyed him with a mixture of loathing and outrage. His presence was an affront, for he represented their most visible
threat: the railroad. He reminded himself that the journey
back to end-of-track would require unusual caution. Another
attempt on his life seemed a distinct possibility.

The noise inside the hall was deafening. Knots of men
scattered around the room were involved in loud and sometimes heated discussion. It occurred to Ryan that whites had
a general misconception about Indians. Contrary to popular
belief, the stoic red man with never a flicker of expression
rarely existed. Indians were prone to play the part around
whites, but in private they were as talkative and expressive
as other men.

A familiar face down front caught Ryan's eye. He saw Major Tappin huddled in conversation with several men. By their dress and features, he took the other men to be of the Creek tribe. Tappin appeared to be lecturing them, emphasizing some point with a sharp, chopping gesture. The listeners nodded, seemingly convinced, their attitude one of absolute respect. With hardly a pause for breath, Tappin went on in a windy monologue.

Watching him, Ryan was struck by an ironic twist. The council hall might well have been a legislative chamber or a congressional assemblage. Except for their color, the men here today were scarcely different from a gaggle of white politicians. Some talked and others listened, and only a very few provided leadership. The art of persuasion was everywhere in evidence, typified by Tappin lecturing the attentive Creeks. The politician's standbys—compromise and trade-off—were equally apparent, and some tribes would fare better than others in the exchange. Ryan found the similarity to whites somewhat disappointing, almost sad. He thought the Indians had learned all the wrong things.

"Well, Mr. Ryan! We meet again."

Turning, Ryan found William Ross in the doorway. As principal chief of the Cherokees and president of the Intertribal Council, Ross was the most influential man in the hall. He was slated to give the opening address, and his speech would set the tone of the meeting. The council, in effect, was an instrument of his will.

Ross was scrupulously polite. Yet he regarded Ryan with casual interest, as though their meeting were a trivial event in an otherwise memorable day. He pointedly made no offer of a handshake.

Ryan pretended not to notice. "Quite a crowd," he said. "Looks like the Nations are well represented."

"And the railroad too," Ross noted. "I assume you're here at Colonel Stevens' direction?"

"Strictly as an observer."

"Naturally the Colonel had pressing matters elsewhere. Otherwise I've no doubt he would have been here himself."

The statement was delivered in a wry tone just short of mockery. Ryan smiled, sensing that the barb was not directed at him personally. He lifted one hand in an empty gesture.

"Tell you the truth, Mr. Ross, I don't think Stevens would be caught within ten miles of Muskogee. He places too high a value on his own hide."

Ross appraised him with a shrewd glance. "Are you implying that Colonel Stevens would not be safe here?"

"Maybe he would and maybe he wouldn't. I'm just telling you how he looks at it."

"And how do you look at it, Mr. Ryan?"

"Well"—Ryan hesitated, still smiling—"let's say he was wiser to send me."

"A diplomatic reply, indeed. Your tact does you credit."

"A man tends to mind his p's and q's when he travels alone."

"Which reminds me," Ross said with a calm, judicial gaze. "I understand your friends won't be here today."

"What friends?"

"Why, Elias Boudinot and Stand Watie, of course."

Ryan was momentarily taken aback. He recalled quite vividly the assassination attempt on the two kinsmen, but he was amazed that Ross would make any reference to their conspiracy with the railroad. However indirect, it seemed a damaging admission.

"What makes you think they're friends of mine?"

"You disappoint me, Mr. Ryan. One minute tactful and the next evasive. Are you denying that you know them?"

"No," Ryan said vaguely. "I'm just saying we're not what you'd call friends."

"Would you say the same for your employer?"

"I don't speak for the Colonel. You'll have to ask him."

Ross allowed himself a reserved smile. "I daresay his reply would make interesting listening. Don't you agree, Mr. Ryan?"

It occurred to Ryan that he'd been given a message. Or perhaps a warning. Ross clearly intended for him to pass it along to Stevens. He inclined his head in a faint nod.

"I'll tell the Colonel you asked."

"Yes, do that," Ross said agreeably. "You might also tell him that Boudinot and Watie make poor allies. Their reputation for double-dealing is well-known."

"Is that why they're not here today?"

"I suspect their reasons are the same as Colonel Stevens'."

There was an implied threat in the reply. Ryan started to pursue it, then changed his mind; there was nothing to be gained in pressing the matter. Better to let things take their natural course. He decided to switch to neutral ground.

"How's Elizabeth these days?"

"Quite well, thank you."

"Give her my regards. I hope to see her again before too long."

Ross examined him with a kind of bemused objectivity. "Would you care to stop over tomorrow night? As our houseguest, of course."

"Well, sure." Ryan sounded surprised. "I'd like that."

"I trust it won't compromise you with Colonel Stevens?"

"If it does, I reckon that's his worry."

"In that event, why not travel with me tomorrow? I have my coach here."

"I don't mind horseback."

"Yes, but why ride alone—on a lonely road?"

Ross' expression was unfathomable. Yet there was no doubt that he'd extended a warning. Once again the deeper purpose was unclear. And once again Ryan decided not to press the issue. Not now.

"Sounds like good advice," he said. "I'll plan on riding with you."

"Excellent."

Ross stuck out his hand. He smiled and shook Ryan's hand warmly. The gesture was hardly lost on the men crowded around the doorway. Nor was Ryan unaware that a message had been passed. The handshake guaranteed his safety while in Muskogee. He pumped Ross' arm once for good measure.

With a nod, Ross walked off. He made his way to the front of the hall, exchanging greetings with several men along the way. Mounting a speaker's platform, he moved directly to the podium. The hall quieted as he took up a gavel and hammered the delegates into silence.

For a long moment Ross just stood there. The silence thickened. Finally, when the crowd was absolutely still, he raised his arms in greeting. His voice flooded the hall.

"Brothers! Delegates to the council. I welcome you as we unite once more in a noble cause. One people, undivided—red men all!"

The crowd responded with a thunderous ovation. Someone loosed a shrill war whoop, and the delegates roared their approval. In that instant every voice there was fused into a single voice. By unspoken agreement all their past differences and the pettiness of tribal politics were set aside. They joined in a confederation of mind and spirit, proudly defiant.

William Ross spoke for nearly an hour. He talked of the railroads and the audacity with which they planned to exploit the Nations. He railed at the conspiracy of white politicians—and certain Indians—who sought to gain control of the red man's domain. He addressed himself to Congress and the federal bureaucracy and their unholy alliance with white power brokers to bring about settlement of Indian lands. His arguments struck to the very marrow of present and future dangers.

And at last, his voice alive with rage, he flung down what was both a challenge and a warning. He predicted an effort to bring about the allotment of their lands in severalty, forcing each of them onto the same 160 acres awarded to homesteaders. When that happened, he promised, there would soon follow the dissolution of tribal governments and Indian Territory as they had known it. Finally, calling the railroad a "greedy cormorant," he warned of a day when 23,000,000 acres of tribal land would be engulfed by a white tide. All that, he concluded, unless the council acted now—today!

Following his speech, Ross opened the floor to debate. Members of each tribe spoke at length, voicing their own concerns. But there was no debate, for every speaker agreed that action—an act signifying resistance—was imperative. By late afternoon a resolution had been drafted to President Ulysses S. Grant. In it the council expressed satisfaction with their own governments and the tribal ownership of land and urged Washington to abide by the provisions of existing treaties. There was nothing in the document to indicate open defiance.

Looking on, Ryan realized that it was all whitewash. The resolution was meaningless, another piece of paper to be ignored by both the President and Congress. But William Ross' speech had nonetheless inflamed the other tribes, incited them to act. Unable to challenge Washington, the Indians would instead strike a symbolic blow. And there was no question as to the closest enemy at hand.

They would attempt to stop the railroad.

CHAPTER NINE

A *morning mist* slowly burned away under the brassy dome of the sky. The coach trundled northward, drawn by a matched pair of carriage horses held to a steady pace by their driver.

Ryan occupied the front seat inside the coach. His horse was hitched to the rear, his saddle deposited in the luggage boot. He was unaccustomed to traveling in style and was impressed by the plush comfort. He thought it befitted an aristocratic Cherokee.

Ross and Tappin were seated opposite him. Earlier, before their departure from Muskogee, Tappin's greeting had been civil but cool. Aside from small talk, there had been little conversation and no reference to yesterday's council meeting. The three men had ridden in complete silence for the past half hour.

Ross appeared preoccupied. He was staring out the window with a faraway look in his eyes, as if toward something dimly visible in the distance. He was clearly pondering a matter of great complexity and seemed unaware of his traveling companions.

Watching him, Ryan was absorbed in thoughts of his own. He wondered why he'd been invited to share the coach. It was entirely possible that Ross wanted to protect him from an assassination attempt. By any estimate most of those attending the council meeting had viewed him as their mortal enemy. And as Ross had implied, a lone horseman on the Texas Road presented a tempting target. Yet that raised a question in Ryan's mind to which there was no ready answer. Why would Ross want to protect him?

No reasonable explanation occurred to Ryan. He had to assume that Ross was responsible for the violence to date. Certainly two assassination attempts had not gone unnoticed by the principal chief of the Cherokees, and it was reasonable to assume that the tribal leader had, at the very least, tacitly sanctioned the attempts. Great men, by their silence, often consigned lesser men to death.

Protection was ruled out, and Ryan was left to ponder exactly why he was jouncing along in the coach today. The obvious conclusion was that Ross wanted something from him. Ryan waited for Ross to make an overture.

Only the leathery creak of the coach broke the silence. As they forded the Arkansas, Ross finally stirred from his spell. Unfolding an oilskin tobacco pouch, he produced a pipe and started to fill it. He glanced at Tappin, who was staring out the opposite window. Striking a sulphurhead, he puffed a billowy cloud of smoke. He at last looked across at Ryan.

"Are you a student of government affairs, Mr. Ryan?"

Ryan shrugged. "Politics never much interested me."

"You're fortunate to have that option. No Cherokee could afford such a luxury."

"No, I reckon not."

"Be that as it may, you're hardly an uninformed man. So perhaps you'd indulge me. I have a question."

"I'll do my best."

"Call it idle curiosity . . ." Ross hesitated, puffing a wad of smoke. "As an observer, what was your opinion of the council meeting?"

"In what respect?" Ryan asked cautiously.

"Quite simply, do you believe we accomplished anything worthwhile?"

"If you're talking about Washington, I'd have to say no. The resolution you drafted won't hardly cause a ripple."

"Another piece of paper to get lost in a blizzard of legislative paper. Is that it?"

"Pretty much."

Ross considered a moment. "Are you aware there's a movement in Congress to force territorial status on the Nations?"

"How's that different than what you've got?"

"All the difference in the world, Mr. Ryan. We would then be a unified territory—with *one* territorial government, not five independent republics."

"Wouldn't that give you a stronger voice in Washington?"

"Hardly," Ross said firmly. "The President would appoint a governor and all the judges. Congress would have veto power over all territorial legislation. And eventually, of course, it would lead to statehood."

"I take it," Ryan said with a smile, "you're not interested in becoming just another state."

Ross laughed without mirth. "Territorial status and statehood would require the dissolution of the Five Civilized Tribes. It would also violate every treaty we have with the United States government."

Ryan rocked his hand from side to side. "Maybe your treaties aren't as ironclad as you thought."

"On the contrary," Ross said. "Our sovereignty was guaranteed for 'as long as water shall flow, as long as grass shall grow.' Hardly equivocal language, wouldn't you say?"

"Sounds permanent, all right."

"Indeed it does. Of course, the coming of the railroad changed all that. As Colonel Stevens once remarked, progress will not be denied."

Ryan nodded. "Even at the cost of a few treaties."

"Let me be frank, Mr. Ryan. You seem reasonably sympathetic to our cause. Am I mistaken?"

"No," Ryan said slowly.

"Then perhaps I might ask a favor. I assume you will deliver a report on the council meeting. Is that correct?"

"Yes."

"When you do, be so kind as to consider something. We might very well strike an accommodation with the railroad if there were a quid pro quo. Some assurance that the railroad would assume a neutral stance—not oppose us—in our struggle for sovereignty. Would you relay that message to Colonel Stevens?"

"I'd be glad to."

"And perhaps," Ross asked pointedly, "argue the merits of such an arrangement for all concerned?"

It sounded to Ryan like an offer to cease obstructing the railroad, but also as though Ross was trying, very subtly, to enlist him as an ally. Or perhaps plant a spy in Robert Stevens' camp. He phrased his reply with care.

"I think cooperation would be to everyone's benefit. That's what I'll tell Stevens."

"What sort of reaction would you anticipate?"

"I doubt he'll go for it. He'd have to burn a lot of bridges in Washington."

"A pity," Ross said ruefully. "Where power and money are concerned, there are no reasonable men. Only winners and losers."

The statement seemed to Ryan a prediction of sorts. He thought the best the Cherokees could hope for was a delay of the inevitable. Stevens would never adopt a position of neutrality where the Nations were concerned. The Katy, as well as the federal government, had everything to gain by the dissolution of Indian Territory. The Five Civilized Tribes were slated for the chopping block.

The coach rolled past the turnoff to Fort Gibson. Tappin, who had taken no part in their conversation, suddenly found his voice. He gestured out the window.

"Up the road is where two Cherokees were killed just about a month ago."

Ryan looked at him, fully alert. Tappin's composure was monumental, and he studied Ryan with an expression of open appraisal. Ross seemed unaware of the byplay. He glanced at Tappin with casual interest.

"Have you determined who was responsible?"

"Not yet," Tappin said, still staring at Ryan. "But whoever it was, he used a shotgun. It's not a common murderer's weapon—among Indians."

"Indians!" Ross repeated sharply. "Are you implying it was done by whites?"

Tappin shrugged, a sourly amused look on his face. "Why not ask our guest? He's a former marshal, and reputedly quite a manhunter." He paused, staring hard at Ryan. "What's your opinion, Mr. Ryan?"

Ryan gave him a wooden look. "Hard to say, Major. Were there any witnesses?"

"No." Tappin eyed him with the same disquieting stare. "Not to my knowledge."

"I never had much luck proving murder without a witness."

"Well, no matter," Tappin said with ominous calm. "Someone will come forward sooner or later. It's only a matter of time."

Ryan sensed the threat. He was suspect and he was being warned that the killings were not forgotten. He kept his features devoid of expression.

Tappin smiled and resumed staring out the window.

Dinner that night provided still another riddle. As an overnight guest, Ryan was treated with great cordiality. The meal, complemented by suitable wines, centered around imported oysters and a haunch of native venison. Afterward, a fine Napoleon brandy was served to the men.

All through dinner Elizabeth seemed elusive. She was obviously pleased by Ryan's visit and extended herself to make him feel welcome, but her attitude, while gracious, was distant.

Ryan pretended to notice nothing, but underneath he felt as though he was involved in some sort of charade. Compared to the last time, when they'd toured Tahlequah, Elizabeth was not herself. Her natural vivacity was muted, and she seemed on edge, curiously tense. He wondered if her father's presence was inhibiting her. He concluded instead that it was attributable to his presence.

Later that evening she confused him even more. Following dinner, Ross engaged him in conversation in the drawing room. Their discussion ranged over a variety of subjects, but they didn't talk of politics and the railroad. Elizabeth listened quietly, rarely offering a comment. Then as she excused herself for the night, she seemed to do a complete turnabout. She invited him to stay over another day on the pretext that he'd not yet seen all of the Cherokee Nation. Her manner was so charming that he readily agreed.

Early the next morning they drove off in an open carriage. Elizabeth wore a fashionable dark blue dress trimmed with gray piping and bone buttons. Her hair was drawn back sleekly, accentuating the contours of her face, and atop her head sat a jaunty little hat. She was animated and sparkling, chattering gaily, her eyes shining like black pearls.

Elizabeth's feelings veered wildly. In Ryan's absence, she'd found herself lost in long reveries about their last ride together. She knew it was witless and silly, for they were separated by his continuing loyalty to the railroad. But now, seated beside him, she was unable to control herself. She felt dizzy with happiness.

Elizabeth took him to see Park Hill. Some five miles south of Tahlequah, the small community was known as the "Athens of the Cherokee Nation." Here were two elegant brick churches, one Methodist and one Presbyterian, both fashioned along the lines of a New England meetinghouse. But most impressive was the Park Hill Mission, which was funded by religious donations. A printing shop operated by the mission produced schoolbooks that were distributed throughout the Nations. Elizabeth was quick to tell Ryan that some books were also printed in the Cherokee language.

Sequoyah's invention of a tribal alphabet had stamped out illiteracy among the Cherokees. In the years that followed, all schools in the Nation were mission operated, sponsored by religious organizations. Then in 1841 the tribal council established a formal educational system, with eighteen elementary schools. Trained schoolteachers were engaged, log schoolhouses were built, and every child was assured an education. The program, Elizabeth pointed out, marked a milestone in Cherokee progress.

Ten years later a system of higher education was established. Seminaries, one for boys and another for girls, were constructed outside Park Hill. The buildings were brick and stone, three stories high, with massive columns on the front veranda. Here, among other subjects, the older children were taught Latin and algebra, grammar and science. While their schooling was conducted in English, they were also grounded in their mother tongue. The most promising students were later sent to colleges and universities back East. In effect, the Cherokee Nation was looking to the future, building from within. The best of each generation was trained in business and law and medicine.

Elizabeth was justifiably proud. She was also somewhat chauvinistic about her people and not the least bit ashamed of it. She boasted that the public schools, particularly the seminaries, surpassed white institutions in both Kansas and Texas. Ryan accepted the statement, for he found himself impressed by the tribe's vision and far-reaching planning. He saw now that these same qualities had been brought to the Cherokees' struggle for sovereignty. William Ross was already planning a generation ahead.

As they turned from Park Hill, Ryan's thoughts took on a personal note. He sensed she was attracted to him, but it was hard to tell with educated women. Particularly one whose moods were so damnably mercurial. A wrong move too early might easily scare her off.

The point quickly became moot. Elizabeth's mood underwent a transformation. Out of the corner of his eye, he saw her expression change. The gaiety was replaced by a troubled look, and her shoulders seemed to tense. Her hands were clenched in her lap.

"John?"

"Yes."

"Would you mind . . . ?" She faltered, then hurried on. "Before we get back to the house, may I ask you something?"

"Of course," Ryan said. "What is it?"

"Father told me about your talk on the way from Musk-ogee. He said he thought you were unusually sympathetic toward the Cherokees."

"I suppose that's a fair statement."

She gave him a searching look. "Were you sincere with him or just being diplomatic?"

"I'm no diplomat," Ryan said, glancing at her. "Either I say what I think or I don't say it."

"Then you meant it?" she asked anxiously. "When you agreed to speak with Colonel Stevens?"

"I'll talk to him. But as I told your father, I doubt it'll change anything."

"It could . . . if you tell him the right thing."

"What's that?"

"Convince him," she said quite intently, "that he will never build the railroad unless he accepts my father's offer. There are men who mean to halt the construction—at any cost."

"You're talking about Cherokees, aren't you?"

"Yes."

"Who are they?"

"I have no idea."

"Does your father?"

Her chin tilted. "No, he doesn't. But he knows they exist, many of them."

"So he put you up to telling me about them—"

"No!"

"—and asking me to pass it along to Stevens."

"Please believe me," she implored, "he has no idea I've told you, and it would make him very angry if he knew." She paused and her voice dropped. "He's ashamed of what they're doing, going back to the old ways. He's trying to stop them."

"How can he stop them if he doesn't know who they are?"

Her voice was barely audible. "I'm afraid he will find out, afraid for him."

Ryan looked deep into her eyes. He read no guile there, and some inner voice told him to believe her. He popped the reins. It seemed important that he return to end-of-track, and quickly.

He had to have a long talk with Stevens.

CHAPTER TEN

Track laying slowed to a virtual halt by early April. Heavy rains turned the prairie into a quagmire, making it impassable for days at a time. End-of-track was scarcely fifteen miles from the Kansas border.

With construction at a standstill, Stevens ordered the supply depot brought forward. A siding was built off the main roadbed, and trains began chuffing back and forth. In a matter of days a mountain of construction supplies and equipment was unloaded on the soggy prairie. The Katy had established its first terminus.

Over the next two weeks the terminus was transformed into an anthill of commerce. Word went out that the Katy had shifted its supply depot, and the race was on. Gamblers, cutthroats, and harlots—all scenting fast money on the wind—arrived by wagon and horseback. Sprawling over the prairie, a shantytown went up as the horde descended on end-of-track.

A squalid, ramshackle affair, the town was constructed of poles and canvas. The street, such as it was, consisted of saloons, dance halls, and gaming dens. The lone hostelry, large as a circus tent, reeked of stale sweat and filthy blankets and charged four bits a night for a rickety cot. Where a grove of trees towered over the prairie, there was a dingy collection of one-room shanties. Among the sporting crowd it was known as Poonville, for it was where the whores practiced their profession. The ladies operating these dollar-a-throw brothels were an enterprising breed, offering something to suit the tastes of any man. Yet they were a ragtag bunch, unkempt and coarse, the lower rung of whoredom. Only the fact that their customers were blinded by lust kept them in business.

On any given night the town was crawling with rene- gades—bandits, cardsharps, wanted killers—a fraternity of rogues seeking sanctuary, whose chief goal in life was to put distance between themselves and the law. Brawls were a sporting pastime. Among men who prided themselves on be- ing ornery as well as tough, any dispute was an excuse for kick-and-stomp. On a nightly basis, cock-of-the-walk squared off against bull-of-the-woods, and blood flowed.

Tonight, with the street axle deep in mud, the town resem- bled an unholy carnival. Huge Studebaker wagons piled with freight and pulled by triple spans of mules clogged the street. Hitch racks outside every shanty were jammed with saddle horses, and raucous laughter from indoors left small doubt that firewater was being dispensed in liberal doses. From dance halls came the sprightly wail of fiddles, and an occasional banjo twanged strident chords. Hundreds of men joined in a rowdy jostling match as they made their way from one dive to the next.

The shantytown was a lure for a particular breed of men who roamed the western plains, men whose appetites ran to fast women, popskull whiskey, and games of chance.

Ryan's job here was a monumental task and constantly dangerous. For all practical purposes, he was the law at end- of-track. Day and night he was required to maintain order among outcasts and outlaws gathered from across the fron- tier, and thus far, only his reputation had prevented a seri- ous outbreak of violence. He'd not yet been forced to kill anyone.

When the sporting crowd arrived, Ryan had quickly laid down a code of conduct. Fisticuffs, even rough-and-tumble brawls, were permissible as long as an altercation did not lead to killing. Theft and robbery, whether by whore or penniless drifter, would result in swift justice. Gunplay, whatever the provocation, would not be tolerated. Anyone who killed or resorted to a gun would be called to answer for it. And it was known that Ryan would exact harsh payment.

Still, throughout the town there was a prevailing attitude of devil take the hindmost. The sporting crowd was comprised of fly-by-night operators, rootless vagabonds. Their interest was in fleecing the railroad workers, not settlement of the land or legitimate business. In fact, any attempt to settle on Indian land was punishable by a federal fine of $1,000. The single exception was for a white man who had intermarried within the Five Civilized Tribes. Such an individual was exempt from normal restrictions and could not only claim land, but found it considerably easier to obtain tribal license for certain types of businesses.

There was no license, however, for trading in whiskey. By federal law spirits in any form, whether liquor, wine, or beer, were illegal in Indian Territory. For selling or bartering, there was a $500 fine. Smuggling or attempting to transport alcohol into the Nations brought a $300 fine. Operating a still for the manufacture of spirits carried a fine of $1,000. Yet no one paid any attention to the law. Popskull and rotgut were stable commodities of trade throughout the tribes.

The crux of the problem was enforcement. Federal marshals were few and far between, due to the reduction in manpower ordered by the Fort Smith court. Whiskey smugglers risked small chance of arrest, and nowhere was the fact more obvious than at end-of-track. Freight wagons loaded with barrels and wooden cases rolled into the shantytown on a regular schedule. All of this compounded Ryan's problem, particularly after dark. Drunks, like vampires, were more active at night.

On only one front had Ryan been allowed a respite. Hampered by the rains, railroad construction was proceeding at a slow crawl. In the last week the track-laying crews had advanced less than a mile, and with the Katy stalled, the threat from the Cherokees had momentarily disappeared. Weather had seemingly accomplished what the Indians wished for most. The white man's iron horse was stopped cold.

Ryan completed his early evening swing through town. He generally made the rounds three times a night, with a break for supper. Tonight there was the usual orderly chaos, with every dive packed to capacity. Off toward Poonville, where red lanterns hung outside the tent bagnios, he saw lines of men waiting their turn. A knot of men gathered outside a saloon fell silent as he walked past. He felt their eyes on his back and imagined what they were thinking. Lots of men would like to be known as the man who killed John Ryan. He wondered how long it would be before someone tried.

Slogging toward the railroad siding, he headed for a meeting with Stevens. Their dealings lately had been very much that of boss and hired hand. Upon returning from Tahlequah, Ryan had presented William Ross' proposal. As he'd expected, Stevens turned it down flat, refusing all discussion. It was obvious that the railroader wanted things his own way. A truce with the Cherokees, at the cost of angering white politicians, was not to Stevens' liking. He clearly believed in leaving his bridges unburned.

Stevens had been angered, too, by what he saw as Ryan's meddling. He failed to understand why Ryan had spent the night at Ross' home and stayed over still another day. Nor was he pleased that Ryan had taken it upon himself to act as a negotiator. While never stating it, he had implied that Ryan had been disloyal. The matter had been dropped, but Stevens plainly hadn't forgotten it. Over the ensuing weeks, he'd treated Ryan with stiff formality.

A conference was under way when Ryan entered the private railroad car. Tom Scullin and Otis Gunn, the construction engineer, were seated while Stevens paced back and forth in front of them. Scullin glanced around at Ryan and rolled his eyes in a gesture of resignation. Stevens caught the byplay and halted, his face screwed up in a frown. His gaze shifted to Ryan.

"Have a seat, John," he said curtly. "I'll be with you in a minute."

"Saints preserve us," Scullin moaned. "Don't you believe it, Johnny m'boy. He's set to talk the whole night, and never a pause for breath."

"Spare me your humor!" Stevens' voice was peevish. He stabbed a finger at Scullin. "I fail to see how you can joke when we're so far behind schedule. And falling farther behind every day!"

"Would you have me wail and gnash my teeth? It's hardly of my choosing."

"Well, it has to improve. No two ways about it, Tom."

"Talk to God," Scullin muttered.

"I beg your pardon?"

Stevens looked as though he couldn't have heard correctly. Scullin shook his head, crossed one massive leg over the other. His eyes were hard.

"You understood me, Colonel."

"Don't get on your high horse with me!"

"Then lower your voice," Scullin grated. "I'll not be talked to in that manner."

A strained silence fell over the car. The two men were locked in a staring contest, glowering at one another. After several moments, Stevens broke eye contact. He massaged his forehead as though he had a headache.

"I didn't mean to snap at you, Tom. It's just that we're running out of time."

"All the same, God's the one who makes it rain. I've no control over the weather."

"No, of course you don't," Stevens agreed. "But that doesn't change our predicament. We have to reach Cabin Creek by the end of the month. That's our absolute deadline."

Scullin pursed his lips. "We'll never make it."

"We must!" Stevens declared loudly. "Otherwise we'll lose the cattle trade for the entire season."

"Would we now? I've always heard that the Texans trail

through the end of September. It seems we've still got a bit of leeway."

"You don't understand. Once they start trailing to Abilene, they'll continue throughout the summer. Texans are like sheep—they follow the leader!"

"I know it's a loss—"

"*A loss!*" Stevens cut him short. "We're talking about tens of thousands of dollars. And keep in mind, we won't get a nickel from the Indians in bond issues. It's a loss that may well drain us financially."

Scullin made no reply. He looked down at his hands with a sorrowful expression. The worry lines on Stevens' forehead deepened, and he seemed at a loss to continue. After a moment he turned to Gunn.

"Otis, you're the engineer. Isn't there some way around the damnable rain?"

Gunn looked pained, as though his teeth hurt. He ran a hand through his thinning hair and shot a glance at Scullin. At last he drew a deep breath.

"No, sir, there's not," he finally answered. "As quickly as the graders get the roadbed leveled, the rain washes it away. We're lucky if we lay track four hours out of the day."

"On top of which," Scullin added, "half the ballast on track we've laid gets washed away. We've got ourselves a hell of a patch job once the rain stops."

The discussion hobbled on awhile longer. None of the men was struck by inspiration, and the rain seemed the clear winner. Several minutes later Scullin and Gunn trooped out of the car. Stevens just stood there a moment, staring dully into space. He finally became aware of Ryan.

"Yes, John," he said absently. "What is it?"

"No idea, Colonel. You sent for me."

"So I did." Stevens slumped into a chair. "How are things going in town?"

"Pretty tame," Ryan said. "Usual fistfights and a couple of stabbings. But nothing too serious."

"I understand Red Baird showed up. Is that true?"

"Yeah, he's here."

"Why didn't you advise me?"

"No need," Ryan told him. "Baird's just another gambler."

"I have it on good authority that among other things he's killed a dozen men," Stevens said shortly.

Ryan smiled, but there wasn't a trace of amusement in his eyes. "Don't believe everything you hear. These gunmen like to boost their reputation by several notches. It makes other hardcases leery."

"The fact remains he's a killer. And he's the sort of man who attracts violence. I want to know how you're going to handle it."

"I've already handled it. When he pulled into town, I had a talk with him. We understand one another."

"Do you, indeed! And what happens if he kills one of our men?"

"He won't."

"What makes you so sure?"

"Because if he does," Ryan said, a touch of irony in his voice, "he knows he'll have to deal with me."

"And you believe that will stop him?"

"Has so far."

"I would prefer something a little more final."

"What'd you have in mind?"

Stevens idly waved his hand. "I suggest you run him out of town."

"Won't work," Ryan said. "If I run Baird off, I'd have to post half the men in town. We'd need an army to make it stick."

"Perhaps it would serve as an object lesson for the others. By posting Baird, you would serve notice."

"Only one problem. Unless he causes trouble, I've got no reason to post him. Not just on his reputation anyway."

"I see," Stevens remarked stiffly. "What if I ordered you to do it?"

Ryan gave him a stony look. "I don't tell you how to run your railroad." He paused, slowly stood. "Don't tell me how to do my job."

"You seem to forget," Stevens growled, "you're working for me."

"No, I haven't forgot."

Ryan walked to the door and let himself out. On the back platform he filled his lungs with air, then let it out slowly. He'd almost lost his temper, and he took that as a bad sign. A damn bad sign, he told himself, for a man in his line of work.

Heading uptown, he realized it was past suppertime. He normally took his meals with Scullin in the car where they both bunked. But tonight he wasn't interested in further talk about the railroad or Robert Stevens. He decided instead to try one of the tent cafés near the center of town.

The street was relatively quiet for midevening. Wooden planks, which were priceless in a tent city, served as a crude boardwalk. As he passed a saloon, Ryan came upon three men standing on the plank byway. The customary practice was for idlers to vacate the boardwalk in favor of passersby. As Ryan slowed, his attention directed to the men, a gunshot sounded from within the saloon.

Turning back, Ryan stepped through the entrance to the saloon. He pulled his Colt and held it alongside his leg, his thumb hooked over the hammer. He stopped just inside the entrance, assessing the situation and those involved at a glance. A man was sprawled on the floor, arms flung wide, blood staining his shirtfront. Standing over him, gun in hand, was a man dressed in a flannel shirt and a battered slouch hat. Beside him was a youngster, similarly dressed, who appeared to be in his late teens. Their backs were to the door.

"Drop it! You're under arrest!"

Ryan's command splintered the silence like a thunderclap. The spectators, who were fanned out away from the killing, froze in a still tableau. The roughly dressed man hesitated for only a fragment in time. Then, crouching low, he whirled and brought his pistol around. All in a split instant Ryan identified the man as Indian and thumbed the hammer on his Colt. A corner of his mind registered amazement; until now, not one Indian had ventured into the shantytown. In that same instant, suppressing conscious thought, Ryan reverted to instinct. The Colt roared, spitting a streak of flame.

The Indian staggered up against the bar. A bright red dot widened on his chest, and the pistol dropped from his hand. He buckled, folding together like an accordion, and slumped to the floor. The youngster, standing not a foot away, reacted even as the older man fell. He stooped low, scooping up the pistol in a swift movement. There was a metallic click as he cocked the hammer and spun back toward the door. His face was contorted with a mixture of rage and fear.

"Don't try it!"

Ryan shouted the order too late. The youngster was already turning, arm extended, the pistol level. Their shots cracked almost simultaneously, indistinguishable twin roars. A slug nicked Ryan's waistband, ripping a belt loop off his pants. Opposite him, the youngster lurched backward, struck dead center below the sternum. Arms windmilling, the Indian youth lost his footing and went down. He fell between the two older men, the pistol still clutched in his hand. His eyes stared into a sightless void.

A leaden moment slipped past. Then Ryan walked forward and stopped before the three bodies. He stared down at the youngster, whose boyish features were set in a rictus of death. His own face went ashen and his stomach knotted in a queasy sensation. The bitter taste of bile flooded his mouth as the truth struck home.

He'd killed a kid.

CHAPTER ELEVEN

The shootings created a momentary sensation. Word of the incident swept through town within the hour. Three dead in itself sparked only minor curiosity; violent death was no stranger to those who worked the frontier. It was the dead men themselves who generated such sharp interest.

The victim was an itinerant cardslick. Something of a loudmouth, he'd objected to the presence of an Indian in the saloon. When he became abusive and put a hand on his gun, he had paid for it with his life. The other man, who was Cherokee, shot him dead. Later it was determined that the Cherokee had wandered in with his son, looking for a drink. The bartender never had a chance to inform him that Indians were not served whiskey. Upon entering the saloon, he'd been braced by the gambler.

There was little surprise generated by the outcome. The sporting crowd knew Ryan to be a man of his word. He had threatened swift reprisal for those who resorted to gunplay, and he'd delivered on the promise. No great importance was attached to the fact that the dead man was an Indian. Everyone agreed that Ryan would just as quickly have tangled with a white man. Nor was there any stigma associated with the killing of a Cherokee boy. Opinion on the youngster, who looked to be about seventeen, was fairly uniform among the sporting crowd. He shouldn't have made a try for the gun.

Ryan was somewhat less charitable about himself. He saw no way to have avoided killing the Cherokee man, and he agreed that the boy had been foolish to take up the fight. But all that failed to absolve him in his own view for killing a kid. He mocked himself for not having faster reactions or greater foresight. He thought he could have handled the situation differently, far more wisely. If he had, the boy would still be alive.

He knew that he was being harsh with himself. His regret was prompted basically by the youngster's age, and by hindsight. Given the circumstances, his reaction was inevitable. Anyone who tried to kill him, man or boy, foreclosed all other options. When the choice was kill or get killed, there was no choice at all. Still, however much hindsight kindled his regret, he couldn't entirely accept the reality. He wished that it had somehow ended differently.

The only positive note to the whole affair was that in the two weeks since the shooting, the town had become almost civilized. The sporting crowd, drifters, and outlaws were on their best behavior. A triple burial of the dead out beyond Poonville had proved highly persuasive. There was even talk that the cardsharp had saved time and trouble by getting himself killed by the Indian. Had he lived, according to local wits, Ryan would probably have shot him anyway. The dark humor contained a moral that escaped no one. Don't start trouble.

Several days later, shortly before sundown, Ryan was on his way to see Stevens. He'd been summoned earlier in the afternoon, but he saw no need for urgency: since the shootout, he'd been left pretty much to his own devices. Apparently Stevens thought the killings proved his ability to maintain law and order. Ryan considered it ironic that men had to die before he was judged to be doing his job.

Neither Stevens nor the manservant was in evidence when Sally Palmer let him into the private car. He thought about leaving but changed his mind. The railroader's mistress was not his worry and certainly no reason to walk on eggshells. He decided to wait.

He accepted her offer of a drink, and as she moved to the whiskey cupboard, he seated himself in one of the armchairs. After pouring a stout shot, she returned and halted behind his chair. She leaned forward, holding the glass in front of him. Her other hand rested lightly on his shoulder.

"Where have you been keeping yourself?"

"Around," he said, taking the glass. "I manage to stay busy."

"You know what they say," she purred. "All work and no play . . ."

"I thought we hashed this out last time."

She leaned closer. Her hands drifted down his chest, and she put her mouth to his ear. Her breath was like warm velvet.

"Foolish man," she whispered. "I told you then it wasn't finished. When I like someone—"

"What the hell's going on here?"

Stevens' voice lashed at them. He slammed the door behind him and strode forward. Sally straightened and took a hasty step back from the chair. She flung an arm at Ryan.

"Blame him!" she declared. "I made him a drink and he grabbed my hands. I was trying to get loose."

Ryan hoisted his glass in a sardonic toast. "Evening, Colonel."

"Well?" Stevens demanded. "Aren't you going to answer the charge?"

"Why bother?" Ryan said, smiling. "You know a fairy tale when you hear one—don't you?"

"Are you telling me she's lying?"

"You be your own judge." Ryan gestured in her direction. "Nobody would ever take that for the look of girlish modesty."

Sally tried to cover her embarrassment with a derisive laugh. Her features only reddened more, and she crossed quickly to Stevens. Her hand gripped his arm.

"Don't believe him, Bob! He got fresh and I just tried—"

Stevens slapped her. The blow was delivered so sharply that her head snapped back. She staggered, blood trickling from her mouth, her eyes round. She looked shocked.

"I should have known," Stevens said hotly. "Once a whore, always a whore!"

"No, honey!" she pleaded. "It's not what you—"

"Go to your room. *Now!* I'll deal with you later."

Sally wavered, slowly turned from him. On the way past she shot Ryan a venomous look. Then, her eyes brimming with tears, she retreated to the bedroom. The door closed with a muted click.

Stevens dropped into a chair. His face was wreathed in a dark scowl and a pulse throbbed in his forehead. There was a moment of oppressive silence as Ryan took a long pull on his drink. Finally, trying for a light touch, he waved his glass.

"Don't fault her too much, Colonel. She just likes to flirt, that's all."

"Indeed?" Stevens snapped. "Am I to understand it's happened before?"

"Would it make any difference if it had?"

"No," Stevens said. "To be frank, I expected it long before this. I knew what she was when I brought her along."

"In that case," Ryan allowed, "you've got no room for complaint. A flirt here and there seems like pretty tame stuff."

"Perhaps," Stevens conceded. "But I didn't call you over here to discuss my personal life. I have an assignment for you."

Ryan permitted himself a smile. "Aren't you afraid the town'll go to hell if I'm away?"

"You'll only be gone two days."

"Whereabouts am I going exactly?"

"Tahlequah," Stevens informed him. "I want you to pay a call on William Ross."

"Oh?" Ryan appeared surprised. "I recollect you told me to steer clear of Ross."

"Necessity dictates otherwise. We're running short of

roadbed ties, and I suspect it's Ross' handiwork. He's not above anything."

"So you want me to negotiate a new delivery schedule?"

"I certainly do," Stevens acknowledged. "First, it was the rain, and now it's the damnable Cherokees. We simply can't afford further delay."

Ryan understood his concern. The rain had finally abated, and the track layers were now within a few miles of Big Cabin Creek. Once there, Stevens would move to lure a vestige of the cattle trade away from Abilene. A steady supply of railbed ties and bridge timber was therefore crucial. And it was obtainable only from the Cherokees.

"You mustn't fail me," Stevens went on. "You have to persuade Ross to live up to his agreement. We must have those ties!"

"Easier said than done," Ryan observed. "What makes you think he'll listen to me?"

"Ross is a pragmatic man. He can use you as a pipeline to me. And vice versa. He'll listen because he doesn't want to lose your . . . services."

Only later that night did Ryan appreciate the irony of it. Lying in his bunk listening to Scullin snore, it occured to him that pragmatism was color-blind. A Cherokee was using him no less than a lily-white railroader.

"Your Colonel Stevens is a fool!"

"I hope that doesn't mean I'm here on a fool's errand."

"Don't bandy words with me, Mr. Ryan."

"Never entered my head. I'm not that good with words."

Ryan had arrived less than an hour ago. He'd been ushered into Ross' study, all the while wondering if Elizabeth was home. After observing the formalities, he had relayed the gist of last night's conversation with Stevens. The reaction was scarcely more than he'd expected.

Seated opposite him, William Ross looked swelled with indignation. His copper complexion was noticeably redder, and his mouth clamped in a tight line. He stared at Ryan with a bemused expression.

"Tell me," he said at length. "Why haven't I heard from you?"

"From me?" Ryan said, genuinely puzzled. "Why'd you expect to hear from me?"

"For one thing, I asked you to carry a message to Stevens. For another, it's been well over a month since I made that request. Simple courtesy would have dictated a reply."

"Stevens wasn't interested in your proposal. I figured it was up to him to tell you so."

"Let me be frank," Ross said in an exasperated tone. "When a week or so passed, it was obvious that Stevens wasn't interested. His failure to communicate that decision was hardly unexpected." He paused and slowly shook his head. "I was very disappointed in you, however. I thought we had an understanding."

Ryan suddenly got the message. In subtle terms, he was being told how the game of diplomacy worked. Delivery on the railbed ties had purposely been delayed. The purpose, aside from impeding construction, was to prompt another visit by him to Tahlequah. So Stevens had been right all along. William Ross would go to great lengths to keep a friend in the enemy camp.

"Next time," Ryan finally replied, "I'll make it my business to keep you informed. As you said, it's nothing more than simple courtesy."

Ross nodded. "Good. I think it will work to everyone's advantage."

"Now"—Ryan cocked his head with an inquisitive smile—"about the ties . . ."

"An oversight that's easily corrected. I'll instruct whoever's reponsible to speed the delivery."

Ross hesitated, fingers steepled in a thoughtful pose. "I understand Stevens has his eye on the Texas cattle trade. Tell me how it's going."

Ryan was quicker this time. He understood that he was being asked to enter into a trade. He would secure Ross' cooperation in exchange for information. And he had no doubt that the crafty old Cherokee knew most of the details anyway.

He told Ross almost everything. What he left out was in deference to the man who paid his wages. He thought Robert Stevens would have approved.

Their discussion drew to a close some minutes later. From Ross' manner it was apparent he had satisfied himself regarding the Katy and the cattle trade. While the financial problems of the railroad had not been mentioned, it was unnecessary to state the obvious. No one had to tell Ross that the Katy was actively seeking a new source of funds.

Toward the end Ryan's thoughts turned to another subject entirely. He waited for Ross to broach the matter of the wild terminus town and the saloon shootout. But there was no reference to the Cherokee father and son now buried alongside a white man. Somewhat gingerly, he finally raised the subject himself.

"You're aware," he said, "that two of your people were killed recently."

"I am," Ross said gravely. "The Light Horse Police keep me very well informed."

There was no need to pursue the statement. Ryan took it as confirmation that the railroad was under constant surveillance. He merely nodded and went on.

"Then you know I'm the one who killed them."

"Yes, I do."

Ross' expression was unreadable. The silence deepened as Ryan waited for him to ask questions, demand the particulars. But the Cherokee sat there, silent and immobile, asking nothing. After a moment Ryan felt obligated to resume.

"I want to explain," he said. "How it happened—and why."

Ross held up a hand. "I require no explanation. I've already been advised of the details."

"Would you mind my asking—"

"Yes, I would," Ross cut him off. "It's not important who advised me. Suffice it to say I am aware of how it happened, and why."

Ryan hesitated, staring at him. "I'd like to hear the verdict. Do you blame me or not?"

"I see no reason to render judgment. That's a matter between you and your conscience."

"What if I said my conscience is clear?"

"As I told you," Ross answered, "I require no explanation. However, you may want to have a talk with Elizabeth."

"Elizabeth?"

"Why do you sound surprised? She's fond of you, and she'd grown to trust you—until this happened."

"Until I killed the boy?"

"Yes," Ross said softly. "As her father, I might offer a suggestion. Give her some rational justification for why it was necessary."

"I appreciate the advice. But I'm not sure I understand it. Why are you so concerned?"

"For the simplest of reasons, Mr. Ryan. Elizabeth is my daughter."

The conversation ended on that note. After a handshake, Ryan walked from the study. He knew he'd been judged by the father, and none too harshly. He wasn't all that certain about the daughter.

He went to look for her.

CHAPTER TWELVE

‑‑‑‑‑‑‑‑‑‑

Stable hands were mucking out the stalls. The interior of the building was dim and musty, ripe with the smell of dung. Outside a late afternoon sun tilted into the westerly quadrant.

Ryan waited near the stables. A house servant had informed him that Elizabeth was off riding. Apparently she was something of a horsewoman and went for a ride every afternoon. Upon hearing that, he'd registered no great surprise. She struck him as someone who would enjoy spirited horses.

South of the stables several horses were grazing in a fenced pasture. Ryan stood with his arms folded over the top rail of the fence, watching them. The horses were clearly blooded stock, with sleek lines and admirable conformation. He thought it very much in keeping with the position and prestige of their owner. Among aristocratic Cherokees, there was none who ranked higher than William Ross. He lacked only a scepter to be king.

Thinking back to their conversation, Ryan was somewhat saddened. In his view William Ross was fighting a losing battle. A valiant effort, with noble ideals, but one that was certain to fail. The forces allied against the Civilized Tribes were too strong, too determined. In a very real sense, the white man held all the cards in a game the Indian was still learning to play. Men such as Ross could postpone the inevitable through diplomacy and transitory political alliances. But delay, even for another generation, would not alter the end result. Eventually the Cherokees, and all the other tribes, would be stripped of sovereignty. Their days of independence were numbered.

Still, as he reflected on it, Ryan couldn't help but admire the Cherokee leader. Ross was a farsighted man of intellect and wisdom. Without question, he saw what the future held for the Five Civilized Tribes. Yet he never flagged in his efforts to outfox Washington and the white power structure. Almost alone, he continued to mobilize the Indians and hammer out a spirit of unity among the tribes. Except for his dogged zeal, his refusal to admit defeat, the battle would have been lost long ago. By sheer force of character, he spurred his people to fight for the next generation.

All of which left Ryan with mixed feelings. His sympathy toward the Indians conflicted with his practical nature. Today, for no apparent reason he'd come very close to forming a private alliance with William Ross. Since it was of no benefit to him, common sense dictated that he should avoid such entanglements. Yet he'd walked a narrow line between his loyalty to Stevens and his affinity with Ross. He wondered why he'd done it, and no ready explanation presented itself. He knew it wasn't conscience, and certainly he was no idealist. So that brought him around to perhaps the only reason that made any sense. He found it difficult to admit that he'd done it for a girl.

Pondering on it, he was tempted to laugh. She had been uppermost in his mind since the day they'd met. Ostensibly, every trip he'd made to Tahlequah had been on railroad business. But beneath a surface of pretext, the underlying reason was of a more personal nature. He wanted to see her, and he had capitalized on every opportunity that brought him to the Cherokee capital. However hard to admit, there seemed no getting around it. Otherwise he wouldn't have waited for nearly an hour like some moonstruck schoolboy and worried all the while about the reception he would receive.

Presently Elizabeth appeared over a low rise of ground. She was riding sidesaddle, and as she approached, Ryan thought she looked more the eastern lady than a young Cherokee. Her clothes were informal, with a short jacket, a pleated skirt, and dark, supple boots. She was bareheaded, her cheeks spanked by the wind.

As she neared the stables, Ryan took a closer look at her mount. A magnificent stallion, the horse was barrel-chested, all sinew and muscle, standing fifteen hands high. His color was blood bay, with black mane and tail, and his hide glistened in the sun like dark blood on polished redwood. She held him to a canter, and he moved with the pride of power, hooves scarcely touching the earth. His nostrils were flared, testing the wind.

Elizabeth reined to a halt before the stables. She glanced at Ryan as he walked forward, and her cheeks seemed to flush even more. Her eyes were curiously impersonal, and she avoided looking directly at him. With casual grace, she dismounted by herself and waited, reins in hand. Ryan tipped his hat, forced himself to smile.

"I admire your taste in horses."

"Thank you," Elizabeth said, not returning his smile. "When did you arrive?"

"A little while ago," Ryan lied. "I had business with your father."

"You're quite the messenger these days."

Her tone stung. There was an edge to her voice just short of sarcasm. Ryan knew he was being rebuffed, and he wasn't sure how to handle it. He tried another smile.

"Truth is, I've been upgraded to negotiator. Stevens sent me down to work out delivery on railroad ties."

"What a shame."

"Beg your pardon?"

"A shame that your construction crews are at work again. We'd hoped the rains would last longer."

"Any more rain and we'd be taking boats, not trains."

"Given the choice, I would much prefer a boat. But then, Cherokees aren't allowed a choice, are they?"

Ryan was saved from a reply. A stable boy hurried outside, and Elizabeth tossed him the reins. The stallion rolled his eyes, prancing sideways, then allowed himself to be led away. An awkward silence was punctured by the thud of his hooves on the stable floor.

"I was thinking—" Ryan stopped and began over. "There's something I'd like to explain to you."

"You owe me no explanation."

"Your father said the same thing. But he wasn't mad at me."

"Nor am I," she said coolly. "I think 'disgust' would be the better term."

"Well, you call it what you want. All I'm trying to do is tell you my side of the story."

"Would it really make a difference?"

"It might," Ryan said earnestly. "You've got nothing to lose by listening."

Elizabeth studied him a moment. "All right," she said. "You can walk me up to the house. I'll listen until we're there."

Ryan fell in beside her. He felt tongue-tied, almost at a loss for words in the face of her anger. But it was a short walk, and he had a lot of explaining to do. He cleared his throat, made a start.

"You blame me for killing the boy, don't you?"

"Should I blame someone else?"

"How about his father?"

She glanced at him, aghast. "You're not serious!"

"Why not?" Ryan countered. "He brought the boy there and he killed a man practically over nothing. The way I look at it, he put the boy in harm's way."

"And that absolves you?"

"No, it doesn't. But it makes it easier to understand what happened."

"What happened requires no understanding. You were simply doing your job, weren't you?"

"Yeah, I was," Ryan said defensively.

"And your job requires you to kill"—her voice dropped, suddenly harsh—"to kill even children."

"Have you asked yourself why?"

"It doesn't matter."

"You're wrong there," Ryan said hotly. "That boy was just about man-size. He had a gun in his hand, and he tried to kill me. He fired first!"

"What did you expect?" she demanded. "He'd just seen you kill his father."

"Who also tried to shoot me!"

"And there was no way to stop him? No way to avoid killing him?"

"None," Ryan said. "He made his play and I had no choice."

"Oh?" Her voice was icy. "Does that mean you chose to kill the boy too?"

"Hell, yes!" Ryan growled. "What was I supposed to do— let him kill me?"

"Why, of course not. That would spoil your record, wouldn't it?"

"What record?"

"Come now, John, don't be modest. I understand you've killed four Cherokees since going to work for the railroad. Or does father and son make it six?"

Ryan gave her a quick, guarded look. "Who told you that?"

"No one you know," she said matter-of-factly. "It's just a rumor I've heard now and again. I hadn't put any faith in it— before."

"But you do now?"

"Yes," she said, staring straight ahead. "I believe every word of it."

"Then I reckon it doesn't matter what I say. You've already got your mind made up."

She stopped abruptly. Her eyes blazing, she turned on him, forcing him to pull up short. Her voice was tinged with scorn.

"You lied to me, John! The first time we met, you told me

you would quit the railroad if it meant policing Indians. Do you remember saying that?"

"Sure I remember, and nothing's changed. I'm not policing Indians."

"Oh, but isn't that a fine distinction. You just kill them, is that it?"

"I kill anyone who tries to kill me. And I don't make excuses for it."

Ryan left her standing there. He strode off toward the stables, calling for his horse. She watched after him a moment, murmuring a low, indelicate curse. Then, slowly, her eyes misted with tears.

She turned and fled into the house.

Some three weeks later the bridge was completed over White Oak Creek. Tom Scullin drove the work gangs relentlessly, starting at dawn the next day. By sundown track had been laid south of the bridge onto a broad expanse of prairie.

Waiting there was Elias Boudinot's town site. Almost two square miles had been fenced off with posts and rough-sawn lumber. Under Cherokee law an individual could claim as much land as he was able to fence and improve. Technically, it was designated his homestead, but there was no limitation on the amount of acreage one man could claim. The law, enacted in a simpler time, had been designed for farmers.

As a Cherokee national, Boudinot was entirely within his rights. The stretch of prairie was situated on unoccupied tribal lands, and his claim, though hardly qualifying as a homestead, was valid. Still, if he had not violated the letter of the law, he had cleverly twisted it in spirit. A sign nailed to a tree identified the site as the town of Vinita. Boudinot had named it after a talented white sculptress who was rumored to be his paramour in distant Washington.

By no small coincidence, the Atlantic and Pacific survey line crossed west to east at this exact spot. While the rival railway was still twenty-five miles short of the juncture, Stevens had taken no chances. He pushed Scullin to span White Oak Creek and thereby disrupt his only competitor.

Boudinot's massive land grab was the icing on the cake, a shrewd and well-orchestrated move. The Atlantic and Pacific would lose a month or more surveying a route around the town site.

Katy representatives had already fanned out through Texas. They carried the message that recently erected loading pens would cut the trail time to railhead by several days. With a bridge over White Oak Creek, the new town site was now being touted as a trade center. Overland freighters, engaged to haul from end-of-track southward, were standing by for the first run into Texas. There the trade goods would be exchanged for cotton and hides and brought back for transshipment to eastern markets. Vinita was already a bright new dot on the map and hardly a day old.

By the second day the town site had assumed a bustling look of permanence. The sporting crowd deserted their shanties up the line and moved bag and baggage to the new railhead. With them came the drifters and the outlaws, a creaking caravan of overland freighters, and the girls who populated Poonville. A tent town sprang up south of White Oak Creek overnight, and it was larger than anything yet seen. Boudinot, for cash in hand, rented lots previously laid out to accommodate the invasion. By nightfall, Vinita was a white settlement deep in the Cherokee Nation.

The existence of a town site had been common knowledge for almost two weeks. Enclosing two thousand acres with sturdy fence had attracted considerable attention. While the work was under way Boudinot had been closely guarded by a squad of Southern Party supporters. Establishment of a town populated with whites left no doubt that he'd cast his lot with the railroad. Opposing forces on the Cherokee council would view it as the supreme betrayal, and another assassination attempt seemed a virtual certainty. He was guarded day and night.

As dusk fell, Boudinot and his followers approached Stevens' private car. Ryan was already stationed there, summoned earlier by Stevens. His orders were to oversee security while Boudinot took supper with the railroader. The dinner was something of a celebration, marking the Káty's first major railhead in Indian Territory. Stevens was determined that the evening would not be marred by unpleasant incident.

Boudinot's followers were already familiar with Ryan. As the man who had saved Boudinot's life, he was something of a celebrity in the Southern Party. Once Boudinot was safely inside, Ryan began posting the men around the car. He stationed them at intervals of ten feet and assigned men to both the front and back doors. Armed with rifles, they were alert and clearly intent on keeping their leader alive. So far as Ryan was concerned, the greater threat was to railroad workers. Anyone who approached the car in the dark risked being shot to ribbons.

The evening progressed without mishap. Sally Palmer joined Stevens and Boudinot and champagne was served. Stevens proposed a toast and they all drank to continued good fortune. At the dinner table there were more toasts, and the conversation was frequently punctuated by laughter. Boudinot, who was something of an actor, treated Sally with the courtly air normally reserved for a lady. She thrived on the attention and failed to notice Stevens' smile.

Outside Ryan could see them through the windows. As the champagne flowed and their laughter grew louder, he wondered if the celebration was premature. Boudinot, who was under a sentence of death, might never live to enjoy his new prosperity. And for all the toasting, Stevens' problems had only just begun. Hostile Cherokees who were willing to kill to protect their land would stop at nothing to halt the railroad. All things considered, the laughter had a false ring to Ryan.

It occurred to him that there would be no celebration in Tahlequah tonight. Elizabeth would no doubt blame him, at least in part, for the new town site. As for William Ross, there was no question that today's events would provoke some sort of drastic action. In Ryan's view it wasn't a matter of whether or not the tribal leader would retaliate. It was only a matter of time and opportunity.

And where it would hurt Stevens most.

CHAPTER THIRTEEN

———————

"Good evening, John."

"Evening, Elizabeth."

Ryan removed his hat and stepped past a servant into the vestibule. Elizabeth stood framed in the doorway of the parlor, hands clasped at her waist. There was an awkward pause as the servant disappeared down the hallway. Then, hat in hand, Ryan crossed the vestibule.

"Sorry for the late hour," he said. "But I need to see your father."

"Doesn't everyone," she replied. "Half the tribal council will be here before the night's out."

"I take it you've heard about Vinita?"

"Yes, of course," she said in a normal voice. "Mr. Boudinot's town site could hardly be called a secret."

"How'd your father take it?"

"Aren't you here to ask him yourself?"

"More or less," Ryan admitted. "Word's out the council went into session today. We're hoping nobody decides to act in haste."

"So you're here with another message, is that it?"

"Yeah, I guess you could say that."

She smiled coolly. "How valuable you've become. Colonel Stevens' eyes and ears in the Indian camp."

Ryan silently conceded the point. Not quite two weeks ago, Stevens and Boudinot had celebrated establishment of the new town site. Since then, the Cherokees had been curiously silent. The track laying went ahead, pushing southward, unmarred by incident or threat. And as yet, no attempt had been made on Elias Boudinot's life.

Then, for no apparent reason, the Cherokee council had been called into session. Earlier in the day, upon hearing the news Stevens had summoned Ryan. Ordered once again to Tahlequah, Ryan had declared it a fool's errand. Still, even as he voiced the objection, he'd known it was a waste of breath. He was being sent not as a peacemaker or with any thought of arranging a truce. He was instead exactly what Elizabeth had termed him: the railroad's eyes and ears. He'd been sent there to gather information.

Now, in the face of her cool anger, he sought another topic of conversation. He wondered what he might say that would restore things between them. At their last meeting she had rebuffed him, severed the relationship. Unless he won her over tonight, he doubted that there would be another chance. Yet for all his resolve, he knew she would not be persuaded easily. She considered him inseparable from the railroad and therefore guilty by association. He saw no simple way around the argument. It was in large measure the truth.

Elizabeth led him into the parlor. Her attitude was polite but distant. She explained that her father was still conferring with council members after spending a day at the Cherokee capital. When, or if, he would be able to see Ryan was open to question. Major David Tappin was expected at any moment.

Once seated, Ryan attempted to steer her onto another subject. He asked about her blood-bay stallion and got a monosyllabic answer. Then, still searching for neutral ground, he inquired as to the source of her father's thoroughbred saddle stock. Her reaction convinced him that it was a futile effort. She stiffened, and her tone was unmistakably crisp.

"You needn't make small talk for my benefit. It won't change anything."

Ryan tried to gauge her mood. "I gather," he said after a moment, "you still hold me responsible for that last shooting."

She averted her eyes. "Why go into it again? We've said all there was to say."

"Maybe so," Ryan said quietly. "But I'd like to think there are other things we could talk about."

"Apart from the railroad, you mean? No, I think not, John. Not anymore."

"Why?" Ryan demanded. "Nothing's any different than the first couple of times I came here."

"I'm different." Her eyes were dark and strangely tormented. "At first I forgot who I was. Who you are."

"And who am I?"

"A *tibo*." Her voice was tinged with sadness. "A white man who works for the railroad."

Ryan gave her a searching look. "Does that make me your enemy? No allowances for anything else?"

Her eyes widened. "Are you so naive? You must know what Stevens and Boudinot intend."

"Nobody's confided in me just yet."

"How convenient! Does that somehow excuse you?"

"Excuse me of what?"

"Working against my father," she said fiercely. "Isn't it obvious that Stevens wants to undermine him—force his resignation?"

"To what purpose?" Ryan pressed her. "Stevens will get his railroad no matter what."

"Perhaps he will," she acknowledged. "But wouldn't it be easier—and quicker—if my father were no longer chief? Or president of the Intertribal Council?"

"You're serious, aren't you? You think Stevens has concocted some elaborate scheme."

"I think he wants Elias Boudinot in—and my father out!"

"Just to speed up the railroad?"

"No!" She spat the word at him. "The railroad is only a

means to an end. The end of the Cherokee Nation! Why won't you see that?"

"And you think Boudinot's the man to get the job done?"

"Why else would he organize a town site? He's forced the issue and ridiculed my father. Forced my father to act!"

Ryan shook his head indulgently. "Maybe Boudinot just wants to get rich. It's not all that odd a motive."

"Do you honestly believe that?"

"I think it's as believable as your version. Stevens just doesn't need a conspiracy like that. Not to build a railroad."

Her voice was barely audible. "Won't you feel foolish when you finally learn the truth."

Elizabeth rose and walked from the room. Staring after her, Ryan realized she'd taken with her the last word. She'd spoken a truth, her truth.

And challenged him to prove it false.

William Ross received him in the study. Upon entering, Ryan was struck by the older man's look of exhaustion. He thought Ross appeared to have aged ten years in the past weeks.

There was no warmth in Ross' greeting. He nodded grimly and motioned Ryan to a chair. Without a word he proceeded to stuff his pipe with tobacco. Then, over the flare of a match, he puffed away for a few moments.

"Forgive me," he said eventually, "but I haven't much time. I'm expecting someone."

"Elizabeth told me."

"Then perhaps you won't mind being brief. It's been a long day."

"And a longer night," Ryan said pleasantly. "From the looks of it, you've still got a ways to go."

Ross ignored the comment. "What brings you here at such a late hour?"

"I have a message from Stevens."

"Do you, indeed?"

The words were spoken around quick spurts of smoke. Puffing furiously, Ross ground the pipe stem between his teeth. His eyes were rimmed with fatigue, but his fiery look indicated he was struggling to control his temper. At last, almost wreathed in smoke, he pulled the pipe from his mouth.

"Very well," he said. "What's the message?"

"Stevens got wind that you called the council into session."

"I made no particular secret of it."

"All the same," Ryan went on, "he's worried you might do something hasty. He thinks it would be to everyone's benefit to arrange a meeting."

"A meeting?"

"Just between you and him. The sooner the better. Wherever you say would suit him fine."

"How accommodating!" Ross snorted. "And what does he suggest we discuss at this meeting?"

"He wants to work out a compromise of some sort."

Ross peered at him owlishly. "I once heard the definition of a white man's compromise."

"Oh?" Ryan said. "What's that?"

"A compromise is when both parties to an agreement feel equally buggered."

Ryan was visibly startled. The crude language was somehow at odds with the man. He thought it revealing that the Cherokee leader, who was normally so dignified, had resorted to a gutter phrase, Whether intentional or not, it indicated the degree of Ross' anger.

"The point being," Ross continued, "a compromise is out of the question. Anything Stevens suggests would not be in the best interests of my people."

"No harm in listening," Ryan insisted. "All it could cost you is a little time."

"Offer declined," Ross said firmly. "Although I will give Stevens credit for audacity. To suggest a compromise after conniving on Boudinot's town site . . ." He paused, shook his head. "Well, you must admit, it takes a certain amount of gall."

"No argument there."

"Shall we move on, then?"

"Beg your pardon?"

"To your next question," Ross chided him. "Stevens wouldn't have sent you all this way merely to request a meeting. What else does he want to know?"

"Now that you mention it"—Ryan smiled, clearly embarrassed—"he told me to find out why you ordered the council into session."

Ross gave him a thoughtful stare. "I suppose it's no real secret. I've asked the council to consider measures which might impede construction of the railroad."

"Impede?" Ryan repeated quizzically. "Are you talking about delaying construction or stopping it?"

"The council has its share of hotheads. They advocate stopping the railroad by whatever means necessary."

"And you?"

"I prefer a more businesslike approach."

"Anything you can talk about?"

"Of course," Ross said easily. "By tomorrow it will be common knowledge anyhow. I intend to raise the tax on cattle to a dollar a head."

Ryan inclined his head in a faint nod. "Won't the other tribes tend to follow suit and raise their taxes?"

"I wouldn't be at all surprised."

"Which means the Texans will go right on trailing to Abilene. Why pay a high tariff just to ship your cows with the Katy?"

"If I were a Texan, I would ask myself that very question."

"Stevens won't like it," Ryan noted. "He's counting on the cattle trade as a source of funds."

"Tell him he'll have to look elsewhere."

"You really think that'll put a crimp in his plans?"

"If it doesn't," Ross said, "then I'll think of something else."

"All right," Ryan said, rising to his feet. "I'll deliver the message."

"One other thing, John."

Ross carefully laid his pipe in an ashtray. He folded his hands on the desktop, staring down as though hesitant to continue. Finally he looked up at Ryan.

"This will be our last visit. I regret to say, you're no longer welcome here."

"Listen, I know Elizabeth—"

"Let me finish," Ross interrupted. "It has nothing to do with Elizabeth. You'll recall I mentioned certain hotheads in the council."

"Yes?"

"Some of them believe I've aided the railroad by my—association with you."

Ryan laughed. "That's pretty farfetched."

"Nonetheless," Ross informed him, "the charge has been made. If I'm to govern effectively, then I've no choice but to put such allegations to rest. I hope you understand."

"Keep the *tibo* at arm's length. Isn't that the gist of it?"

"Yes, it is." Ross smiled ruefully. "A practical man sometimes has to bend before the political wind. I'm genuinely sorry."

Ryan accepted his handshake. Then, aware that there was nothing left to say, he walked to the door. Outside, still somewhat dazed, he proceeded along the hallway. It occurred to him that Elizabeth must have known of her father's decision. And yet in their earlier conversation she'd said nothing. He wondered why.

As he crossed the vestibule, a servant hurried to open the door. Then, abruptly, he stopped short. Major Tappin stepped through the entryway, removing his hat and handing it to the servant. He gave Ryan a jaundiced look.

"We meet again, Mr. Ryan."

"Just passing through, Major."

"Good. I'm pleased to hear it."

Ryan started around him, then turned back. "What's that supposed to mean?"

"I'd think it's obvious. After all, *I* am a peace officer, Mr. Ryan."

"I still don't get your drift."

"Tell me," Tappin said, watching him with undisguised hostility, "killed anyone lately?"

For what seemed a sliver of eternity, their eyes locked.

Then, his expression murderous, Ryan took a grip on his temper. Only a fool allowed himself to be baited on ground of another man's choosing. And Tappin was clearly trying to bait him.

He smiled and stepped through the open door.

CHAPTER FOURTEEN

———◆———

By the middle of June, end-of-track had progressed to within a few miles of Pryor's Creek. The winding tributary lay fifty miles south of the Kansas border, and halfway to Fort Gibson.

The summer heat cloaked the land like a shroud. Track laying, even in the early morning hours, became a grueling and sometimes maddening business. Swarms of flies and mosquitoes fed on the work gangs with a ravenous appetite for blood. Heat and festering insect bites slowed construction to a torturous pace.

Approaching Pryor's Creek, the survey line had been laid three miles west of the Texas Road. The purpose was to avoid an irregular stretch of hilly terrain, and thereby speed construction. Yet the Irish Brigade was forced to slash their way through dense canebrakes, with the ground underfoot like muddy, jungle sloughs. What had originally seemed a good plan gradually evolved into a nightmare of agonizing labor. Everyone cursed the survey crew and the mosquitoes alike.

With all their other problems, the work gangs gave little thought to the Indians. Hardly a day passed without a party of Cherokee horsemen being spotted on a distant hill. But the riders never lingered, and the nearest village was ten miles to the east, on the banks of the Neosho River. Out of sight was out of mind, and the beleaguered workmen ceased to think of the Indians as a threat. The swampy bottomland and a sorching sun became the enemy.

Still, for all the construction delays Robert Stevens was very much aware of the Cherokees. He convened a war council on a muggy evening, not long after Ryan's meeting with Ross. The section chiefs, led by Tom Scullin, trooped into the private car and took seats. Ryan, who had returned from Tahlequah that afternoon, was the last to arrive. He'd made his report earlier, and he already knew that Stevens was in a foul mood. He stood by the door, separating himself from the others.

Stevens waited until the men were settled. Then, in a carefully measured voice he related the details of Ryan's meeting with William Ross. He paused and allowed the news to percolate a few moments. Finally, when no one spoke up, he went on in a somewhat harsher tone.

"The bastard intends to cripple us financially. A dollar a head would sound like a death knell to the Texans."

Scullin cleared his throat. "You think we'd lose the cattle trade, is that it?"

"Hell, yes!" Stevens said roughly. "The other tribes play monkey see, monkey do with the Cherokees. Before it was over, every cow would be taxed three dollars—maybe more!"

Scullin swapped a look with Otis Gunn. The engineer glumly shook his head, obviously disturbed. His gaze shifted to Stevens.

"Is there any way we could reason with Ross? Maybe he could be persuaded to withdraw this plan."

Stevens gestured toward the rear of the room. "How about it, John? You're the one who spoke with Ross. Will reason work?"

The other men turned in their chairs. Ryan stared back at them and was all too aware that he'd been put on the spot. He was also aware of the answer Stevens expected. Yet he saw nothing to be gained by hedging.

"No," he said levelly. "You could talk yourself blue in the face, and it wouldn't matter. Ross won't budge."

Stevens arched one eyebrow. "While you're at it, give the boys the benefit of your thinking. How far would Ross go to stop us?"

Ryan's face was impassive. He wrestled with himself a moment, then shrugged. "I think he'll go the limit. Whatever it takes, that's what he'll do."

"Thank you, John."

Stevens took a furled map off a nearby table. Holding it overhead, he stopped before the seated men. His mouth curled in an odd smile as he let the map drop open. In the lamplight was revealed a large-scale rendering of the Cherokee Nation.

"Here's how we deal with William Ross!"

Tracing an inked line on the map, Stevens' smile turned to a smug grin. His finger skirted Tahlequah, then leaped past Fort Gibson to the Arkansas River. His eyes blazed with excitement.

"We're going to bypass Ross and his damned Cherokees! We'll lay track on a beeline to the Creek Nation."

"God's blood!" Scullin protested. "Are you sayin' you mean to bypass Fort Gibson?"

The question claimed everyone's attention like a clap of thunder. Fort Gibson, apart from being a key military post, was the only white settlement in the Cherokee Nation. To bypass it seemed unthinkable, perhaps impossible.

Stevens uttered a low, gloating laugh. "We'll leave the Cherokees high and dry. Their one and only railhead will be Boudinot's town site—Vinita!"

"Jesus," Scullin muttered. "I'd think the army might take a different view. They'll not appreciate being tossed aside so lightly."

"I intend to discuss that very thing with General Sherman."

Stevens grinned and stuck his thumbs in his vest. The men stared at him with a look normally reserved for sword swallowers and magicians. At length Scullin managed to recover his voice.

"And where would you be seein' the General?"

"Fort Gibson," Stevens said. "He arrived yesterday."

"Well now, that is a piece of news. Do you think he'll actually go for your idea?"

"What I intend to propose will be to everyone's benefit, including the Army. I think General Sherman will approve it quite readily."

At the rear of the room, Ryan looked on with a grudging sense of admiration. He thought Stevens had all the moral scruples of a hungry spider. Yet there was no denying the man's cunning and his commitment to a vision. The railroad would be built despite all obstacles. There was simply no stopping it.

Still, the irony of the situation was not lost on Ryan. Bypassing Fort Gibson might well be viewed as a mixed blessing. For William Ross and his supporters were about to see a dream partially realized.

The Katy would make only one stop in the Cherokee Nation.

At dawn Stevens and Ryan departed for Fort Gibson. They traveled by horseback, and their route generally followed the Texas Road. Ryan, as he had before, acted as bodyguard and guide. He rode with his shotgun laid across the saddle.

Stevens was in a talkative mood. He dwelled at length on a plan he'd formulated overnight. At Three Forks, where the major rivers of Indian Territory converged, he would build a sprawling railhead. There, without interference from the Cherokees, he would construct as well a vast complex of shipping pens. All of which placed him even closer to the Texans and their herds of longhorns. The cattle trade would still fall to the Katy, although a bit later than he'd calculated. In so many words he congratulated himself on turning adversity to advantage.

Ryan marked again the voice of an ambitious man. He'd always considered such men to possess an equal mix of arrogance and pride. He understood them as well as their motives. Ryan realized that to a lesser degree he had many of the same traits. He took pride in his work, prided himself on being better at it than most men. And there was a certain arrogance involved when he bet his life that he could outwit— or outshoot—robbers and killers.

Ryan was disturbed by these similarities. Yet in the end he believed there was an essential difference between himself and Robert Stevens. He was content with the respect of other men and the satisfaction of a job well done. Stevens was driven to build empires and would never know contentment. His reach would forever exceed his grasp.

They rode into Fort Gibson just before sundown. Several such garrisons, built following the Civil War, were scattered across Indian Territory. Part of a containment strategy, the purpose of these outposts was to hold hostiles such as the Kiowas and Comanches within established boundaries. Generally manned by cavalry with supportive infantry units, the forts were crude wilderness bastions. No one lived well, or comfortably, serving on the frontier.

General of the Army William Tecumseh Sherman had appropriated the post commander's office. An aide-de-camp ushered Stevens and Ryan through the door with starchy formality. Sherman rose and came around the desk, his hand outstretched. He and Stevens traveled the same circles in Washington and neither of them was a stranger to the White House. Their handshake was cordial, almost fraternal.

Watching them, Ryan's first impression of the General was one of surprise. Sherman was a stocky bulldog of a man, rather short in stature. His face was square and pugnacious, covered by a wiry beard, and there was a rocklike simplicity in his manner. His badly fitting tunic gave him a curiously unmilitary appearance. Yet his piercing eyes and commanding presence left little doubt as to who or what he was.

The Plains Tribes called him the Great Warrior Sherman and the sobriquet aptly suited the man. Sherman had led the legendary Union march through Georgia, which split the Confederacy and hastened the end of the Civil War. His peacetime command was at first the Division of the Missouri, which embraced the Great Plains. Then he had been appointed General of the Army and ordered to "pacify" the hostile tribes. Blunt and brutally practical, his instructions to his cavalry commanders were typical of the man. "The more Indians we kill this year, the less will have to be killed the next. . . ."

The Bureau of Indian Affairs branded his policies as genocide. Sherman simply labeled the bureaucrats "rosewater dreamers" and went about his business with total indifference to public opinion. Sherman argued that the Army's duty was to protect American citizens and not nomadic savages. The current U.S. President and Sherman's former commander, Ulysses S. Grant, sympathized with the view. Sherman operated with the ruthless tactics of a soldier bent on destroying an enemy army.

Sherman's fame had only recently gone up another notch. A band of Kiowas and Comanches had gone on a bloody rampage through Texas, and Sherman had assumed personal command of their pursuit and capture. The upshot was several dead Indians and their leaders sentenced to life in prison. Wholly in character, Sherman had urged that the leaders be hanged in the most expeditious manner. Afterward, he'd undertaken a tour of frontier outposts which brought him to Fort Gibson.

Intrigued by the General, Ryan was a rapt observer as the discussion got under way. It occurred to him that Sherman and Stevens were very much birds of a feather. Both men were obsessed by their own visions of the future, and their ambition, by any yardstick, was remarkable. Moreover, they shared a mutual trait that bonded them like brothers. Their contempt for Indians was absolute and immutable.

As the conversation progressed, Ryan sensed that Stevens was employing verbal sleight of hand. The railroader first recounted all his previous difficulties with the Cherokees. Then he elaborated on William Ross' latest ploy to undermine the Katy. From there, he raised the specter of what would happen if the Katy folded and the Five Civilized Tribes prevailed. He underscored the logistical threat to the Army if rails could not be laid through Indian Territory and on into Texas. On that patriotic note, he concluded, awaiting a reaction.

Sherman gave him a hard, wise look. "You've made your case, Bob. Suppose you tell me what it is you want—specifically?"

"For several reasons," Stevens said forcefully, "I want your permission to bypass Fort Gibson."

"Forget several," Sherman growled. "Give me *one* good reason."

Stevens leaned forward, very earnest now. "The Cherokees are the greatest single threat to western settlement. William Ross, by his high-handed manner, sets a bad example for all tribes. And it's an example that breeds resistance and encourages hostility. He has to be stopped!"

"Not a bad argument," Sherman said slowly. "A bit overstated but still fairly believable. So how do I justify bypassing one of my key forts? How does that put the quietus on Ross?"

"It bypasses him!" Stevens said triumphantly. "We leave Ross and his Cherokees to wither on the vine. No railheads, no towns, no money pouring in! The other tribes will see the light soon enough."

Sherman mulled it over a moment. When he finally spoke, his tone was calculating and military. "How would you adjust the survey line? Keep in mind it has to be done with no detriment to the Army. We're still a long way from pacifying the hostiles."

Stevens popped out of his chair. He moved to a large operations map mounted on the wall. With his finger he traced a line from the present end-of-track to a stretch of high ground situated above Three Forks. He rapped the spot with his knuckles.

"There!" he thundered. "On that spot I'll build you a railhead and supply depot bigger than you ever imagined. We'll centralize all military shipments"—his finger skipped westward on the map—"supplying Fort Sill as well as the Texas posts. It will be the hub of military operations!"

Sherman's eyes crinkled with what passed for a smile.

"By jingo!" he said. "That's a sound plan. You've just cut my logistics problem by half."

"Then you'll approve the new survey line?"

"Well"—Sherman hesitated, gave him a conspiratorial look—"one of my commanders won't be too happy. What you're proposing pretty much consigns Fort Gibson to the ash heap."

"And the Cherokee Nation!" Stevens added with vinegary satisfaction. "William Ross will have no more influence than a toadstool. He'll be silenced!"

"So he will," Sherman agreed. "All right, Bob, get to it. I approve."

Ryan knew he'd just witnessed a turning point in the railroad's fortunes. His thought was borne out not quite two weeks later. On June 28, with the bridge completed, track was laid over Pryor's Creek. The drive was on to the Creek Nation.

Looking back, Ryan was no less impressed by the meeting with Sherman. Yet even as the rails extended southward, a vestige of doubt still remained. Stevens' words had seemed too optimistic, almost overconfident. Ryan was certain that they hadn't heard the last of William Ross.

Or the Cherokee assassins.

CHAPTER FIFTEEN

━━⊶ ⊷━━

Ryan was bored. To him, idleness was all but intolerable, and there suddenly seemed no need for the services of a special agent. He found himself with time on his hands.

One reason was the relative quiet that had settled over the Cherokees. By imposing a stiffer cattle tax, William Ross had apparently stilled his opposition. The tribal council, after approving the measure, appeared to be awaiting some counter-move by the railroad. As yet, of course, no one knew of the decision to bypass Fort Gibson. The Cherokees were sure to retaliate in some fashion when it became public knowledge. But for now neither side seemed in a rush to provoke the other.

Apart from the Cherokees, there was still another reason for the period of calm. The work gangs were now laying track seven days a week. There had been no respite and therefore no opportunity for a tent town to spring up around end-of-track. As a result the sporting crowd hadn't moved forward from Vinita. The absence of whiskey and whores in particular seemed to have put a damper on violence. After dark the railroad camp was quiet as a church, and almost as peaceful. No one had the time, or the energy, to hunt trouble.

For Ryan it was sheer tedium. He tried to stay busy by following a normal routine. Morning and afternoon he scouted ahead of the track-laying crews but found nothing to report. He silently prowled the camp at night but was aware that the effort was largely wasted. With time to spare his thoughts dwelled more and more on Elizabeth and her distant attitude. He brooded on the obstacles separating them and gradually worked himself into a disgruntled state of mind. His temper grew even shorter when he was forced to admit an uncomfortable truth. However hard he tried, he was unable to forget her.

A reprieve of sorts came three days after track had been laid across Pryor's Creek. Stevens sent for him shortly before suppertime. He found a meeting underway at the private car. Otis Gunn, the chief engineer, and George Walker, head of the survey crew, were huddled around a map with Stevens.

Sally Palmer intercepted him as he entered. She was wearing a low-cut gown that was almost an exact match for her china-blue eyes. Unwittingly, she put a hand to her hair, patting a stray curl. It occurred to him that her vanity was curiously inward. She resembled a cat admiring itself in a mirror. She smiled and offered him a drink, and he was aware that he'd arrived sooner than expected. She was attempting to distract him until the meeting ended. He politely declined the drink.

Looking around, Stevens rather abruptly ended the meeting. He rolled up the map and turned from the table with the other two men. Gunn and Walker seated themselves, and Stevens motioned Ryan forward. His manner seemed almost jolly.

"Evening, John," he said, smiling. "Hope I didn't pull you away from supper."

"It'll keep till later."

"Good. Have a seat, join us."

Ryan lowered himself into an armchair. Gunn and Walker bobbed their heads in greeting, all smiles. Some inner voice warned him that things were not as they appeared. The pleasantries and the smiles, particularly on Stevens' part, were overdone. There was a strong scent of snake oil in the air.

"I need your help," Stevens went on. "You're familiar with Colbert's Ferry, aren't you?"

"I've been there," Ryan acknowledged.

"Are you acquainted with Ben Colbert?"

"Only in passing."

"What does that mean?"

"Couple of years ago I was on the trail of a whiskey smuggler. I stopped overnight at Colbert's place."

"Did he know you were a marshal?"

Ryan shook his head. "I never went out of my way to advertise the fact. Indians tend to get closemouthed when they know they're talking to the law."

"So it's true, then?" Stevens asked. "Colbert really is part Chickasaw?"

"No, not part," Ryan said. "He's a full-blood."

The Chickasaw Nation lay at the extreme southwestern boundary of Indian Territory. Ben Colbert was something of a backwoods businessman who operated a ferry across the Red River. Apart from natural fords, it was the only way back and forth between Texas and the Nations. Colbert's name was known all along the frontier.

"Since you've met him," Stevens continued, "let me ask your opinion. Would you consider him a shrewd trader?"

"Hard to say," Ryan allowed. "I only met him the one time."

"Is he an educated Indian?"

"Not to hear him talk."

"Do you think he'd remember you?"

"Probably not. Lots of people pass through there every day."

"I see."

Stevens exchanged a look with Gunn and Walker. Then, still smiling, he glanced back at Ryan.

"I'm sending Otis down to have a talk with Colbert. I'd like you to act as his guide."

"We've had this conversation before."

"I know," Stevens conceded. "But for the most part you'll be traveling outside the Cherokee Nation. There shouldn't be any trouble this time."

"I seem to recall that's what you said last time. And I ended up killing two men."

"Which we all regret," Stevens said with exaggerated gravity. "Suppose I threw in a bonus—say five hundred dollars. Would that change your mind?"

"Why so much," Ryan said skeptically, "if you're not expecting trouble?"

"To insure your discretion. You and Otis will be traveling incognito."

"You'll have to spell that out."

"For the time being, we want Colbert kept in the dark. There's to be no mention of your association with the railroad."

"Why not?"

"Everything will become obvious once you're at Colbert's Ferry. Until then, let's just say it's privileged information."

Stevens paused, nodding to himself with a cryptic smile. Ryan was confused, but he'd long since ceased being surprised by the railroader's convoluted schemes. The man was like a Chinese box, a puzzle within a puzzle.

"Trust me for now," Stevens insisted. "You won't regret it. You have my word."

Ryan shifted his gaze to Otis Gunn. He stared hard at the engineer a moment. "How about it, Otis?" he said at length. "Any chance I'll regret it?"

"Not on my account," Gunn said with a weak smile. "We're going there to talk, nothing more."

Ryan mulled it over awhile. Then, finally, he shrugged. "All right," he said. "I could use a change of scenery anyway."

"Excellent!" Stevens said, grinning. "I knew you wouldn't let me down, John."

Sally Palmer walked forward, joining the men. She caught Ryan's eye for an instant, then looked quickly away. There was a trace of amusement hidden in her expression. And that, more than anything else, bothered Ryan.

He wondered if he'd been snookered again.

The water appeared dark against the washed blue of a plains sky. A massive ferryboat stood docked on the north bank of the river. Above it, dotting the shoreline, were the outbuildings of Colbert's Ferry.

Ryan, with Otis Gunn at his side, rode into the compound about midafternoon. Their trip had consumed four days, traversing the lands of the Creeks, Choctaws, and Chickasaws. The Texas Road, which angled southwestward through the Nations, brought them directly to the ferry landing. On the opposite side the Texas shoreline provided a backdrop for the Red River.

Grimy with trail dust, Ryan and Gunn passed themselves off as butt-sore travelers. They found Ben Colbert on the porch of the main house. He was a grizzled character, with a broad, good-humored face and a shock of white hair. His jaw was stuffed with tobacco and a quart of whiskey rested beside his chair. He informed them that he was now a man of leisure and the overseer of the operation. A gaggle of relatives attended to running the ferry.

Gunn engaged the old man in conversation. With little prompting, Colbert drifted off into a recollection of days past. In 1858, with hardly a nickel to his name, he'd obtained a tribal license to operate a ferry. At the same time he had claimed a Chickasaw head right of several hundred acres. The land included a wide stretch of river frontage and fanned out northward from his homestead.

The venture had prospered from the outset. Wagon trains loaded with heavy freight were ferried back and forth. The Butterfield Stage Line, with coaches operating between Missouri and Texas, used the ferry on a regular basis. Before long a small town appeared on the Texas side directly above the ferry landing. The inhabitants grandly named it Red River City, even though its principal commerce was the sale of rotgut whiskey.

And through it all, like a link in a chain, the ferry remained the connecting tie between Texas and Indian Territory.

"Bad times or good," Colbert concluded, "everybody needs a way across the river. I've done right well for myself over the years."

"You surely have," Gunn beamed. "Tell you the truth, I'm surprised you don't have competition. How come another ferry never got started?"

Colbert squirted a jet of tobacco juice over the edge of the porch. He wiped his mouth and let go a wheezy chuckle. "Only one license ever gonna be granted, and that's mine. I got blood kin on the Chickasaw council."

"Just the same, you have a real moneymaker here. I'd imagine lots of people have tried to buy you out."

"Not so many. Even then, most of 'em tried to steal it. Figgered me for one of them ignorant Injuns."

"Their mistake," Gunn said, his voice bland as butter. "If you'd been offered a fair price—who knows? You might very well have been tempted."

Colbert cocked his head, appraising the other man with a crafty look. "You talk like you got somethin' on your mind. Whyn't you toss 'er out and let's have a look-see?"

Gunn gave him a slow nod. "My partner and I," he said, gesturing at Ryan, "like the looks of your operation. We might just make you an offer to buy it, lock, stock, and barrel."

Colbert shifted his quid to the off cheek. "You talkin' about the land too?"

"I certainly am. We'd want the land, the house—everything."

"You're out of luck, then. A Chickasaw can't sell land to a white man. Only thing for sale is the ferryboat license."

"Not necessarily," Gunn said cautiously. "I've heard there are ways around tribal laws."

"Yeah, there are," Colbert said with a lopsided smile. "If you're willin' to marry yourself a Chickasaw woman."

"If not me," Gunn advised him, "then one of my associates. We can always find a man who's eligible and willing."

Colbert chortled out loud. "You're serious, aren't you? You come here to talk a deal!"

"I'll do more than talk, Mr. Colbert. I'm prepared to put my money where my mouth is."

Colbert turned out to be a shrewd haggler. After an hour or so of hard bargaining, they finally struck a deal. The figure agreed upon included Colbert's land, all the buildings, and the ferry. Only one item in the negotiations remained tentative. Gunn would have to arrange for a bridegroom before the deal could be finalized.

Some while later the conversation ended with a round of handshakes. Gunn and Ryan collected their horses and rode back the way they'd come. A short distance up the road, Ryan finally succumbed to curiosity. He fixed the engineer with a thoughtful stare.

"It's his land you're after and not the ferry, or did I miss something?"

"No, you're right, it's the land. The Katy certainly doesn't need a ferryboat."

"What's so important about his land?"

Gunn laughed heartily. "A small fortune, John. Some might even call it a bonanza."

As they rode, Gunn briefly explained the details. Stevens' goal was to secure large tracts of land on both sides of the river wherever the Katy crossed the Red. The arrangement would be kept secret until all the railroad's plans were completed. To that end three different survey lines would be run to the river. No one would know where the Katy actually intended to cross until it happened.

"I don't get it," Ryan said when he finished. "Why three survey lines?"

"Town sites!" Gunn announced. "We'll run one line upriver to Preston. Another will be downriver, somewhere around Sherman. And the third to Colbert's Ferry."

"Then you'll play one off against the other, Sherman against Preston, is that the idea?"

"On the button," Gunn admitted. "Whoever makes the

most land available, that's where we'll cross the Red River. We intend to sell a world of town lots."

Ryan gave him the same disquieting stare. "So your offer to Colbert wasn't legitimate. You're just hedging your bet?"

"Colbert's Ferry is our ace in the hole. If things fall through elsewhere, we've always got Colbert on tap. Not to mention Red River City."

"What about it?"

"We could buy the whole town dirt cheap—and own both sides of the river!"

"Why not do it, then?"

"We want to create a boomtown atmosphere. And that's easier done where a town already exists. Preston or Sherman, either one would do very nicely."

Ryan shook his head. "Stevens must've lost a lot of sleep figuring that out."

"Never underestimate him, John. He's as shrewd as they come."

"And tricky too."

"I beg your pardon?"

"Nothin'," Ryan said. "Just thinking out loud."

Gunn gave him a funny look. "Well anyway, we're on the verge of something great. And you're part of it, John! Just think of that."

"I am thinking. All the time."

Ryan's thoughts would have surprised Gunn. He felt no triumph in the railroad's progress, only sympathy for the old Chickasaw. One way or another, he told himself, Ben Colbert was out of business. Whether the railroad crossed at Colbert's landing or elsewhere was immaterial. Ferryboats were about to become a thing of the past. Ryan understood that Colbert's only hope was Gunn's ace in the hole: a breakdown in negotiations with all the other towns along the river, which would leave the railroad no choice but to cross at Colbert's Ferry.

Ryan silently cast his own vote for the old Chickasaw.

CHAPTER SIXTEEN

A searing midday sun beat down on the work gangs. Graders cursed their mules while laborers wrestled railroad ties into place on the roadbed. The men's faces were streaked with a mixture of sweat and choking dust.

Ryan rode past on his horse. The morning, like so many other mornings, had been spent scouting ahead of the construction site. As he'd come to expect, there was nothing out of the ordinary, no sign of trouble. He hadn't seen a Cherokee for the last three days.

The grind of a daily routine was again starting to wear on him. Over a week had passed since his return from Colbert's Ferry. As yet, there was no clue that the railroad was slated to bypass Fort Gibson. Soon enough, however, the tracks would take a sharp turn to the southwest and angle toward Three Forks. Then, without question William Ross and the Cherokees would discover Stevens' plan.

What would happen at that point was anyone's guess. After another tedious morning, Ryan was in no mood to forecast the future. His mind turned instead to the noonday meal as he neared the supply train. He was contemplating a hot cup of coffee when he spotted Sam Irvin. The marshal stood talking with another white man whose strident voice carried up and down the roadbed. Crowded around them were a half dozen Cherokees, listening intently. All along the tracks, railway workers had paused to watch.

Several things went through Ryan's mind. He wondered what brought Irvin to end-of-track. Even more, he questioned why a deputy U.S. Marshal was traveling in the company of six dour-faced Cherokees and a white man who appeared mad with rage. He wasn't at all sure that he wanted to hear the reasons.

Approaching them, Ryan inspected the group closely. The white man was lean and rawboned, with shifty eyes and sleek, glistening hair. He wore mule-eared boots and a slouch hat, and strapped around his hip was a Remington pistol. The Cherokees were armed with an assortment of carbines and vintage muskets and appeared ready to take the warpath at any moment. Their features were taut with barely constrained anger.

Ryan dismounted, hitching his horse to the end of a flatcar. As he started forward, the marshal looked around and saw him. Irvin silenced the white man with a gesture and turned away. He hurried along the roadbed, motioning Ryan to stay back. His expression was a mix of disgust and simmering exasperation. He stopped where Ryan waited beside the flatcar.

"Howdy, John."

"Sam." Ryan nodded, cutting his eyes toward the white man. "Who's your friend?"

"Friend, hell!" Irvin grunted. "He's a shiftless no-account by the name of Bud Wilson."

"And the Cherokees?"

"They're relatives. Or maybe in-laws would be better. He was married to a Cherokee woman."

"What do you mean *was*?" Ryan inquired.

"His wife's dead," Irvin replied. "Got herself killed pretty near a week ago."

"Well," Ryan sighed heavily, "I guess I'm going to hear it anyway. So go ahead and tell me. Who killed her?"

Irvin told the story quickly, without frills. Bud Wilson and a Cherokee man, Frank Proctor, were enemies of long standing. A chance meeting in Tahlequah led to an exchange in results, and Proctor pulled a gun. In the ensuing melee, Wilson's wife was mortally wounded while Wilson himself managed to escape unharmed. Proctor was arrested by the Light Horse Police and charged with murder.

"Sounds reasonable to me," Ryan remarked when he had finished. "What's the problem?"

Irvin looked pained. "Proctor goes to court tomorrow. Word leaked out that the charges will be dropped."

"Any truth to it?"

"Who knows?" Irvin said sourly. "But if he is released, I've got a federal warrant for his arrest."

"On what charge?"

"Attempted murder."

"You're joking!"

"Wish I was," Irvin muttered, lowering his eyes. "He killed a Cherokee woman, and it rightly belongs in a Cherokee court. But if he goes free, then it falls in my jurisdiction. His intent was to murder a white man—and that's a federal crime."

Ryan was silent a moment. "How'd you get tangled up with Wilson and his in-laws?"

"Sorry bastard," Irvin swore. "He's worried Proctor will slip loose and run. He tagged along to make sure I get the job done."

"And brought reinforcements just to make double damn sure. Why was he giving you a hard time when I rode up?"

"Hold your hat," Irvin said wearily. "The sonovabitch wants me to deputize him and that bunch of Cherokees. He says I'll need a posse to get Proctor away from the Light Horse."

"You'd be a fool to deputize them."

"Christ, wouldn't I! But that won't stop them from trailing me into the courtroom tomorrow. I'm liable to have a hell of a lot more than I can handle alone."

Ryan stared at him, eyes narrowed. "I've been waiting for you to get around to it."

"Hell, John," Irvin said lamely. "I can't ride herd on Wilson's bunch and the Light Horse and still arrest Proctor. I'm only one man."

"Last time you asked my help, I ended up getting shot at."

Bud Wilson suddenly took a step toward them. His features were flushed, and his voice went up a couple of octaves in an angry shout. "What d'ya say, Marshal? We're tired of coolin' our heels. Is he gonna lend a hand or not?"

Irvin groaned and rolled his eyes. He looked back over his shoulder. "Keep your shirt on, Wilson. I'll be with you in a minute."

"Time's awastin'," Wilson said defiantly. "You let my wife's murderer get away and there'll be hell to pay. I guarantee it!"

"So you keep telling me."

Irvin turned back to Ryan, wagging his head. Wilson and the Cherokees began talking among themselves in low monotones. Watching them, Ryan got an odd sensation about the white man. He looked at the Marshal.

"Lemme ask you something, Sam. You think Wilson's playing with all his marbles?"

"No, I don't," Irvin said crossly. "The man's a goddamn half-wit. Why?"

"Half-wits sometimes go off half-cocked. He's liable to start something you'll have to finish."

"All the more reason I need your help. He'll be in that courtroom tomorrow, no matter what I say. I'd feel easier knowing you've got me covered."

"Hell, why not?" Ryan grinned. "I've got nothing better to do."

"Won't cause you any problem with Colonel Stevens, will it?"

"No problem at all, Sam."

Ryan felt as confident as he sounded. He'd come to the conclusion that Stevens needed him more than he needed the job. Which tended to switch the leverage in their dealings on to his side. The thought made him smile.

Early next morning they rode into Tahlequah. The stores were already open, and the square was crowded with people. Several paused to stare as the armed column rode past.

Marshal Irvin and Ryan, who now wore a badge, were in the lead. Behind them rode Wilson and one of his brothers-in-law. The other family members rode three abreast and two in the rear. All of the Cherokees had their long guns propped against the saddle, muzzles pointed skyward. Their bearing was that of determined men, prepared to fight.

Ryan saw a squad of Light Horse Police up ahead. There were four out front and four in the rear, with a lone civilian sandwiched between. On foot and armed with Spencer lever-action carbines, the Light Horse were escorting the civilian to the courthouse. Ryan figured the man to be Frank Proctor, the accused murderer. He also counted the Light Horse again, puzzled by their number. So many police to guard one man seemed to him a bad sign.

Ryan dismounted before a hitch rack on the street. Looking up, he saw a Light Horse with sergeant's stripes on his sleeves glance in their direction. The sergeant barked a command and hurried the squad and their prisoner up the steps and into the courthouse. A moment later the sergeant and another Light Horse returned, positioning themselves on either side of the door. Behind them, Major David Tappin stepped outside onto the landing. He stood with his hands clasped behind his back.

Irvin mumbled something unintelligible under his breath. He swapped a worried look with Ryan, then moved around the hitch rack. Ryan fell in beside him and they started up the walkway to the courthouse. Bud Wilson and the Cherokees formed a wedge immediately behind them. Passersby on the square watched curiously as the small phalanx of men trooped forward. Irvin halted them at the bottom of the steps. He nodded curtly to Tappin.

"You're blocking my way, Major."

Tappin smiled, a mere baring of his teeth. "We're in Tahlequah, not Fort Smith. What business do you have here today?"

"Frank Proctor," Irvin said. "I understand he's scheduled to appear in court."

"A Cherokee court," Tappin remarked. "On a tribal murder charge. You have no jurisdiction here."

"I do if he's released."

"Why would he be released?"

"Good question," Irvin said flatly. "But if it happens, I've got a federal warrant on him."

"And the charge?"

"Attempted murder." Irvin jerked a thumb over his shoulder. "You know Bud Wilson, don't you?"

Tappin bristled, his eyes dark as slate. "Have you any proof that the shot was meant for Wilson?"

"I only arrest people, Major. Juries decide whether or not there's enough proof."

"The juries in Fort Smith," Tappin said viciously, "always find enough proof when it's an Indian."

"You're entitled to your opinion. All the same, I've got a job to do, and I intend to do it."

"So it appears," Tappin said, indicating the other men. "Quite a show of force, Marshal. Are these your deputies?"

Irvin gave him a dull stare. "Mr. Ryan's been duly sworn. Wilson and the others asked to come along. You might say they're interested parties."

"Too interested," Tappin observed. "How do I know they won't start trouble in the courtroom?"

"It's your courtroom, Major. You're welcome to stop them from going inside."

The Light Horse sergeant stepped away from the door. His face looked as though it had been hewn from rough walnut, with an angular nose and cold, brooding eyes. His thumb was hooked over the hammer of his carbine, finger on the trigger. He stared directly at Wilson.

"Nobody moves," Ryan said with chilling calm. "Major, do yourself a favor. Call the sergeant off."

Tappin gazed down at them a moment. Then he motioned the sergeant to move back beside the door. His eyes finally settled on Ryan.

"You've chosen the wrong side again, Mr. Ryan. It seems to be a habit."

"Some habits are hard to break."

"Are you here under Colonel Stevens' directions?"

"I'm here," Ryan said through clenched teeth, "because the Marshal asked. No other reason."

Tappin's voice was alive with contempt. "Any excuse will do so long as it involves Indians. Is that it?"

"I'm here, and I'm sworn. You make what you want of it."

"One day," Tappin said ominously, "you'll regret this. You have my solemn promise on that, Mr. Ryan."

Tappin wheeled around abruptly and walked into the courthouse. The sergeant and the second Light Horse followed a pace behind. Irvin glanced at Ryan, one eyebrow raised in a questioning look. When Ryan said nothing, the Marshal proceeded up the steps. Ryan and the others trailed him through the door.

They moved along a central corridor inside the courthouse. Halfway down they turned left into the open door of the courtroom. Irvin was in the lead when he suddenly halted, his expression tense. The others crowded in behind him and were jammed together in an aisle between rows of benches. Irvin's tension was contagious, and Ryan went stockstill, his every sense alerted.

An oppressive sense of violence hung over the courtroom. There were no spectators occupying the benches, and the jury box was empty. Frank Proctor, who stood beside his lawyer at the defense table, looked terrified. The prosecutor sat at another table across from them and nervously fanned through a sheaf of papers. The Light Horse Police were spread out between the front row of benches and the defendant. They formed an armed line across the middle of the room.

At the center of the line, Major Tappin was engaged in a one-sided conversation with the Light Horse sergeant. While Tappin talked, the sergeant listened and slowly nodded his head. After a moment Tappin turned, no longer talking, and looked directly at Ryan. The sergeant followed his gaze and both men stared at Ryan. Then the sergeant's eyes became hooded, his face devoid of expression. He nodded once.

Instinct told Ryan he'd been marked for death. He watched as Tappin turned and moved through a door at the rear of the room. Several moments passed, then the door opened and a man attired in a frock coat entered. He walked straight to the judge's bench and stopped in front of a high-backed chair. His gaze shuttled around the courtroom before fixing on Sam Irvin. He glared down at the lawman.

"Marshal Irvin," he intoned, "I order you to remove yourself and those men from my court. If you refuse—"

"*No!*"

Bud Wilson's strangled scream echoed off the walls. He leaped past Irvin, his Remington six-gun extended at arm's length. The pistol roared and Proctor staggered backward into the defense table. He clutched at his throat and blood poured through his fingers. He made an ugly gurgling sound and dropped to the floor. In the next instant gunfire became general throughout the courtroom.

Ryan acted on reflex alone. He saw the Light Horse sergeant's carbine aimed directly at him. Ryan's arm moved like light in a mirror, blurred motion. The Colt appeared in his hand and spat a sheet of flame. The slug impacted beneath the sergeant's breastbone and jerked him sideways. His arms flailed wildly and the carbine slipped from his grasp. He pitched raglike into the front row of benches.

A hail of lead whistled across the room as the Light Horse Police exchanged shots with Wilson and the Cherokees. The ranks of both sides were winnowed as though chopped down by a giant scythe. Three of the Cherokees were hurled backward, splattered with blood. Another dropped, then another, and finally Wilson staggered. He slumped to the floor without a sound.

Only two Light Horse were still standing in the courtroom. The others were sprawled in death or wounded. Sam Irvin and one of the remaining Light Horse fired on each other almost simultaneously. The Light Horse collapsed to his knees and toppled over like a felled tree. Irvin stiffened, a gaping hole blown in his shirtfront, and his eyes went opaque. His knees buckled and he folded at the middle. He fell dead across Wilson's body.

Ryan was vaguely aware that he'd been wounded himself. His shirt was wet and sticky, and there was a faint buzzing in his ears. He turned, drawing a quick bead on the last Light Horse left standing. The man fired, and Ryan felt a burning sensation sear his left arm. He touched the trigger and the Colt bucked in his hand. A whoosh of breath exploded from the Light Horse as he let go of the carbine and clutched his stomach. He took a step sideways, then slowly pitched forward on his face.

There was an instant of tomblike silence. Through a haze of gunsmoke, Ryan sensed all around him the carnage of a bloodbath. He realized for the first time that the judge and the defense attorney were down. A moan caught his attention, and he saw the prosecutor sitting beside the jury box, cradling a shattered arm. It came to him that no one was left on his feet. He was standing alone.

His vision suddenly dimmed. The stench of death mixed with the sweet smell of blood was overpowering. The courtroom blurred before his eyes and the gun dropped from his hand. Slowly, all feeling gone, he folded to the floor. He lay perfectly still.

CHAPTER SEVENTEEN

———❦———

The toll from the courtroom shootout was eleven killed and eight critically wounded. Among the list of dead were the judge, the defendant and his attorney, and Bud Wilson. The Cherokees filed a formal protest with Washington, which was studiously ignored. The death of deputy U.S. Marshal Sam Irvin apparently balanced out against five dead Light Horse. No federal warrants were issued on the Cherokee survivors.

Nor were any federal charges preferred against Ryan. He'd been a duly sworn officer of the federal court at the time of the shootout. His actions were in the discharge of duty and therefore both legal and defensible. Because he was white, the Cherokee Nation was unable to prefer charges of any nature. But there was little doubt that he'd been judged and found guilty by certain factions within the tribe. For all practical purposes, he was under a sentence of death.

Grievously wounded, Ryan had barely survived the shootout itself. At William Ross' order, he'd been tended for several days by a Cherokee physician. A bullet had been removed from his side, and only after forty-eight hours had the danger of infection been dismissed. The wound in his left arm, which passed clean through, had presented no complications.

Three days after the shootout, he had been moved by wagon to end-of-track. There, under the watchful eye of Tom Scullin, he'd been nursed back to health by the camp's cooks.

On July 20 end-of-track crossed the northern border of the Creek Nation. The Katy was now sixty miles deep in Indian Territory, roughly a third of the way to the Red River. Texas and the Great Southwest no longer seemed a pipe dream.

Robert Stevens and his section chiefs breathed a collective sigh of relief. Behind them lay the land of the Cherokees and nearly five months of bitter strife. Bypassing Fort Gibson would surely provoke some act of reprisal from William Ross. Yet there had been a curious silence out of Tahlequah and the Cherokee council. No one believed it would last indefinitely.

Still, there was a sense of deliverance throughout the camp. The lowliest track layer was aware that a crisis had been averted. While the Creeks were by no means allies, they were notably less antagonistic toward white men. The Creeks were perhaps more fatalistic than the Cherokees. The iron horse was treated somewhat like a natural disaster: regrettable but unavoidable. The tribal council effectively turned a blind eye to the railroad.

The Creek Nation represented a personal haven for John Ryan as the long weeks of his convalescence passed. At first, while confined to his bunk he'd had plenty of time to reflect on the shootout. His principal regret centered around the death of Sam Irvin. He had genuinely liked the lawman, and he felt somehow diminished by the passing of a friend. There was, as well, an idle thought that his presence might have jinxed the entire courtroom affair.

Violence seemed to have followed wherever he went since he first arrived in Indian Territory. Looking back on the men he'd killed—which now included two Light Horse—he began thinking of his job as a sort of death work. He was the lightning rod that drew the Cherokees' fire almost as if he'd been destined to attract violence and death. And he wondered if it had been Irvin's misfortune to share his ill luck.

Lying in his bunk, he had brooded about it for several

days. Whether or not his luck had rubbed off on Irvin would remain an unknown. But there was no question that he'd spent too much time on the killing ground. Nor was it entirely happenstance that the men he'd killed over the past several months were Cherokee. The tribe he admired most seemed somehow slated to be his deadly antagonist.

However much he pondered on the problem, the reason eluded him. There was no explanation for why he and the Cherokees had been brought to a common killing ground. But all his pondering led to a seed of thought that slowly took root. As though drawn to it, he had years ago chosen a line of work that dealt largely with death. Now with newfound clarity, he saw something he'd been blinded to in the past. Despite the best of intentions, death work was too often indiscriminate. The man who performed it was seldom given choices. He killed almost by random lot, for by the nature of his work he killed anyone who tried to kill him.

In that respect, there was still a score to be settled. Ryan knew that the courtroom shootout and the death of the Light Horse sergeant had changed nothing. Major David Tappin had personally marked him for death, and the sentence would not be withdrawn. There was no court of last resort, no appeal. Tappin would simply pick another executioner, and if he failed, then another, until the job was done. To save himself, Ryan would have no option but to respond in kind. He would have to kill Tappin.

Oddly, the thought of killing always brought to mind Elizabeth. He had entertained the notion that she might visit him after the courtroom shootout. While he was under the care of the Cherokee doctor, he'd finally come to his senses. She wouldn't look in on him or inquire about his condition, and she had an excellent reason. Of the eleven dead men, nine were Cherokee, all of them her people. She would assign at least part of the blame to him, and no explanation would alter the judgment. In a sense, the Tahlequah courtroom had been his last bridge. And he'd burned it to a cinder.

The realization gave Ryan some long and restless nights. Still, for all his regrets he was not a man to dwell on the past.

By the third week of his recovery, he was able to hobble around on a cane, and he was getting restless. Tom Scullin, returning one night to the bunk car they shared, found him cleaning his guns. The Irishman shook his head with a look of amusement.

"By all the saints! What d'ya think you're about here?"

"Just what it looks like. I'm cleaning a shotgun."

"Are you daft?" Scullin rumbled. "You're not yet mended!"

Ryan ran a swab through the off-hand barrel of the scattergun. He held the open breech to the lamplight and peered down the bore. Satisfied, he began swabbing the other barrel.

"You'd make a hell of a wet nurse, Tom. Only you're not exactly built for it."

Scullin huffed indignantly. "Full of piss and vinegar, aren't you?"

"I've felt worse," Ryan commented. "And you can stop treating me like I'm an invalid. I threw the cane away today."

"Did you now? I suppose you'll tell me next you're ready to start work?"

Ryan smiled. "You must be a mind reader."

"God's teeth!" Scullin rumbled. "We've not had a speck of trouble since you were shot. What's the rush?"

"I figure it's time I earned my keep. Besides, I'm tired of you hovering over me like a mother hen."

"You're an ingrate, John Ryan. And a poor excuse for an Irishman too!"

Ryan inspected the bore against the light. Then he snapped the breech closed and leaned the shotgun in a corner. He finally looked up at Scullin.

"Tomorrow"—he paused, grinning—"I think I'll ride out and scout around. What do you say to that?"

"Jesus, Mary, and Joseph!"

Toward the end of August, the railroad reached Three Forks. The track stopped on the north bank of the Verdigris River, awaiting a bridge. But the delay was momentary and lasted only one night.

Scullin and his work gangs forded the stream early next

morning. Behind them a caravan of wagons hauled construction supplies to the opposite shore. By noontime the graders
had started a roadbed and the track crews were hard at work.
Not quite four miles ahead lay the Arkansas River.

From the Verdigris crossing point, the muddy stream curved
south to mingle with the Arkansas and the Neosho. The con-
fluence of these three great rivers, along with the stretch of
land between the Verdigris and the Arkansas, was the famed
Three Forks. A small Creek settlement located where the
waters met served as the tribal headquarters. The area had
been the commercial hub of Indian Territory scarcely four
decades ago.

Keelboats and shallow-draft paddle-wheelers plied upriver
to the landing at Three Forks in the 1830s. Vast shipments
of baled furs were assembled at Chouteau's Trading Post.
Boatloads of the valuable cargo were transported downriver
to New Orleans and eventually to the fur market in St. Louis.
At the time Sam Houston, who later led Texas to independence, lived in a wilderness area near Three Forks. His log
cabin, which he called Wigwam Neosho, was a gathering
place for officers stationed at Fort Gibson.

Three Forks had fallen on lean times with the decline of
the fur trade. But there was a new explosion of activity with
the arrival of the Katy. A terminus, which was quickly dubbed
Gibson Station, was located on high ground north of the Verdigris crossing. The station depot was completed, and daily
passenger service began operating between Kansas and Indian Territory. Track sidings and a turntable were installed,
and shortly afterward loading pens were erected to serve the
cattle trade. The first herd of longhorns trailed in from Texas
a week later.

The freight of military and civilian goods further intensified the boom. Army detachments hacked a wagon road
through the wilderness from Fort Gibson to the terminus.
Caravans from Overland Transit, which had obtained the contract for hauling government supplies, began departing with
quartermaster stores and Indian allotments for transhipment
throughout the Southwest. Towns in northern Texas were also

quick to take advantage of the new railhead. From the south long wagon trains bulging with cotton were soon strung out along the trail between Gibson Station and the Red River.

A hastily constructed warehouse was packed to overflowing within days of being built. Mountains of freight, awaiting available wagons, lay stacked in the rail yard and along the tracks. Almost five hundred tons of materials were offloaded for transshipment to military posts in Indian Territory and Texas in a matter of weeks. Swamped by the flood of supplies, Overland Transit scarcely put a dent in the massive piles at end-of-track. The problem quickly added to the already herculean task of organizing and policing a wilderness settlement.

Spanning the barriers of the Verdigris and Arkansas rivers was expected to delay railroad construction for several months. As a result Gibson Station was designated the Katy's base of operations and main supply depot. Trainloads of construction materials were brought down from Pryor's Creek and dumped beside the mounds of government goods. Following close behind was the sporting crowd from Elias Boudinot's town site. Gamblers and saloonkeepers, whores and grifters simply packed up and deserted the Cherokee Nation en masse.

Gibson Station began to take on a look of permanence within a fortnight. A tent town of more than fifty structures sprang to life around the depot. The ladies of Poonville opened for business, and raucous music blasted from a row of dance halls and saloons. Texas cowhands and outlaws, along with the usual assortment of cardsharps and footloose wanderers were thrown together with the roughnecks of Scullin's Irish Brigade. Added to this volatile mix was a new element: full-bloods and breeds who were drawn to the hurdy-gurdy boomtown. The Creeks, unlike the Cherokees, evidenced a great curiosity about the white man's ways.

Gibson Station was like an elixir to Ryan. By now completely recovered, he needed a stimulant, some new challenge to seize his interest. He quickly laid out rules of conduct for the sporting crowd as he had at previous railheads. Word spread that gunplay and mayhem would not be tolerated by the Katy's special agent. His reputation alone, which had been enhanced greatly by the courtroom shootout, served to dampen the rowdier element's enthusiasm. No one made even a halfhearted attempt to hoorah the town.

The military supply dump was an altogether different matter. The jumble of crates, stuffed with every imaginable type of goods, proved to be a magnet for thieves and looters. At Ryan's suggestion Stevens telegraphed the railroad's main office, ordering armed guards to be hired in Kansas and rushed south. The Fort Gibson commander also detached a platoon to act as sentries. The sight of soldiers patrolling the rail yard quickly had the desired effect. Thieves soon began to give the supply depot a wide berth.

Early in September Ryan got the first real challenge to his authority. Word reached him that Brad Collins, a whiskey smuggler and desperado, had drifted into town. Collins was a half-blood Cherokee outcast, renounced by his own tribe and posted from the Cherokee Nation. A federal warrant was still out on him for shooting a deputy marshal. He traveled with a pack of cutthroats and robbers, vicious breeds who to a man were wanted by the law. To date, none of them had been arrested.

Ryan walked uptown. He carried the shotgun under the crook of his arm, proceeding along the rutted street at a deliberate pace. A knot of men loafing outside one of the saloons quickly took their business indoors. Several tents farther down, he turned in at the Acme Saloon and Gaming Parlor. He moved through the door and stopped.

Brad Collins stood at the bar. He was whipcord lean, light-skinned for a half-breed, with a hard smile and empty eyes. His men were gathered around him and listened attentively when he spoke. Three of them flanked him on one side and two on the other, and their deferential attitude was a message in itself. Even a casual observer could readily spot the gang leader.

Ryan moved to the end of the bar. He laid the scattergun across the countertop and eared back both hammers. The metallic snick brought the saloon to a sudden standstill. Several men along the bar eased to the opposite side of the room. Hands on the bar, the gang members waited for Ryan to make his play. Collins watched him with a frozen smile.

"Hello, Collins," Ryan said, nodding. "Figured we ought to have ourselves a talk."

Collins returned his stare levelly. "You're Ryan, ain't you? The one they call the Indian Killer."

Ryan's look betrayed nothing. "I reckon some people call me that."

"Well, what can I do for you, Indian Killer? You sorta busted up our party."

"I'm here to deliver a warning. Behave yourself and you're welcome at Gibson Station. I'll even overlook the federal warrant on you."

"You sure make it sound hospitable. But lemme ask you—what happens if I get out of line?"

"Don't," Ryan said in a low, dangerous voice. "Otherwise I'll have to kill you."

"Yeah?" Collins snarled. "It'd take more'n you and that shotgun to get the job done."

"Then go ahead and try me."

A leaden silence descended on the saloon. Collins' eyes flicked down at the shotgun and back to Ryan. He kept his hands in plain sight.

"You're bluffin'! No way you'd get us all. Not even with that!" Ryan lifted the snout of the shotgun. He centered the barrels on Collins' head. "I'm tired of talking. Either we've got a deal or we don't. Which is it?"

Collins swallowed, thinking hard. "You won't try to ride herd on me and the boys?"

"Not unless you cause trouble."

"And you won't take sides with the *tibo* marshals? I got your word on that?"

"You've already heard me say it."

"Awright, then," Collins said, bobbing his head. "You got yourself a deal."

"Don't break it. I won't try to talk you around next time."

"What next time?" Collins laughed. "Here, lemme buy you a drink. Just to prove there ain't no hard feelings."

"No, thanks."

Ryan walked to the door. His head was turned slightly, watching the bar out of the corner of his eye. As he went through the door, the metallic whirr of his shotgun's hammers being lowered sounded through the saloon. He passed from view onto the street outside.

Brad Collins took a long sip of whiskey. His eyes fixed on the middle distance in a thoughtful stare, and his mouth tightened at the corners. He smiled to himself.

CHAPTER EIGHTEEN

—◁◁◁◍▷▷▷—

William Ross stood at the window in his study. A pipe was clamped in his mouth and tendrils of smoke drifted slowly toward the ceiling. His gaze was abstracted and far away.

Over the past several weeks he had aged visibly. There were dark rings under his eyes and worry lines creased his forehead. His features appeared tight, almost stretched, like those of a man who has experienced a sudden loss of weight. His shoulders were unnaturally stooped and he looked somehow defeated.

Ross had led his people for five years. Not once in all that time had there been serious opposition to his policies. As principal chief, he had ruled the tribal council by sheer force of character. Even Elias Boudinot and the Southern Party had conceded Ross' preeminence among the Cherokees. He had never been challenged in the political forum.

All that had changed with the advent of the railroad. Political opponents such as Boudinot and Stand Watie had denounced him as backward and uninformed. Worse, a schism had developed within the ranks of his own followers. A silent conspiracy which advocated violence and bloodshed had arisen. Assassins once more roamed the land of the Cherokees.

The identity of the leader, or leaders, of the conspiracy was an absolute mystery. Whoever issued the orders was a master of secrecy and thus far an invisible presence. The organization itself indicated a brilliant mind at work behind the wall of silence. Nothing was known about the band of assassins or their objectives, for there had been no public pronouncement. Their intent was made clear only by the names of those they tried to kill.

The assassins appeared to be Ross' allies. Their enemies— the railroad and the Boudinot faction—were his enemies as well. Yet he was opposed, both philosophically and on general principle, to their activities. They advocated a return to the old tribal customs by resorting to violence. Ross thought their methods were a return to the savagery of bygone times. He'd let it be known that such men were to be considered renegades. He would not countenance cold-blooded murder.

Opposing the assassins had done nothing to improve Ross' political position. There was a faction within the tribal council that openly supported violence. Until now, despite their rebellious attitude he'd been able to hold them in check. But events of the past few weeks had forced him into an extremely tenuous situation. When the railroad bypassed Fort Gibson, he'd lost still more influence with council members. The courtroom shootout, though not directly related to the railroad, had further undercut his support. The tribal council, to a man, declared it the work of *tibo* interlopers.

Ross agreed with the allegation in principle. Every problem besetting his people stemmed in one way or another from the railroad. But he'd considered it futile to prefer charges against the railroad's special agent, John Ryan. He had further fanned the flames of discontent by providing medical care for Ryan. A vote of censure in the tribal council had been averted by the narrowest of margins.

Ross saw little reason for optimism as he stared out the window today. His leadership of the Cherokee Nation was still in great jeopardy. One more misstep, and there was every likelihood he would be driven from office. He resolved not to let that happen at any cost. He knew his people would need him even more in the years to come.

There was a knock at the door. Ross squared himself up, shoulders back and head erect. He turned as Major Tappin entered the study. He nodded briskly in greeting.

"Good afternoon, David."

"Good afternoon, sir."

Ross waved him to a chair. He crossed the room, halting at the edge of his desk as Tappin seated himself. He chose to remain standing.

"What can I do for you? Your message sounded urgent."

"Are you aware," Tappin asked, "that the council plans to meet tomorrow?"

"I am."

"Do you plan to address them?"

"No, I do not."

"May I ask why?"

"Because my presence would serve no useful purpose. I think it's best to let them get mired down in the routine conduct of business."

"Then you haven't heard," Tappin said. "There's talk that you'll face another vote of censure tomorrow."

"On what grounds?" Ross demanded.

"Failure to act in the tribe's best interests. Specifically, your failure to convene an emergency session of the Intertribal Council."

"I wasn't aware an emergency existed."

"Perhaps you should be," Tappin said pointedly. "It's been three weeks since the railroad entered the Creek Nation."

"To date," Ross observed, "I've heard no complaint from the Creeks."

"The Creeks are not at issue. We're discussing your people, what the Cherokee council wants."

"And what is that?"

"Some form of retaliation. At the very least, an act of defiance. We've been made to look the fools."

"On the contrary," Ross informed him. "Our prohibitive cattle tax drove the railroad from Cherokee lands."

Tappin laughed too loudly. "Stevens lost nothing in that bargain. He's shipping trainloads of cows from Three Forks."

"Precisely my point! As a practical matter, there is only one railhead in the Cherokee Nation. And I understand Boudinot's town site is all but deserted."

"Boudinot's another matter entirely. A majority of the council believes he deserves the death sentence. If it's ever put to a vote, he's as good as—"

"No!" Ross announced. "I will not be a party to barbarism."

Tappin studied him with a thoughtful frown. "You would do well not to state that opinion in public. By tribal law, Boudinot is subject to the extreme penalty."

"Times change," Ross said. "Ancient laws sometimes have no place in a modern world."

"I suggest you keep that opinion to yourself as well."

"Your advice was much the same regarding John Ryan. What would have happened if I hadn't voiced my opinion then?"

"He would have been killed," Tappin said harshly. "Or allowed to bleed to death. Which was exactly what he deserved."

Ross looked at him inquisitively. "Could you have let him bleed to death?"

"He killed two of my men!"

"You haven't answered the question."

Tappin was seething inside. He took a grip on his anger, forced himself to appear outwardly calm. "I suppose no man deserves a slow death. But that's neither here nor there. We're talking about the council."

"Yes, so we are."

Ross stuffed his hands in his pockets, moved behind the desk. "You know, of course, that Fort Gibson will eventually be closed down."

"Why do you say that?"

"It's a burdensome expense and serves no useful purpose. Unless, of course, we create an incident to justify its existence."

"An incident involving the railroad?"

"Precisely," Ross affirmed. "By biding our time, we end up with no military posts and only one railhead. We can then devote our energies to the critical engagement—the fight for Cherokee independence."

"Well . . ." Tappin said doubtfully, "I'm not sure the council would be persuaded. You're talking long-range, and they tend to be very shortsighted."

"Then we'll give them a short-term solution. Suppose an incident were to occur in the Creek Nation. Would that suffice?"

"What sort of incident?"

"You know the Creeks as well as anyone here does. What would you suggest?"

Tappin considered a moment. "I received a report that Ryan had some trouble with Brad Collins and his gang. Perhaps I can arrange an incident through Collins."

"No harm must come to John Ryan! You would have to make that clear to Collins."

"I think he'll listen to reason."

"Have I your assurance on that point?"

"Leave it to me," Tappin said, grinning. "Outlaws can always use friends in high places."

After Tappin had gone, Ross slumped wearily into his chair. He scrubbed his face with his palms but was unable to erase his dour expression. For all practical purposes, he'd just struck a bargain with the devil. And for little more than momentary political gain.

He knew he'd sold himself cheap.

The rose was dark magenta in color. Elizabeth clipped it with shears, careful to avoid the thorns. She held the flower to her nose and breathed deeply.

The aroma was faint, barely detectable. She lowered the rose and looked around the garden with a melancholy expression. At the height of the summer, the flower garden was a riotous explosion of colors and hues. But now it was early September and only a few of the rosebushes were still in bloom. Windswept petals, already dry and faded, littered the earth.

Elizabeth dreaded the passing of summer. A short autumn inevitably led to a long, dreary winter. The rain and sleet brought with it a dank, bone-chilling cold that sapped her spirits. An occasional snow, particularly at Christmastime, relieved the monotony. But the seemingly endless months of dismal weather left her dispirited and out of sorts. Her vivacity returned only with the arrival of a new spring.

Her mood today was only partly caused by summer's end. Even the dying roses were a reflection rather than the source of her low spirits. Hard as it was to admit, she was lost in a morass of conflicting emotions. One minute she prided herself on having driven John Ryan away. In the next, she ached for the sight of him.

The courtroom gun battle had provided her with an almost painful emotional confusion. She'd rushed to Tahlequah upon hearing that Ryan had been wounded. There, heedless of public reaction, she had spent the night at Ryan's bedside. Elizabeth surprised herself with the strength of her concern for him but felt strangely glad that he couldn't see her clutching his hand and very close to tears. Although the operation had gone well, he'd been heavily sedated with laudanum and therefore unaware of her presence. When the crisis ended the next morning, she had undergone another shift in mood. She departed before he'd regained consciousness.

She had been revolted by the aftermath of the shootout. The final count of eleven dead and many others wounded left her sick at heart. She rejoiced that Ryan had survived, and would recover in time. Yet she couldn't ignore the fact that he'd again taken sides and killed two more Cherokees. Once again she found herself torn between loathing and a compulsion to be with him. In the end, unable to live with half measures, her conscience had prevailed. She restrained herself from seeing him again.

For all her restraint, she never tried to deceive herself. She was concerned for his welfare and vitally interested in his recovery. Through her father she was able to gather bits and pieces of information. She heard that Ryan was up and around and walking with a cane. A short time later she learned that he was practically fully recuperated. While the news relieved her anxiety, it also left her saddened. She knew he would soon resume his work with the railroad. For all her fear and worry, nothing had changed.

There was one small consolation. The railroad, and Ryan, were now in the Creek Nation. She thought it unlikely that he would be thrown into another confrontation with Cherokees. The Creeks were somewhat less rigid in their attitude toward whites, so it seemed to her a remote possibility that Ryan would kill anyone else. She wanted to believe that he resorted to a gun only when provoked.

Yet she was not altogether sanguine. She couldn't help being depressed by the growing distance between herself and Ryan. The deeper tracks were laid into the Creek Nation, the more isolated she felt. With each passing day, Ryan was farther away, moving inexorably southward. She knew he would be gone forever once he crossed the Red River. All that might have been between them would then become a bittersweet dream.

Her reverie was suddenly broken by the sound of her name. She turned and saw her father on the veranda. He moved down the steps, then proceeded along a path to the flower garden. She waited, still holding the rose.

"Well, well," Ross said, halting beside her. "The last rose of summer, hmm?"

"Don't tease," she said seriously. "You know the thought of winter depresses me."

"Winter?" Ross asked. "Nothing else?"

"Why do you say that?"

Ross took a moment to light his pipe. He snuffed the match and ground it underfoot. Finally he looked up.

"Major Tappin was just here."

"Oh?" she replied without interest. "What new calamity did he have to report?"

"You shouldn't be so hard on him. Tappin is a very capable administrator."

"I'm sorry, Father. I just don't like the man. He's too . . ."

"Unsociable?"

"Worse than that. He's always impressed me as being very insensitive. I know it sounds silly, but somehow he . . . Well, he frightens me."

Ross smiled, puffing on his pipe. "I suppose Tappin frightens many people. But then, policemen are seldom loved. It's part and parcel of the job."

"Perhaps you're right," she said with a shrug. "What brought him here today?"

"Among other things, he had a bit of news about John Ryan. I thought you might be interested."

"Maybe I am," she said indifferently, "and maybe I'm not. What is it?"

Ross was aware that she'd begun plucking petals off the rose. He suppressed a chuckle, forcing himself not to look at her hands. "According to Tappin's information, Mr. Ryan is back on the job. In fact, he recently had words with Brad Collins."

Her eyes widened. "The outlaw? *That* Brad Collins?"

"Don't worry," Ross reassured her. "As such things go, it was rather inconsequential. Ryan simply warned Collins to behave himself."

"Why would I worry?" she murmured uneasily. "Apparently he's happy doing what he does best."

Ross could see the hurt deep in her eyes. He gently touched her arm, saying nothing more. At length she nodded, then smiled a little. As he turned to leave, she found her voice.

"Father."

"Yes?"

"Is he still at Three Forks?"

"So far as I know. Why do you ask?"

"No reason."

Ross wisely let it drop. As he walked toward the house,

Elizabeth glanced down at her hands. She saw that the rose was completely bare of petals. Nothing remained but the stem and sharp thorns. Her mouth softened in a wan smile.

Winter seemed distant and yet so near. She suddenly felt cold.

CHAPTER NINETEEN

"I want your personal guarantee."

"No soap, Colonel."

"You refuse?"

Ryan's jawline tightened. "I'm telling you there's no way to guarantee any man's safety. The best we can do is whittle down the odds."

"Odds?" Stevens repeated. "Are you saying something's bound to happen?"

"The sporting crowd's a rough bunch. None of them has any particular love for politicians. That goes double for the Indians."

"You refer to Collins and his gang of half-breeds."

"Not altogether," Ryan corrected him. "Any Indian—Creek, Cherokee, Choctaw—they've all got a bone to pick. A Washington bigwig makes a pretty inviting target."

"Target!" Stevens said incredulously. "Good God, you sound like he's certain to get shot!"

"You want my best advice, Colonel? Wire Secretary Cox and make some excuse. Tell him you've had to postpone the ceremony."

"Absolutely not! Cox is one of our most influential

supporters. And we need all the clout we can get with Congress. I just won't risk offending him!"

"Then I suggest you ask the Army for some help. Surround him with soldiers and maybe nothing will happen. It's your best bet."

Stevens shook his head adamantly. "Everyone would think we're incapable of safeguarding our own railhead. We can't afford that kind of publicity."

Ryan spread his hands. "Can you afford to have someone take a shot at the Secretary of the Interior?"

There was a prolonged silence. Stevens seemed to stare at him and past him at the same time. For a moment Ryan thought he intended to ignore the question. At last Stevens appeared to rouse himself. His voice was edged, almost raspy.

"Put out the word," he ordered. "We *will not* tolerate troublemakers. And that's final!"

"When you say *we*, you're actually talking about *me*, aren't you?"

"John, your job is to maintain peace and order. I expect you to do no less."

"It's just about even money," Ryan warned. "You go through with this and somebody's liable to get himself killed."

"Make sure it's not Secretary Cox."

"I'll do my damnedest, Colonel."

Ryan told himself it was a hell of a way to run a railroad. Later that night, lying awake in his bunk, it seemed even more asinine. He thought it likely that his damnedest might be too little and too late. Lots of people in Indian Territory would consider it an honor to kill the Secretary of the Interior. Some of them would willingly sacrifice themselves for that honor.

The occasion for the Secretary's visit was the completion of the Verdigris River bridge. The trestles were in place and engineers estimated the river would be spanned by the middle of September. Across the muddy stream, four miles of track had been laid to the next barrier, the Arkansas River. Scullin and his work gangs were idle while awaiting construction of both bridges. Stevens saw the slack time as a golden opportunity, capable of garnering wide publicity in the east-ern press. He planned to stage a celebration around the Verdigris River crossing.

To mark the event, a ribbon-cutting ceremony would be held on September 18. Secretary of the Interior Harold Cox had been invited to officially open the bridge and afterward deliver a speech. An astute bureaucrat, Cox jumped at the chance to make an appearance in Indian Territory. The at-tendant publicity would benefit everyone involved, himself included. As an added sweetener, Stevens laid on a special train to transport Cox, and his retinue, westward. The event promised to make front-page news.

Ryan viewed the ceremony, at best, as a calculated risk. Harold Cox, as Secretary of the Interior, was directly respon-sible for the Bureau of Indian Affairs. No friend of the red man, the Bureau was largely a tool of robber barons and rail-road czars. To a great extent, the Katy was traversing Indian Territory under the auspices of the Bureau. Moreover, should the Five Civilized Tribes lose their independence, it was the Bureau that would bring it about. So Harold Cox was vili-fied by the Indians as the most visible symbol of *tibo* greed. His appearance in the territory would serve as a goad to those who felt victimized.

Ryan believed it was entirely possible that someone would attempt to kill the Secretary. He'd gone to Stevens voicing his concern for Cox's safety. The upshot was that he'd been appointed to play guardian angel. Just before going to sleep, he reminded himself never again to volunteer an opinion. By doing so, he'd gone from the frying pan to the fire.

He already felt singed around the edges.

The special train arrived on schedule. The ribbon-cutting cer-emony was set for high noon at the north end of the Verdi-gris River bridge. To add to the festivities, all the railroad workers had been awarded a day off.

Harold Cox detrained at Gibson Station like Caesar tri-umphant. He was a short, rotund man, completely bald, with watery eyes and a bogus smile. He wore a cutaway coat, striped pants, and a shiny top hat. His retinue consisted of several bureaucratic flunkeys and his own personal press contingent. A newspaperman from Washington and a journalist for *Harper's* magazine trailed him like hounds on a fresh scent. Following close behind was a photographer with camera and powder box.

Their arrival created an immediate sensation. A crowd of almost five hundred people gathered around the depot. Tom Scullin and his Irish Brigade, cheering lustily, were positioned in the front rank. Behind them was the sporting crowd, gamblers and whores tricked out in all their finery. On the fringe of the assemblage were an assortment of Creeks and Cherokees who were drawn by the spectacle. A brass band, drafted piecemeal from the dance halls, thumped a sprightly tune. Bunting and streamers decorating the stationhouse lent an exuberant, carnival air to the scene.

The festive atmosphere continued on the walk to the bridge. The band led the way and was followed by the dignitaries and their party. The procession resembled a circus parade. Ryan maintained a position close beside Stevens and Secretary Cox. Spread out around them were armed railway agents who normally performed guard duty at the warehouse. Wary of the crowd, Ryan constantly scanned the sea of faces. His unease was heightened by the fact that Cox was built like a bale of cotton. He thought the Secretary made an inviting, and almost unmissable, target.

Stevens delivered a short and somewhat flowery introduction at the bridge. Then Secretary Cox posed with Stevens for the photographer. Ryan thought the Secretary looked like a trained bear. Cox and Stevens' handshake, as well as the ribbon cutting, was immortalized with several explosive flashes of the powder pan. When Cox actually cut the ribbon, the Irish Brigade, led by Scullin's bull-like roar, broke out in a fresh round of cheers. As planned, the special train then chugged onto the bridge, halting halfway across. The last car groaned to a stop where the ribbon drooped on the tracks.

Secretary Cox mounted the rear platform. With Stevens

beside him, he launched into a speech commending the railroad. His reedy voice was punctuated by a powder flash, which caused him to pause and hold an artificial pose for the camera. Oblivious to the crowd's laughter, he then resumed with an ornate tribute to Colonel Robert Stevens. He hailed the railroader as "a giant of a man, leading the vanguard in America's march to progress."

"*Bullshit!*"

A voice from the crowd cut the bureaucrat short. Cox halted, sputtering and red-faced, suddenly dumbstruck. Ryan, who was positioned on the car steps, searched the crowd. Toward the rear he spotted Brad Collins and the gang of half-bloods. The outlaw's eyes were lighted by a cold tinsel glitter, and he seemed to be staring straight at Ryan. His mouth curled in a ferocious grin.

"Goddamn *tibos*!" he shouted. "You're robbing us blind, stealing our land!"

The Indians standing nearby muttered agreement. Scullin and the Irish Brigade, as well as the sporting crowd, turned angrily toward the voice. Then off to one side there was a flash of sunlight on metal. Out of the corner of his eye, Ryan saw a man raise a cocked pistol. He had only a moment to identify the man as a breed and wonder why he was separated from the Collins gang. In the next instant the pistol roared and Harold Cox's top hat went spinning into the air.

Stevens grabbed Cox and threw him down on the platform. Drawing as he turned, Ryan leveled his Colt, sighting over the barrel. He feathered the trigger, holding dead on the man's chest. The Colt leaped and the half-breed seemed to suck in a great lungful of air. A starburst of blood spread across his shirtfront and he went down like a stone.

Wheeling around, Ryan once more searched the crowd. Off in the distance, he saw Collins and the gang of breeds hightailing it toward town. The Irish Brigade, led by Scullin, had formed a protective circle around the car. The armed railway guards clambered aboard the rear platform amid shouts and panicked confusion. As Ryan sighted on Collins, one of them jostled his arm and spoiled his aim. He slowly lowered the Colt, all too aware that the gang was racing for their horses. For the moment there was nothing to be done.

Ryan holstered his pistol. He heard Stevens consoling Harold Cox, who was blubbering in a high-pitched, hysterical voice. Then, turning on the steps, he looked down at the dead half-breed. It occurred to him that someone had, after all, risked suicide in an attempt to commit murder. But the man had not acted alone or on his own initiative.

He'd been sacrificed by Brad Collins. A stalking horse used to kill and then be killed.

The crowd slowly dispersed. Their festive mood was gone, replaced by sober amazement. What they had witnessed left them in a total quandary. No one could figure the dead man's motive.

Ryan ordered the body removed. With Secretary Cox safely inside the car, the special agent then turned his attention to security. Another assassination attempt seemed to him highly unlikely. Yet, given the number of Indians in town, he saw no reason to take chances. He quickly stationed the railway guards around the train.

A short while later he entered the rear door of the private car. He found Stevens and Cox seated opposite one another. Cox was slumped in an armchair, a brandy glass clutched in one hand. His face was pasty and beads of perspiration glistened on his forehead. His hand trembled as he drained the last of the brandy.

"Madness," he said in a shaky voice. "Why would anyone want to kill me?"

Stevens nodded sympathetically. "Who can say, Mr. Secretary? All Indians are deranged savages anyway."

Cox looked at him blankly. "The man was Indian?"

"A half-blood," Stevens said. "But a dead one, now. You've no reason to concern yourself further."

"I—" Cox faltered, passed a hand over his eyes. "I don't feel so well."

"Perfectly understandable. Why not lie down for a while? We can talk later."

Stevens assisted him to the bedroom. There was a murmured conversation, and then, closing the door, Stevens returned to the parlor. He angrily bit off the end of a cigar and lit up. Inhaling deeply, he gave Ryan a sideways look.

"You were right. I should have called it off."

"We got lucky," Ryan said. "All the same, if I were you I wouldn't push it."

"What are you suggesting?"

"Get him out of here *muy pronto*. Our luck might not hold next time."

"You think someone else might try?"

"I'd just as soon not find out."

Stevens' expression was grim. "It all happened so fast. Who was the gunman?"

"One of Collins' gang."

"Well, that's a hell of a note! Why weren't you watching him?"

"You seem to forget," Ryan said evenly. "Collins had everybody distracted, including me. The way he rigged it damn near worked too. His man got a little nervy and rushed the shot."

"Why would Collins try to kill Cox? It makes no sense."

"I've been thinking along those lines myself."

Stevens was thoughtful a moment. "Perhaps it was revenge of sorts. After all, you did put him on warning, and in open public."

"I tend to doubt it. He could have killed me easy enough out there. But the whole thing, start to finish, was aimed at Cox."

"And?" Stevens said, puzzled. "What are you saying?"

Ryan moved to the window. He stared down, looking past the bridge timbers to the muddy river below. Then, as though talking to himself, he spoke in a slow, pensive tone.

"It's got the smell of a put-up job. Collins is small-time. He runs whiskey and robs people. Why would he turn assassin all of a sudden?"

Stevens looked surprised. "Are you suggesting that someone paid him to do it?"

"Tell you what I think," Ryan said, turning from the window. "Collins never dreamed that up on his own. Unless I'm way off, somebody put the idea in his head."

"Yes, but who?"

"We keep asking ourselves the same question, don't we?"

"Christ," Stevens muttered. "You think whoever tried to kill Boudinot is behind this too?"

"Anything's possible. Like I said, Collins is no assassin."

"Perhaps not. But we don't know who put him up to it. At the moment he's our only lead."

"I wouldn't argue that."

"Well, then . . ." Stevens hesitated, puffed a cloud of smoke. "How soon can you get on his trail?"

"Why borrow trouble? Half-breed or not, Collins is still an Indian. We'd have to start a war to smoke him out."

"You intend to do nothing?"

"No," Ryan said in a flinty voice. "If he shows up here, I'll kill him. Otherwise, it's a job for federal marshals or the Army."

"I don't care for that," Stevens grumbled. "It looks like we're trying to pass the buck."

"Seems to me it's out of our jurisdiction. The Secretary of the Interior works for the government, not the railroad."

Stevens' mouth hardened. "Perhaps I haven't made myself clear. We have to take care of our own dirty laundry. I want you to find Collins."

"No can do, Colonel."

"What?"

"Before I got to Collins, I'd have to fight my way through half the Creek Nation. I want him as much as you do, maybe more, but I'm tired of killing Indians."

"What the hell does that have to do with anything?"

"It says all I've got to say."

"Are you refusing a direct order?" Stevens demanded. "Because if you are, don't think you can't be replaced!"

Ryan smiled. "It's your railroad, Colonel."

Stevens seemed on the verge of saying something more. Then, as though to halt the words, he stuffed the cigar in his

mouth. He made a brusque, dismissive gesture with his hand
and turned away.

Outside the car Ryan stood grinning to himself. What he'd
only suspected before was now a hard fact. Stevens needed
him more than Ryan needed the job.

He went down the steps whistling a lively tune.

CHAPTER TWENTY

The weather was unseasonably warm. A forenoon sun reflected off the Verdigris in ripples of orange and gold. The tent town of Gibson Station appeared almost lifeless in the late morning hour.

Weather dominated conversation in the railroad camp. Even though the days were balmy, the temperature dropped sharply at night. There was a hint of frost in the air during the darkness hours; potbellied stoves in the bunkhouse cars were being stoked shortly after dusk. No one expected the warm days to last much longer.

Robert Stevens' forecast was especially pessimistic. He viewed the weather as a capricious and sometimes menacing adversary. The chilly nights left him convinced that winter would arrive early. Drizzling rain, followed in the harshest months by snowfall, would severely hamper railroad construction. He was determined to make the most of what promised to be a short autumn.

Delay on the Arkansas River bridge was particularly worrisome. To span the river required an immense structure at least 840 feet in length. It was by far the largest bridge yet attempted by Katy engineers. The latticework of trestles and

support beams gave it the look of a gigantic spider's web. By
the very nature of its complexity, it was a slow and tedious
project. With maddening regularity, the estimated completion date was revised time and time again.

Stevens had been temporarily distracted from his worries
by the Verdigris River bridge opening. Following the attempted assassination and Secretary Cox's hasty departure,
there was a lull before things returned to normal. By the third
day, however, Stevens' attention focused once more on the
Arkansas River crossing. Track laying through the Creek
Nation had been brought to a standstill until the barrier was
surmounted.

Tom Scullin was summoned to the private car. There Stevens informed him that the Irish Brigade was being pressed
into service. Scullin and his work gangs, idle now for almost
a week, were to report to Otis Gunn. The chief engineer
would assign them jobs alongside his bridge-building crew
and thereby speed the completion date. Scullin readily agreed
and expressed the opinion that his Irish Brigade would show
Gunn a thing or two about spanning a river. At Stevens' in-
sistence he further agreed to place himself at Gunn's command. No rivalry, Stevens told him, would be tolerated over
leadership of the project.

The first construction train was loaded by late morning.
There were two flatcars, one stacked with supplies and rough-
hewn timbers, and the other carrying fifty men. Scullin
placed one of his foremen in charge, ordering him to report
with the work gang to Otis Gunn. As for himself, Scullin
planned to supervise loading of the second train, then bring
it forward to the river crossing. The first train pulled out of
the rail yard shortly after eleven o'clock. A caboose that had
been converted into a kitchen car was coupled on at the last
minute.

On impulse, Ryan swung aboard the caboose. He generally visited the construction site once a day, covering the four
miles by horseback. He decided to make the trip by train
today for no particular reason. The shantytown was of no
immediate concern since it seldom came alive before dark.

He'd be back by then, as one of the supply trains always returned before nightfall.

A brakeman boarded from the opposite side as the train was switched onto the main track. Ryan looked around, nodding to him, then once again turned his attention forward. His senses suddenly alerted when the locomotive picked up speed and rolled onto the Verdigris River bridge. A loud creaking noise like trees swaying in the wind sounded over the rumble of the locomotive's driving wheels. An instant later there was an earsplitting *crack* from somewhere beneath the bridge.

Ryan saw the center span of the bridge buckle. Beams and splintered timbers flew like matchsticks as supporting trestles collapsed underneath the weight of the locomotive. In an eerie sort of slow motion, the two-hundred-foot-long center span simply vanished. Too late, the engineer cut the throttle and slammed on the brakes. The locomotive screeched forward, showering sparks along the rails, and teetered on the edge of the chasm. Slowly, hissing steam and smoke, it nosed over the last upright trestle.

As it hurtled downward, the locomotive jerked the entire train forward. Ryan felt the sudden acceleration in speed even as he saw the tender and the first flatcar disappear. Directly ahead, men were leaping off the second flatcar, arms and legs akimbo as they slammed into vertical beams on both sides of the bridge. One man missed completely, sailing through the opening between beams, and plummeted to the riverbed fifty feet below. A dozen or more of the work gang rode the flatcar over the shattered roadway.

Ryan jumped, landing hard on his shoulder beside the bridge rails. He rolled, stopping himself against a beam, and looked up as the caboose toppled over the edge. He saw the brakeman on the rear platform, paralyzed with terror, unable to move. The man's eyes were bugged, his mouth frozen in a silent oval, as he vanished from sight. The sound of rending steel filled the morning as one car after another crashed into the water. A moment later the firebox in the locomotive exploded with a thunderous roar.

The blast struck Ryan with cyclonic force. A towering fireball leaped skyward, shooting through the chasm of the center span. The heat singed Ryan's eyebrows and pocked his shirt with tiny, smoking holes. For an instant it was as though the air had been sucked from the earth, and he couldn't get his breath. Then, with an effort of will, he levered himself to his feet. His breathing returned with a ragged gasp, and he stumbled away from the heat. His eyeballs felt seared, but his vision, oddly enough, had never been more acute.

He saw Tom Scullin running toward the bridge.

The riverbed resembled a funeral pyre. Twisted steel and burned timbers were fused in a mound of smoky rubble. The locomotive, at the very bottom of the debris, looked like an incinerated dinosaur.

Scullin directed teams of men searching through the wreckage. On the riverbank the bodies of the engineer and the fireman, charred beyond recognition, were covered with blankets. Nearby lay the body of the brakeman, broken and torn as though trampled to death. Eighteen of the work gang had been found, and miraculously, none of them were dead. All the men were seriously injured and many had not yet regained consciousness. Three of them clung to life merely by a thread.

Overseeing the operation, Stevens moved back and forth between the injured and the rescuers. His features were sallow and his eyes glowed with a feverish look. He paused to watch several whores and dance hall girls tending the injured with bandages and kindness. His mouth went dry as a man with a compound fracture moaned in agony. It occurred to him that more men would die unless they received medical attention. Turning away in disgust, he tried not to think of the truth. The nearest hospital was in Topeka, Kansas.

As Stevens stared toward the rescue operation, he happened to spot Ryan. He'd noticed Ryan earlier, standing knee deep in the river, looking up at the bridge. But now, to his amazement he saw Ryan some ten feet above the water, wedged in among the trestles. As he watched, Ryan inched along a crossbeam and stopped underneath the yawning gap of the center span. It seemed to him that Ryan was inspecting one of the first trestles to have collapsed.

After a time Ryan began making his way down the understructure. Stevens walked along the shoreline and waited for him near the north end of the bridge. Ryan splashed through the water, skirting the last masonry piling, and waded ashore. His eyebrows were gone, replaced by two ugly red streaks. He appeared otherwise uninjured as he halted in front of Stevens. The look in his eyes was flat and cold, somehow chilling.

"What's wrong?" Stevens asked.

"The bridge gave way awful damn fast. Too fast, for my money. So I had a look around."

"Yes, go on."

"It wasn't an accident."

"Sabotage!" Stevens said hoarsely. "Are you certain?"

Ryan stared at him. "No doubt about it. Somebody cut halfway through the trestles and the support beams. I figure it took at least two men with a crosscut saw."

"My God! Someone did that—killed all these men. Why?"

"No mystery about that. You've made yourself some powerful enemies, Colonel."

"The Cherokees," Stevens grated. "William Ross finally got his revenge. That scheming bastard!"

Ryan looked skeptical. "Why should he wait until we're in the Creek Nation? He could've started a war a long time ago."

"Because everything else failed! I outfoxed him at every turn, made him look the fool. Now he's evened the score, and very cleverly too! Suspicion will just naturally fall on the Creeks."

"Maybe," Ryan said slowly. "Seems like a mighty big coincidence, though. Three days after an attempted assassination and a bridge suddenly collapses. Good timing, wouldn't you say?"

Stevens' brow furrowed questioningly. "You think Brad Collins did this—was ordered to do it?"

"Yeah, I sure do," Ryan said flatly. "One thing failed, so they tried another. I'd say the same man's behind both."

"And you don't think that man is William Ross?"

"It's not Ross' game. He's tough, but he doesn't kill people. He'd never deal with scum like Collins."

Stevens averted his eyes, thoughtful a moment. Finally he let out a deep breath. "We've no proof either way, so it's a moot point. For the moment, however, I hope you're right. I need a favor from Ross."

"What sort of favor?"

Stevens gestured to the injured workers. "Some of those men will die unless they get medical attention. The nearest doctor is in Tahlequah, but he won't come without Ross' approval. I want you to arrange it."

"I'll do my damnedest," Ryan said. "No guarantees, but I'll try."

"Good," Stevens said, nodding. "In the meantime I'll lay on a train for Topeka. With or without the doctor, we have to get those men to a hospital."

Ryan consulted his pocket watch. "It's going on twelve now. I ought to make it back here by dark."

"Tell Ross I'll do anything he asks. Just so he sends the doctor."

"Sounds like an invitation to write his own ticket. How far should I go?"

"Anything within reason, short of closing down the railroad," Stevens said. "I have an obligation to these men, and I'll stick by them."

"I'll deliver the message."

Ryan turned to leave. Stevens caught his arm, stopping him. "One other thing, John. After today Brad Collins has to pay the piper. I want him dead."

"I want the man who pulls Collins' strings. Once I've got him—"

"Yes?"

"Then," Ryan said, walking away, "I reckon I'll kill Collins."

* * *

A midafternoon sun streamed through the study window. William Ross sat behind his desk, fingers steepled, in thought. Across from him Ryan was seated in a wing-back chair, waiting. The older man finally lowered his hands to the desktop.

"You couldn't be mistaken?"

"No," Ryan said with conviction. "Somebody used a cross-cut saw to weaken the bridge."

"Even so," Rose inquired, "how can you be so positive about Collins? From what I gather, the sabotage was done at night. No one actually saw Collins."

Ryan gave him an odd look. "Why all the interest in Collins?"

"It seems out of character for him. I understood Collins was just a garden-variety bandit."

"So did I," Ryan said, "till he tried to assassinate the Secretary of the Interior."

Ross' expression was bland, unreadable. Yet on the inside he was boiling with anger. He'd already spoken to David Tappin about the assassination attempt, but Tappin had shrugged it off, saying Collins had acted on his own initiative. Now, after hearing about the bridge, Ross was even more troubled. He made a mental note to question Tappin thoroughly, and soon.

"Unfortunate," he said softly. "Good men, red and white, dying for no reason."

"More will die," Ryan added, "unless you send the doctor. For once you've got Stevens over a barrel."

"He actually said he'll grant anything I ask?"

"Well, almost anything. He won't shut down the railroad."

"Perhaps there's hope for Stevens yet. At least he appears to have feelings for his own men."

"I don't mean to press," Ryan said, "but time's short. What's your price for the doctor?"

"Nothing," Ross informed him. "I don't trade in men's lives. I'll give you a note to Dr. Porter."

Ryan was visibly impressed by the gesture. But he thought the lesson in humanity would be lost on Robert Stevens. He watched as the older man hastily penned a short note.

Finished, Ross folded the sheet of paper and pushed it across the desk.

"There is a price," he said quietly. "I understand that today was an emergency. However, you will oblige me by not coming here again."

"Some things don't change, do they?"

"We are who we are, Mr. Ryan. If I weren't accountable to the tribal council, things might be different."

Ryan tucked the note in his jacket pocket. He rose, nodded acceptance of the condition, and walked from the study. He proceeded along the hallway to the vestibule and abruptly stopped. Elizabeth was standing beside the central staircase.

"Hello, John."

"Afternoon, Elizabeth." He moved forward, trying for an offhand manner. "You're not waiting for me, are you?"

"As a matter of fact"—she paused, her eyes sad—"I wanted to tell you how sorry I am. It's just terrible . . . all those men."

"How'd you hear about it?"

"Moccasin telegraph," she said, smiling. "The Creeks and the Cherokees keep each other very well informed."

"So your father knew all along. He just let me talk to hear my version, is that it?"

"Why, is there more than one version?"

"Not so far as I'm concerned."

"Your eyebrows!" she said, suddenly staring at him. "Were you hurt in the accident?"

She would learn soon enough that it was no accident. Ryan saw no reason to correct her. "Nothing serious," he said. "I got off luckier than most."

"I . . ." She faltered, groping for words. "I'm glad you're all right. I really am."

"Would it have made any difference?"

"Yes, John. Whatever you may think, it would have made a great difference—to me."

Ryan searched her eyes. What he saw there sparked a faint hope. "Elizabeth, let me ask you something. Your father says

I'm not welcome here, regardless of the reason. How do you feel?"

For a moment it seemed as though she would reach out to him. Then, her voice almost inaudible, she lowered her eyes. "I never contradict my father."

A moment of stark silence passed between them. Ryan waited, willing her to look up at him. But she kept her eyes fixed on the floor, saying nothing. He walked out without another word.

CHAPTER TWENTY-ONE

The death toll mounted. By morning three more men had succumbed to their massive injuries. Of the remaining survivors, four were in critical condition.

Shortly before sunrise, the hospital train pulled out of Gibson Station. Dr. Frank Porter, who had worked through the night, agreed to accompany the injured to Topeka. The men of the Irish Brigade treated him with respect and deference and appeared unmindful of the fact that he was a Cherokee. Several of their comrades were alive only as a result of his efforts.

The bridge collapse was a monumental setback for Robert Stevens. The loss of a locomotive, not to mention a score of seasoned workers, was catastrophe enough. But the greater reverse was the bridge itself. To rebuild it before winter arrived became an imperative of the first order. All railroad construction was stymied until the Verdigris was once again spanned.

Under Otis Gunn's supervision, Scullin took charge of the project. Gunn meanwhile hopped back and forth between the Arkansas River bridge and the Verdigris. Within the week, with both crews working fourteen-hour days, there was modest reason for optimism. The Arkansas crossing was nearing completion, and the Verdigris bridge was progressing faster than anyone had dared anticipate. Gunn estimated an overall completion date of late October.

On October 1 Stevens sent for Ryan. Entering the private car, Ryan noted that the railroader was in an agitated state. A cigar stuck in his mouth, Stevens trailed a cloud of smoke as he paced the floor. Sally Palmer sat quietly in one of the armchairs and watched him with an apprehensive look. She glanced at Ryan and rolled her eyes in mock fright. Then, without waiting to be asked, she retired to the bedroom.

Stevens motioned Ryan to a chair. He continued pacing, all the while puffing his cigar as if it might go out. He put Ryan in mind of a mad bull hooking at cobwebs, frustrated and angry. Finally he halted at the window and turned to Ryan.

"It's showdown time!" he said, waving his cigar. "I've just found out who sabotaged the bridge."

"You have?"

"I have, indeed! It was that mealymouthed back-stabber, Andrew Peirce."

"Who?"

"Andrew Peirce!" Stevens growled. "Head of the A&P. Here, read this."

He handed Ryan a telegraph form. It was a wire from the station agent at Vinita. The message briefly related that the Atlantic and Pacific Railroad was within a few miles of the Katy right-of-way. All indications were that the A&P would intersect the Katy roadbed some three miles north of Vinita. On that spot, the station agent advised, A&P crews were constructing what appeared to be a depot.

Ryan recalled that the Katy charter granted a north-south right-of-way through Indian Territory. The A&P grant, as stipulated by Congress, was for an east-west right-of-way. It was further stipulated that the two lines were to intersect somewhere in the Cherokee Nation. Within the past month word had leaked that the A&P was about to gain control of the Missouri Pacific Railroad. The move was a direct challenge to Robert Stevens and the Katy.

As Ryan was aware, the Missouri Pacific was a main artery into St. Louis and points eastward. Should the A&P gain control of that line, it would represent a coup of major proportions. In effect, Stevens' working arrangement with the Missouri Pacific would be voided; the end result would be to block the Katy from direct access to eastern markets. The A&P, at that point, would then command all trade with the Southwest.

"Sounds like trouble," Ryan said, looking up from the telegram. "But what's all this got to do with the bridge?"

"Everything!" Stevens snorted. "Andrew Peirce is a black-hearted scoundrel. He makes the Cherokees look like Good Samaritans."

"And you think he's behind the sabotage?"

"Who else has a better reason? We'll end up a month behind schedule because of that bridge. By the time we get moving again, he'll have track laid halfway across Indian Territory. Jesus Christ, just think of it."

Ryan pondered a moment. "Would Peirce kill all those men just to get a jump on you?"

"*Would he?*" Stevens parroted. "He'd cut his own mother's throat! The man is morally bankrupt."

"But would he kill?" Ryan insisted. "Have you ever known him to resort to violence, calculated or otherwise?"

"Well . . ." Stevens hesitated, munching his cigar. "No, I suppose not. But that doesn't mean a goddamn thing. We're playing for table stakes here! Murder wouldn't stop him."

"Maybe not," Ryan allowed. "All the same, I'd still tap Brad Collins for the honors. It's more in his line of work."

"Whether it is or isn't doesn't matter. The fact remains that Peirce and his railroad are on our doorstep. I want you to leave for Vinita on the next train."

"What's in Vinita?"

"The A&P!" Stevens thundered. "Or at least they're only three miles away. You go up there and nose around. See what they're up to."

"What makes you think they're up to anything?"

"Because I know Andrew Peirce! The man's middle name

is 'devious.' So don't argue with me about it. Just get on up there and keep me informed."

Ryan boarded a freight train that afternoon. His horse was stalled in a boxcar, along with his camping gear. As the train rolled out of Gibson Station, his attitude toward the trip darkened. He figured it for a wild-goose chase.

Vinita looked like a ghost town. Apart from the stationhouse, the community consisted of three frame structures. The buildings were slapdash affairs, crudely constructed, and appeared to be deserted. There was no one in sight.

Ryan dumped his gear on the ground after unloading his horse. Asa Johnson, the station agent, wandered over as the train got under way. Johnson was a cadaverous man, all knobs and joints, with a loose-gaited stride. He gave the impression that life held no surprises, aside from a sudden attack of constipation. He halted, nodding as though it were an effort.

"You'd be Ryan," he said. "The Colonel wired me you was on your way."

Ryan began saddling his horse. "Looks sort of lonesome around here."

"Yep," Johnson said laconically. "Nobody but yours truly."

"Who belongs to those houses?"

"Boudinot owns 'em," Johnson said. "Empty now, though. Have been since everybody pulled up stakes for Gibson Station."

"That a fact?" Ryan tied off the latigo and began strapping his saddlebags into place. "When's the last time you saw Boudinot?"

"Hell!" Johnson cackled. "Been so long I plumb forgot. He lit out with everybody else."

"What's new with the A&P?"

"I dunno much more'n I telegraphed the Colonel. Only got wind of 'em late yesterday."

"You said they're about three miles north of here?"

"Yeah, 'bout that."

Ryan stepped into the saddle. "Much obliged, Asa. Enjoyed our little chat."

"You ridin' up there for a look-see?"

"That's why I'm here."

"Take some free advice," Johnson said. "Don't try to ask questions. Them boys ain't too friendly."

"Gave you a hard time, did they?"

"Told me to haul ass and don't look back. Bastards meant business too!"

"I'll keep it in mind."

Ryan reined the gelding around. As he rode off he pulled the shotgun from the saddle boot and laid it across his lap. The station agent impressed him as a man who spoke between the lines and left a great deal unsaid. He decided to take the warning the way it was meant.

A short time later Ryan halted the gelding in a stand of trees. He had followed the railroad tracks two miles or so and then turned off into the woods. His approach had been unobserved, and he was now concealed by the treeline. What he saw convinced him that it was no wild-goose chase.

To his immediate front a passenger depot was situated within twenty feet of the Katy tracks. Nearby a crew of carpenters were hammering together what appeared to be a freight warehouse. The location of the buildings left no doubt that the A&P tracks would cross east to west at that point.

Far in the distance a dust cloud smudged the skyline. With the sun at his back, Ryan was able to make out the figures of men and animals. The dust cloud was raised by graders who were carving a roadbed from virgin soil. Behind them work gangs were methodically laying track on a line almost due west. Smoke from the engine of a construction train was dimly visible even farther away. The distance to the graders appeared to be something more than two miles.

The sound of voices suddenly broke the silence. Startled, Ryan peered through the woods and saw a work gang beyond the treeline. They were pulling fence posts from a wagon and planting them on a north to south line. Looking closer, he spotted another crew working east to west on a perpendicular line. By rough estimate he judged that the fence, when joined on four sides, would enclose at least a thousand acres.

The meaning of what he saw was all too clear. Within a few days, three at most, the A&P track would intersect the Katy right-of-way. The purpose of the fencing operation was clearly to establish land for a new town site. Once in place, with the track crossing on the map, the A&P's town site would totally overshadow Vinita. It was apparent that Andrew Peirce meant to steal a march on the Katy.

Yet however clear the intent, there was a riddle attached. The A&P, being owned by white men, could not organize a town site on Indian land. Only a Cherokee, exercising tribal head right, could claim such a vast homestead. So the conclusion was inescapable. A Cherokee was in league with the A&P.

Ryan thought it an ironic joke. Stevens, with great cleverness, had seduced Elias Boudinot. And now, borrowing the tactic whole, Andrew Peirce had bought himself a Cherokee. All that remained was to turn up the name of the newest Judas.

Ryan reined about and rode back through the woods.

Ryan camped late that night outside Tahlequah. After hobbling his horse, he built a small fire for warmth. His supper was cold vittles from his saddlebags and creek water. The meal finished, he crawled into his bedroll and went to sleep.

He broke camp and rode out before sunrise. He skirted Tahlequah, avoiding roads and people. His course was generally southeast, traveling cross-country through woodlands and rolling hills. He was some five miles south of the Cherokee capital by full light. He halted in a grove of trees overlooking William Ross' home.

Around ten o'clock he saw Elizabeth walk to the stables. A few minutes later she rode out on the blood-bay stallion. He marked her general direction, and then, sticking to the woods, he followed on a parallel course. His appearance bothered him, for she'd never seen him unshaven and grubby from a night on the trail. He wondered how she would react.

He intercepted her on a stretch of open ground a mile from the stables. Her hair was upswept and she wore a pale doeskin jacket over her riding habit. The sight of her quickened his pulse, and he tried to smile. She looked him over like he was a bearded highwayman, unwanted company. She held her stallion to a prancing walk.

"Morning," Ryan said. "Mind if I join you?"

She stared straight ahead. "You seem intent on ignoring my father's wishes."

"No choice. Leastways not if I want to see you."

"Then I suggest you consider my wishes in the matter." She turned her head just far enough to look at him. "I don't want to see you, John. I thought you understood."

"Oh, I hear you," Ryan said with a wry grin. "I just don't believe you."

"Well!" she sniffed. "Aren't you the vain one. I believe you overestimate yourself, Mr. Ryan."

"Suppose we save that discussion for another day. I'm not here on a personal call—it's business."

"Now you do presume! Your business affairs are the least of my interests."

"Your father wouldn't agree."

"Then speak with him."

"After last time," Ryan commented, "I doubt I'd get past the front door."

"In that case," she said haughtily, "why should I bother listening to you?"

"Because it involves your people. The Cherokees."

"How ominous. Are you trying to frighten me?"

"Maybe I am," Ryan admitted. "Unless you help me, it'll go bad for everyone."

"What do you mean, go bad?"

"A railroad war," Ryan told her. "A battle royal between Stevens and the Atlantic and Pacific—with the Cherokees caught in the middle."

She reined to a halt. The stallion acted skittish and cast Ryan's gelding an evil eye. Ryan kept his distance, waiting while she considered his statement. Finally, as though somehow resigned, she agreed to listen.

Ryan quickly explained the problem, expressing no uncertainty about the A&P's intentions.

"In a nutshell," he concluded, "Stevens won't roll over and play dead. He'll start a shooting war to stop Peirce."

"And if he did?" she asked. "It would be a white man's war. How does that involve my people?"

"Boudinot rigged a land deal with the Katy. Now some other Cherokee has sold his soul to the A&P. Town sites mean big money. So it won't stay a white man's war for long."

"All right," she conceded, "you have a point. What do you want of me?"

"A name," Ryan said. "Whoever threw in with the A&P has to be convinced he made a bad deal. I need his name."

"So you can persuade him to deal with the Katy, is that it?"

Ryan spread his hands. "Sounds better than people shooting at one another."

She seemed to look through him. At length she smiled with a touch of mockery. "Well, why not? All we're talking about is which railroad controls the town site. Isn't that so?"

When Ryan nodded, she went on. "I've heard rumors, nothing definite. Apparently there are members of the tribal council who will go to any lengths to destroy Stevens and the Katy. They've made their peace with Elias Boudinot."

"Boudinot?" Ryan repeated. "What's he got to do with it?"

"From what I hear, his allegiance no longer belongs to Stevens. He abandoned the old town site, and he's now filed claim on a new plot of land—for the A&P."

"Well, I'll be . . ." Ryan's voiced trailed off. He shook his head with amazement. "Boudinot's even trickier than I thought. He sold himself to the highest bidder."

"So it would appear," she said. "Of course, he had support this time. It seems there are other Cherokees willing to sell their birthright."

"Any names?" Ryan asked. "You said they're members of the council."

"The only name mentioned was Boudinot's. I assume the others don't want their names tarred with the same brush."

"Probably not."

Ryan paused and his expression underwent a change. His features softened under the dirt and beard, and his eyes were warmer. "Look, we've made a pretty good start today, haven't we? Don't you think we could—"

"No!" she interrupted. "You said you wanted to talk business and we have. Don't read anything personal into it."

"Who are you trying to convince—me or yourself?"

"Good-bye, John. Let's make this the last time."

She wheeled the stallion sharply about. Ryan sat there motionless as a statue and watched as she rode away. His eyes registered nothing.

CHAPTER TWENTY-TWO

───※∭Ω∭※───

Ryan stood in the dark shelterbelt of the woods. An owl hooted somewhere and farther away a dog barked. He slowly scanned the yard around Stand Watie's home. Finding nothing, his eyes moved to the front of the house. He spotted a guard on the porch.

Earlier, he'd struck out cross-country again after talking with Elizabeth. Traveling almost due south, he had sighted Webbers Falls late that afternoon. He'd skirted the village, still avoiding people and roads, wary of being seen. By sundown he had secreted himself in the woods behind Stand Watie's farmhouse.

So far as Ryan knew, Elias Boudinot was there now. Boudinot, when not off politicking in Washington, stayed with his uncle. The trick would be to get past the guard and inside without raising an alarm. Surprise was vital to what Ryan had in mind.

The moon went behind a cloud. He stepped from the trees as darkness momentarily cloaked the land. His nerves were strung wire tight and his hearing seemed painfully acute. He catfooted to the side of the porch. There he waited until the guard turned toward the opposite side of the house. Timing his move closely, he stepped onto the porch with the Colt raised. He thunked the guard over the head and caught him before he fell. A minute's work left the man bound with his own belt.

Ryan eased through the front door. He gently closed it behind him, hesitating in the darkened hallway. The layout was familiar from his previous visit, and he proceeded to the lighted parlor entrance. A quick look located Boudinot seated at a small desk, writing a letter. There was no sign of Stand Watie.

Ryan lingered a moment longer in the hall. His interrogation of Boudinot would not take long, perhaps ten minutes at the most. He felt confident that all questions would be answered to his satisfaction. Yet he wanted no surprises, and it seemed risky to begin until he knew the whereabouts of Boudinot's uncle. He also wondered about women and children in the house.

A door at the rear of the parlor opened. Stand Watie entered, wearing a floppy nightshirt out over his pants. His hair was mussed and he padded barefoot to the fireplace. He yawned, stood with his back to the flames, and idly watched his kinsman. Finally his voice intruded on the scratch of pen on paper.

"I'm going to bed."

"Good night," Boudinot said without looking up. "Sleep well."

"Don't stay up all night."

"I just want to finish this letter to Vinnie."

"Humph!" Watie snorted. "Bad enough you named a town after her. You don't have to act like a lovesick puppy."

"We've been through that before."

"Well, I still think it's damn foolishness. You've got no business chasing after a white woman!"

"Precisely the point," Boudinot remarked. "It's my business, no one else's."

"She'll never marry you. You know that, don't you?"

"Whether she does or doesn't alters nothing. She provides

an entrée into the proper Washington circles. I'm satisfied with the arrangement."

"Still say it's damn fool nonsense!"

Boudinot smiled, dipping his pen in the inkwell. He resumed writing with an amused glance at his uncle. Watie muttered something, then turned from the fireplace.

"Hold it right there."

Ryan stepped into the room. His voice was low, but the words were a whipcrack command. The pistol was extended at waist level, covering Watie. He wagged the barrel in Boudinot's direction.

"Over by your uncle."

Boudinot rose, dropping his pen. He crossed to the fireplace, halting beside Watie. His features congealed in a scowl.

"What's the meaning of this?"

Ryan ignored him, glancing at Watie. "Where are the women and children?"

"In bed," Watie said sullenly. "What happened to the man I had posted outside?"

"Nothing much. He'll wake up with a lump on his head."

Watie glowered at him a moment. Then his eyes went dark and vengeful. "You've got more trouble than you bargained for. I'll see to that personally."

Ryan smiled without warmth. "I'll remember you warned me. Tonight's not your night, though. I'm here to talk with your nephew."

"About what?" Boudinot demanded.

"The A&P," Ryan said. "I understand you've made a deal with Andrew Peirce."

"Who told you that?"

"Do you deny it?"

"No," Boudinot's voice was guarded. "It wouldn't have remained secret long anyway."

Ryan regarded him with contempt. "Stevens will be disappointed in you."

"I had no choice!" Boudinot said with a sudden glare. "My life was threatened. I had to go along."

"Way I hear it, you didn't lose anything. You've still got a town site."

"No, that's not true. I only have a share—a small share—in this one."

"Who are your partners?"

"That's none of your business."

"I just made it my business. Suppose you tell me the whole story."

"And if I refuse?"

Ryan cocked the pistol. "You know what the Cherokees call me?"

"The Indian Killer," Boudinot said weakly.

"Don't make me prove it."

Boudinot stood immobilized, as though frozen in place. Ryan looked to him like the image of death itself. He wondered if Stevens had sent the man here to kill him. A moment slipped past, then he sighed and hung his head.

"What do you want to know?"

"Who's behind it?" Ryan asked. "And don't tell me it's a bunch of council members. It has to be someone with authority."

Boudinot's eyes fell before his gaze. "It was Tappin."

"Tappin?" Ryan said, astonished. "Tappin threatened your life?"

"I swear it's true!"

"And Tappin is your partner?"

"No," Boudinot said in a shaky voice. "Several council members are involved. Tappin wanted it that way so it would appear more legitimate to the tribe. He took nothing for himself."

"Why?" Ryan pressed him. "What's he got to gain?"

"Tappin wants to destroy Stevens and the Katy. He feels the A&P is the lesser of two evils."

"What about William Ross?"

Ryan was alert to the slightest reaction. He watched the other man's eyes, looking for anything hidden or uneasy. Boudinot met his gaze steadily.

"I never met directly with Ross. But, of course, that means nothing in itself."

"Why not?"

Boudinot shrugged. "Tappin is a loyal bootlicker. He wouldn't visit the outhouse without Ross' permission."

Ryan wasn't all that sure he agreed with the assessment. Yet his purpose was to glean information, rather than start a debate. He went on to a more relevant point.

"Think back," he urged. "Did Tappin ever say Ross was involved in the A&P deal?"

"No, he never actually said it. But he certainly implied as much. Why do you ask?"

"I like to know who my enemies are."

Watie grunted aloud. "You've made one here tonight. No man forces his way into my home without paying the price."

Ryan fixed him with a harsh stare. "Do yourself a big favor. Stay out of my way."

Boudinot silenced his kinsman with a gesture. "Forget what he said, Ryan. We're in no position to be threatening people."

"Glad to forget it," Ryan said, his eyes impersonal. "Just don't get crosswise of me, or I'm liable to remember."

Boudinot and Watie looked at him without speaking. Still covering them, he backed through the entryway and into the hall. A moment later the front door closed.

Gibson Station was still going strong. Midnight had come and gone, but the street was crowded with men. Drunken laughter mixed with discordant strains of music echoed from the dives and saloons.

Ryan forded the river south of town. He bypassed the construction camp and rode directly to the livestock pens. Then, after turning the horse into an empty stall, he fetched water and an armload of hay. He thought the roan had earned his keep.

Approaching the rail yard, he noted that the lights were out in Stevens' private car. He mounted the steps and rapped on the door. Several seconds passed before a lamp was lighted. Attired in a nightshirt and dressing robe, Stevens made his way through the car. His eyes were gummy with sleep and a whiskery stubble covered his jawline. When he opened the door, he looked both irritated and surprised.

"Ryan!" he said in a phlegmy voice. "Where the devil have you been?"

"Here and there," Ryan replied. "I just now rode in."

"Why didn't you telegraph me? I wired the station agent at Vinita and he said you'd disappeared."

"Figured you'd better hear this in person."

"Hear what?" Stevens said, motioning him through the door. "Have you turned up something?"

"It's a long story."

Ryan took it step by step. He first related what he'd seen at the A&P construction site. Then he explained why he had called on Elizabeth Ross and what he'd learned. He ended with a recounting of his unannounced visit to Stand Watie's farmhouse. He stuck to the facts, voicing no conclusions.

As he talked, all the color drained from Stevens' face. The railroader seemed turned to stone, his mouth set in a grim line. At one point he bolted from his chair and began pacing the floor with jerky strides. Finally he pulled himself together and once more sat down. When he spoke, there was an undercurrent of rage in his voice.

"Goddamn Boudinot!" he said hotly. "After all I've done for him, and he stabs me in the back. The miserable bastard!"

Ryan nodded. "That pretty well pegs him."

A vein pulsed in Stevens' forehead. "You were right about him being a turncoat. He betrayed his own people easily enough—so why not me?"

"Probably easier with you than it was with the Cherokees. After all, you're a *tibo*."

"Well, as someone once said, hindsight makes the most ignorant of men wise. I won't make the same mistake twice."

"I don't follow you."

"No more side deals with Indians," Stevens declared.

"We'll finish building the railroad and get the hell out of the Nations. Whoever called these people civilized had a strange sense of humor."

"Speaking of that," Ryan added, "Major Tappin has had himself a horse laugh at our expense. One way or another, we ought to have the last laugh."

"Tell me," Stevens asked, his eyes grave. "Do you think Ross authorized the A&P deal? Or was it solely Tappin's handiwork?"

"Hard to say," Ryan remarked. "I know Ross has lost some of his influence over the tribal council. But whether Tappin would pull this on his own is another question."

"And in the end," Stevens said in a disgusted tone, "it probably doesn't matter. We've been forced into a fight with the A&P, and it's dog eat dog. We have to take countermeasures."

Ryan looked at him. "What'd you have in mind?"

"Go get Tom Scullin. Roust him out and tell him I said chop, chop! We need to hold a war council."

Ten minutes later Ryan returned with Scullin. The Irishman was half dressed and looked grumpy as a soretailed bear. But his mood underwent an abrupt turnaround when Stevens began talking. Stevens' eyes were fierce and his voice was clipped.

"Tom, I want the Irish Brigade ready to roll by dawn!"

"*Dawn?*"

"You heard me!" Stevens said. "Every man jack of them, bright-eyed and bushy-tailed."

Scullin gave him a sharp, sidelong look. "And where might we be rollin' to?"

"Vinita!" Stevens announced. "Or to be more precise, three miles north of Vinita. I intend to raid the A&P terminal."

"You *what?*"

"A guerrilla raid!" Stevens rasped. "We'll rout their work gangs! Close down their operation!"

Scullin's eyes took on a bright, madcap gleam. "You're serious, are you? You plan to hit them head-on?"

"I do indeed! I want the depot and the warehouse torn down. When you're through with that, pull up all their fence posts—"

"*All* of them?"

"—and build a bonfire to light up the Cherokee Nation. I want the bastards put on warning. We will not tolerate interference!"

Scullin turned to Ryan. "What d'you think, John? Are we within our rights?"

"It's not legal," Ryan ventured, "but possession is nine-tenths of the law. Who's to stop us?"

"Andrew Peirce," Scullin said, glancing at Stevens. "You know him yourself, Colonel. The man's a terrible dirty fighter. He'll not take it lyin' down."

"Let him come!" Stevens said vindictively. "We'll rout him *and* his railroad. No quarter asked and none given!"

"So it's war, then?"

"Yes, goddammit! How many times do I have to say it? A war to the finish!"

"Aye," Scullin said with a harsh bark of laughter. "And we'll be the ones to finish it."

The Irishman turned toward the door. He smote Ryan across the shoulder, grinning broadly. "C'mon, Johnny. We'll give 'em a shellacking they'll never forget!"

"Tom, I wouldn't miss it for all the tea in China."

Scullin roared a great belly laugh.

CHAPTER TWENTY-THREE

The operation was conducted like a military campaign. Throughout the remainder of the night, Scullin attended to logistical matters. His manner was that of a general preparing to occupy a foreign country.

Arms were the first consideration. By company edict railroad workers were not allowed to possess personal firearms. In Scullin's bunk car were several rifles and pistols, which were rotated on a nightly basis among the railway guards. Wary of starting a shooting war, he decided to keep these weapons under lock and key.

Scullin was a seasoned campaigner. He'd fought in railroad wars back East, and he knew that fists were not the weapon of choice. Men determined to inflict injury and rout their opponents selected weapons suitable to the task. Accordingly, he ordered several crates of replacement parts brought up from the warehouse. Every member of the Irish Brigade was then armed with a stout pickax handle.

Stevens appointed himself commander-in-chief. He was neither a physical man nor a warrior. To him violence was merely another business tool to be used with judicious application. His preference was to outmaneuver an opponent, wits over force. Mayhem, while not necessarily repugnant, simply wasn't his strong suit. He wisely left the fighting to Scullin and the Irish Brigade.

Scullin accepted the responsibility with a certain brutish glee. He was a blooded scrapper himself and was confident that his men would make a good showing of themselves. Any true son of Erin fancied pugilism over diplomacy, and all of Scullin's men still spoke with a brogue. He had no doubt that they would carry the day.

Ryan was appointed second-in-command. The men respected him, and they were by now fully convinced of his fighting ability. Apart from being coolheaded, he was chosen as well for his experience in outwitting wanted men. Scullin knew the battle with the A&P would be decided as much on stratagem as on brute force. He thought Ryan would advise him well.

The construction train was revamped for battle. All flat-cars and boxcars were shunted into the rail yard. What remained were the bunk cars, which would serve as troop carriers, and a well-stocked kitchen car. Stripped to essentials, the train was capable of highball speed and quick maneuver. It would carry more than two hundred men and sufficient victuals to feed them for three days. Coupled to the rear was the private car of Robert Stevens.

The Irish Brigade worked through the night. Hours were consumed in the rail yard, breaking down the train and then reforming it into a sleek war wagon. Scullin constantly exhorted the men to move things along. No one resented his badgering, for they were all caught up in the contagion of an impending fight. Like all good troop commanders, he also knew that an army travels on its stomach. An hour before dawn the men were fed a hot breakfast.

At first light the train got under way. The girls of Poon-ville turned out to cheer them on with fluttering hankies and ribald hurrahs. Pickax handles thrust overhead, the Irish Brigade responded with a bellowing roar.

* * *

Asa Johnson felt the tracks vibrate. He checked the depot clock, noting that it was a few minutes past nine. No train was scheduled through Vinita until late morning.

Walking outside, Johnson peered down the tracks. He saw the smoke, then the engine, and finally he heard the clickety-clack of steel on steel. He idly wondered why the engineer wasn't sounding the whistle, but his curiosity turned to amazement as the train pulled into the station. He saw it was an entire trainload of Micks. Scullin and his Irish buffoons.

And all of them waving ax handles!

The private car was speedily uncoupled. At Scullin's in-sistence, Stevens was to establish a command post in the de-pot. There, with access to the telegraph, he could open lines of communication with Gibson Station. Otis Gunn and his bridge builders could be rushed north if reinforcements were needed.

Stevens, looking properly military, took over Vinita sta-tion. Asa Johnson was pressed into service and ordered to clear the telegraph line southward. By half past nine, with the private car shunted onto a siding, the command post was in operation. Stevens stood on the depot platform as the train chuffed away, gathering speed. He waved even though no one waved back.

Some ten minutes later the train topped a small rise. Ahead lay the A&P depot, and nearby the freight warehouse. At the cardinal points of the compass, work crews were putting the finishing touches on a post-and-rail fence. To the east, obscured by a haze of dust, the track-laying gangs were perhaps a mile away. Not more than thirty men were still working around the depot itself.

Surprise, which was critical to Scullin's plan, appeared to be complete. Hanging from the engine cab, he scanned the depot and shot Ryan a wide grin. His primary objective was to occupy the terminal before significant resistance could be mounted. By the look of things, no one expected an aggressive move, much less an invasion from the Katy. For the moment he had superiority in numbers and a jump on the A&P's main force. He meant to press the advantage without delay.

The engineer throttled down, quickly set the brakes. Groaning and squealing, the train eased to a stop directly in front of the depot. Scullin hopped onto the platform with Ryan at his heels. Behind them the Irish Brigade poured out of the bunk cars like a horde of blue-eyed Mongols. With leaders appointed earlier and the Brigade already split into four companies, the men moved out smartly. In less than a minute, the depot and warehouse were completely surrounded.

The stationhouse door banged open. Lon Kellett, foreman of the depot operation, stalked out onto the platform. He was a tough ox of a man with scarcely any neck, his head fixed directly on his shoulders. He knew Tom Scullin on sight, though they had never before tangled. He looked decidedly unimpressed today.

"What the hell's the idea, Scullin?"

"Why, it's simple enough," Scullin said pleasantly. "You're trespassing on private property. I'll have to ask you to clear out."

"Trespassin'!" Kellett rumbled. "You've got rocks in your head. This here's A&P property!"

"No, Lon, *you're* mistaken. You've built your depot on Katy right-of-way. I want you out—now."

Kellett glared at him, baffled. "That just ain't possible! We can't be on your right-of-way!"

"You are," Scullin said with finality. "And I'll not argue the matter further. So be a good lad and vacate the premises."

"Like shit!" Kellett growled. "The graders are gonna be here after noontime. They're all set to put in the crossing."

"Not today," Scullin informed him. "Until things are put right, there'll be no crossing. Tell Mr. Peirce to stay clear of our tracks."

"Stick it up your ass! I ain't going nowhere."

"That's your last word on it?"

"Goddamn right!"

Scullin hit him. The blow caught Kellett flush between the

eyes, staggered him backward, and he dropped to one knee. Uncommonly agile for his size, Scullin shifted and took a quick step forward. He lashed out, exploding two splintering punches on the other man's jaw. Kellett went down like a wet sack of oats. He was out cold.

Grinning wickedly, Scullin dusted his hands and glanced around at Ryan. "Some men just won't listen to reason. And wouldn't you know, I gave him the straight of it. He is on our right-of-way!"

"No doubt about it," Ryan said, smiling. "You were entirely justified, Tom."

"Oh, indeed I was! Can you imagine the man's gall? Tellin' *me* to stick it! Blood of Christ!"

The A&P work crew was herded up to the depot. Three wagons were brought around, with mules already harnessed, and Lon Kellett was loaded aboard. He regained his senses just as the wagons took off across the prairie, headed toward the distant track-laying operation. Wobbling to his knees, he rose and shook his fist in the air. Scullin laughed uproariously, waving good-bye with his hat.

The Irish Brigade went to work with a cheerful vengeance. One company began dismantling the depot while another assaulted the warehouse. With wagons and teams the two remaining companies set out to destroy the fence. Ryan thought they looked like overgrown boys pulling an outlandish prank. It all seemed so good-natured and playful, some sort of jest.

Then his gaze shifted to the A&P end-of-track. He wondered how Andrew Peirce would enjoy being made the butt of the joke. He knew the answer wouldn't be long in coming.

There was now a gigantic bonfire where the station once stood. Already the wreckage of the depot and the warehouse had been consumed, reduced to ashes over the afternoon and early evening. Fence posts were being fed a wagonload at a time into the roaring blaze. Sparks showered the air and great tongues of flame leaped skyward.

Scullin and Ryan stood near the tracks. They were amused

by the men's antics, watching quietly as another load of posts fueled the fire. The beefy track-layers whooped and shouted, not unlike Indian braves engaged in a war dance. Their exuberant cries filled the still night air.

Scullin had ordered the bonfire rekindled after the men had been fed a hot supper. Several lookouts were posted atop the train and told to keep a watchful eye on the A&P camp. But Scullin's confidence seemed to ebb as the night wore on. He'd waited all afternoon for Andrew Peirce to retaliate. He had felt certain the roaring bonfire would provoke the other side. Yet now he'd begun to have his doubts.

"Hell of a note," he said gruffly, holding his pocket watch to the light. "Going on midnight and still no sign of them. Where are they?"

Ryan was silent a moment. "Maybe Peirce doesn't like the odds. It's possible he's got something else in mind."

"Such as?"

"Well, for one thing, there's the law. He might've sent to Fort Smith for a marshal."

"What would that accomplish?"

"If nothing else, it'd be a standoff. They were trespassing, but we destroyed their property. The law would order us to move out of their way—let them lay track."

"Oh, we'll not stop them from laying track. Peirce has a federal grant and nothing to be done about that."

Ryan looked at him. "Then why not pull back to Gibson Station? You've wrecked their depot and warehouse. What's left?"

"Nothing," Scullin said. "Unless Peirce still has some notion of organizing a town site. If he does, then we'll sit here till doomsday."

"How will you know whether he does or not?"

Scullin smiled. "If he wants a town site, then he knows he'll have to drive us off. It's a case of might makes right. To hell with the law!"

"What about Boudinot? From a legal standpoint, the land belongs to him and his new cronies."

"The Colonel will hold Boudinot to the original deal.

Assuming, of course, that nobody kills him in the meantime. How do you feel on that score—will they try?"

"Hard to say," Ryan allowed. "We still don't know who they are."

"You're talking about the assassins?"

Ryan nodded. "Boudinot crawled in bed with Tappin, and that might help him some. We'll just have to wait and see."

"Jesus," Scullin grunted. "It makes you wish for the good old days. Building a railroad used to be a damnsight easier."

Ryan chuckled. "Some folks call it progress, Tom."

Scullin's reply was cut short. One of the lookouts whistled and caught their attention. Standing on top of the nearest bunk car, the man rapidly motioned eastward. They crossed the tracks and halted in front of the locomotive. Their eyes were drawn to movement far out on the prairie.

Moonlight bathed the landscape in a pale glow. The distant movement slowly became distinct human forms. Looking closer, Scullin and Ryan were able to make out a large body of men. As the gap narrowed and the figures became more distinguishable, their number appeared to be something over two hundred. They were carrying pickax handles and lengths of chain and approaching at a determined stride.

Scullin laughed and spat on his hands. "Well now, it appears we've got ourselves a donnybrook!"

"In spades," Ryan added. "Where do we meet them?"

"Where else? On our own right-of-way!"

The Irish Brigade was mustered in a matter of minutes. With Scullin and Ryan in the lead, they took up position on the east side of the tracks. After the long wait, the prospect of a skulldusting contest seemed to raise the men's spirits even higher. They began shouting catcalls, slapping their pickax handles into open palms. Behind them the bonfire cast a shimmering light across the tracks.

Lon Kellett was in the vanguard of the A&P track layers. He carried a three-foot length of logging chain and his eyes glinted with cold ferocity. The men around him closed ranks. They advanced in a burly wedge, weapons gripped tightly. As they approached, the catcalls died off and the Irish

Brigade fell silent. There seemed no reason to talk, nothing left to negotiate. Whatever was to be settled would be settled by force.

Leaping out front, Kellett snarled a murderous oath and swung the logging chain overhead. Scullin went to meet him, ducking aside to let the chain whistle past. He clouted Kellett square in the knee with the pickax handle, and there was a loud crack. As Kellett screamed and toppled sideways, the A&P tracklayers surged forward. A roar went up along the tracks, and the Irish Brigade jumped into the fray. The earth seemed to quaver under the impact as the two sides collided head-on.

Ryan waded in to join Scullin at the forefront. Together, almost shoulder to shoulder, they clubbed and hammered in a blurred flurry. The men of both sides battered their way into the center of the action like ancient warriors, hurling themselves at one another with savage abandon. The struggle quickly became a contest of brute strength, a barbarous melee of ax handles and swinging chains. Over the grunts and curses came the dull whump of blows, and louder still the strangled cries of those struck down.

The battleground soon turned wet and slick with blood. The mushy thump of wood on flesh and the crunch of shattering bone beat a steady tattoo in the otherwise still night. Men fell in increasing numbers, trampled and crushed underfoot, reduced to bleating, terrified animals. Yet the struggle raged on, never slackening as the strongest ones hacked their way toward each other. Neither side wavered, and no man backed off.

The momentum of the battle slowly shifted as foot by foot the A&P tracklayers were forced to give ground. The Irish Brigade smelled victory and their ax handles flailed faster. Kellett's men broke ranks and scattered before the attack. Once the retreat began, a sense of panic swept through the A&P forces. Those in the rear quietly deserted their comrades, fleeing across the prairie. The few who still fought on were quickly hammered into the ground.

The battle ended with abrupt suddenness. Breathing hard,

Ryan stepped back from a man he'd just clubbed on the head. The special agent lurched, wobbling unsteadily, pinwheels of light flashing before his eyes. Blood oozed down over his cheekbone and an ugly cut split his lower lip. His hat was gone and one side of his jacket was ripped across the shoulder. He dimly remembered the blows, the punishment he'd absorbed. But he had lost count of the men who had fallen before his ax handle.

Ryan became slowly aware of his surroundings. He was some thirty yards beyond the railroad tracks, with no recollection of how he'd gotten there. The moonlit earth was littered with fallen men, many of them severely injured and moaning pitifully. Others lay sprawled where they'd been struck down, unconscious and bleeding, perhaps dead. Those still standing were the men of the Irish Brigade. Their breathing was ragged, frosty spurts in the chill night air, and most of them had already cast aside their ax handles. They looked curiously unlike victors.

Ryan turned, then suddenly stopped. He saw Scullin a few yards away, bent down on one knee. The Irishman was matted with blood, his scalp laid open along the hairline. He seemed dazed, blinking his eyes as he surveyed the carnage. After a moment, as though he sensed Ryan's stare, he looked around. Their eyes met, and Scullin seemed to gather himself. His mouth twitched in a game smile.

"We whipped 'em, Johnny. Whipped 'em good!"

CHAPTER TWENTY-FOUR

The light of day was sobering. All the exhilaration of the fight seemed to have evaporated overnight. There was little talk in the Katy camp, and a somber mood prevailed. No one crowed victory or slandered the vanquished.

As the sun rose higher, men paused to look at the battleground. Sometime during the night a string of torchlit wagons from the A&P camp had collected their injured. One of the bunk cars had been converted into a hospital and quickly filled with the Irish Brigade's casualties. Before the moon waned, all those struck down had been removed.

To Ryan's amazement, no one had been killed. He'd worked late into the night helping tend some of the fallen men. Broken arms and legs were the most common injury. Several men, their heads split open and their features horribly mangled, were in serious condition. None would die, but weeks, perhaps months would pass before they were once again whole. The price of victory had been extreme.

Ryan considered himself lucky. Compared to some in the Irish Brigade, he'd come through almost unscathed. Fleeting images of the night before were still with him, and he found himself in a dark, introspective mood. Violence was part and parcel of his work; over the years he'd killed more men than he cared to admit, but some aspect of last night's struggle left him reflective and vaguely troubled. While the Civil War raged, he had taken part in many of the bloodiest battles. He'd seen death in every known form, from grapeshot to entrails spilled by a cavalryman's sword. Later, as a marshal he had killed swiftly and without regret. But now, for some reason he was unable to identify, he felt demeaned by what he'd done last night. He didn't understand it, and more to the point, he didn't understand himself. He wondered if a man might somehow become tired of violence and bloodshed the way he might become surfeited with rich food. The question nagged at him and that bothered him all the more.

Stevens walked into camp late that morning. Advised of the battle's outcome, he had hiked the three miles from Vinita. His attitude was triumphant, and he lavished high praise on Scullin as well as Ryan. But then, as he marched around congratulating the Irish Brigade on their victory, a strange thing happened. The men avoided his eyes, nodding wordlessly, their manner distant. Unspoken, though felt by everyone, was the thought that Stevens, like his rival, Andrew Peirce, had sat out the fight in safety. He was therefore not one of them, and the men resented his Johnny-come-lately camaraderie. Stevens was obviously wounded by the men's coldness and withdrew in confusion and embarrassment. He looked like a general who had arrived late and missed the parade.

Around one o'clock the train departed for Gibson Station. There was a brief stop in Vinita, where Stevens' private car was hooked on to the rear. Scullin and Ryan both declined an invitation to join the railroader for the balance of the trip. Instead, they rode in the hospital car, assisting those who had volunteered to look after the injured. Scullin, whose head was wrapped in a bloody bandage, seemed particularly sensitive to the needs of the hurt men. He acted very much like someone with a guilty conscience.

Ryan became absorbed in watching Scullin. He wondered if the Irishman was having second thoughts similar to his own. The idea intrigued Ryan for Tom Scullin was no stranger to bloodshed. Nor was he known for putting the welfare of his men before the dictates of the railroad. He tended to see the world in bold black and white even more than Ryan, and the demands of the job took precedence over all else. Still, he looked troubled today and ministered to the wounded men as though he'd smote them down himself.

Some miles down the road, Ryan moved to the open door for a breath of air. He was lost in his own thoughts when he became aware that Scullin had joined him. The Irishman filled a pipe from his tobacco pouch and cupped his hands into the wind to shield a match. He puffed smoke, saying nothing, and seemed content to share the silence. After a while he gave Ryan a sidelong glance. Then he nodded back into the hospital car.

"I've been thinkin'," he said in a muted voice. "All these boys crippled and hurt—it's a hell of a price."

"During the war," Ryan remarked, "I heard it called the aftereffects of battle. Once the fighting's over, you get to wondering whether it was worth it—who really won."

"God help me," Scullin said half to himself. "Last night I did my damnedest to kill somebody. And a blessed wonder I didn't too! I had a taste for blood."

"Nothing unusual in that. It happens to lots of men in the heat of a fight."

"Do you think so, John?"

"I know it for a fact. I've seen it too many times to doubt it."

"Well, I don't mind tellin' you, it's new to me. I've busted heads, fought rough and tumble all my life. But I've never killed a man—never wanted to—till last night."

"It's the way of things," Ryan said quietly. "One day you do it and the next day you wish you hadn't. I reckon you just got lucky."

Scullin puffed thoughtfully on his pipe. He'd heard a rueful note in Ryan's voice, and he was suddenly tempted to ask a question that he had always avoided. He hesitated even now, fearful the younger man would take offense. But the compulsion to ask, regardless of the consequences, was too great. After last night he had to know.

"We've known each other how long, John? Eight months or thereabouts?"

"Close enough," Ryan said. "What makes you ask?"

"Because I'm about to trade on friendship. I want to ask you a personal question."

"Go ahead."

"Well . . ." Scullin paused, then rushed on. "So I'll quit wonderin', I'd be obliged if you'll tell me. What's it like to kill a man?"

Ryan wasn't offended. Had it been anyone else, he would have responded curtly. But he'd shared a bunk car and a great many confidences with Tom Scullin. And he'd never forgotten the Irishman's genuine concern following the courtroom shootout. He decided to answer the question.

"The first time," he said evenly, "you get a little queasy at your stomach. It's like you've suddenly learned what death means—it's not pretty."

"And the next time?" Scullin asked softly.

"Unless you're a mad-dog killer, it never gets easier. You're able to do it without a whole lot of thought while it's happening. But afterward you always wish there'd been another way."

Scullin searched his eyes. "And the man you've killed, what do you feel for him?"

"Anger," Ryan said simply. "You wonder why the damn fool forced your hand. You want to jerk him up and box his ears good for making you do it."

"Are you bothered by it later?"

"Your conscience isn't bothered. You're sorry and you wish it'd turned out different. But what you think about mostly is whether you did it quickly and cleanly. Your biggest regret is if you didn't and he suffered."

"So it's not all that cold-blooded, is it?"

"No," Ryan told him. "It's damn personal. Just as personal as you'll ever get with another man."

Scullin considered a moment. "When it's happenin', are

you ever afraid, Johnny? Do you think about the other man killin' you?"

Ryan nodded, as though it was a question he'd already asked himself. "You don't think about anything. You trust your instincts and you get the job done the best way possible. When you start thinking, you're almost certain to get yourself killed."

Scullin realized his pipe had gone cold. He stared out the door, watching the countryside rush past. He thought he had never heard anything sadder than what he'd just been told. And he was sorrier for John Ryan than any man he'd ever known. After a time, he looked around.

"Thank you, John," he said genuinely. "You've done me a service. I'll go out of my way to avoid that first time."

"You could do worse, Tom. A hell of a lot worse."

Neither of them spoke again. They stood there, warmed by the sun, while the train rattled southward. An hour or so later they crossed into the Creek Nation.

Gibson Station celebrated their return. Stevens magnanimously gave the men of the Irish Brigade a bonus and awarded them two days off. Those of them who were able to walk beat a path first to the saloons and then to Poonville. The girls welcomed them like a conquering army.

Early the next morning Ryan rode out of camp. After a restless night, he'd decided to resolve the mystery of Elias Boudinot. There were unanswered questions in his mind, and he knew he'd heard only one side of the story. He told no one where he was going, for he considered it a personal matter. Outside town he turned his horse northeast, toward Tahlequah.

Autumn was slowly settling over the land. Frosty nights and cool days were gradually chilling the wooded terrain. Trees already gave promise of leaves turned umber and gold and fiery red. Yet Ryan saw nothing of the burgeoning splendor, for his mind was preoccupied with other matters. As he rode he tried to organize his thoughts, phrase the questions that needed to be asked. He decided on the direct approach, rather than cat and mouse. He'd had his fill of diplomacy.

An hour before noontime he sighted William Ross' home. When he stepped out of the saddle, the stable boy took his horse with a great show of reluctance. At the door one of the house servants admitted him as though he was unwelcome. Some twenty minutes passed while he cooled his heels in the vestibule. At last, without apology, he was shown into the study. By then Ryan himself was not inclined to be tactful.

Ross received him with austere civility. He looked openly displeased. There was no offer of a chair, even though the older man was seated behind his desk. Nor was there any pretense of welcome, or a handshake.

"I can only assume," he said formally, "that you've chosen to ignore my wishes. I thought I made myself clear the last time you were here."

Ryan halted in front of the desk, hat in hand. "You did, but there's no way around it. I need a question answered, and you're the man to ask."

"Indeed?" Ross replied. "Why should I answer anything put to me by Colonel Stevens' emissary?"

"I'm not here for Stevens or the railroad. I'm here to satisfy myself about something."

"And what might that be?"

"Elias Boudinot."

Ryan let the name drop, then waited. There was no flicker of reaction on Ross' features. He merely sat there unsmiling, returning Ryan's stare. At length he made a noncommittal gesture.

"Very well—ask your question."

"I braced Boudinot," Ryan said. "According to him, Tappin rigged the A&P land deal. The new town site was a put-up job, start to finish."

"Go on," Ross said faintly.

"Tappin threatened Boudinot to make him cooperate. Scared him so bad that he agreed to betray Stevens and throw in with the A&P."

"You still haven't asked a question."

"Tappin's your man." Ryan paused, looking him straight in the eye. "I want to know if he was following your orders."

"Is that what Boudinot told you?"

"Yeah, more or less. He said Tappin doesn't hop unless you say 'frog.'"

Ross appeared bitterly amused. "Whether I gave the order or not seems somewhat academic. What does it matter to you?"

"Let's just say it matters. Are you going to answer me or not?"

Ross grew silent, staring at a shaft of sunlight filtering through the window. His expression was abstracted, a long pause of inner deliberation. Finally he glanced up, motioned to Ryan.

"Please sit down, John."

Ryan took a chair. He was keenly aware of the abrupt change in Ross' manner. The tension between them seemed to melt away.

"When I was younger," Ross said in an avuncular voice, "I thought a strong leader could impose his will on an entire people. In time I learned that it's sometimes necessary to turn a blind eye and exercise pragmatism."

"So you knew," Ryan ventured, "but you didn't actually issue the order. You just let Tappin go ahead with it."

Ross inclined his head. "I had little choice in the matter. Had I attempted to stop him, I would have been accused of taking sides with Stevens. Any hint of that would destroy my influence with the tribal council."

"Weren't you worried about what Stevens would do? You must've known he wouldn't let the A&P get away with it."

"I'm not responsible for what Stevens does or doesn't do."

"Yeah, but you're responsible for what Tappin does."

"In a sense, I condoned it with my silence. So, yes, you're right."

"And that got a lot of good men hurt the other night. Some of them could've been killed."

Ross looked at him squarely. "A number of my people *have been* killed."

"There's a difference," Ryan said with studied calm. "They went looking for a fight and found it. You forced Stevens' hand—and got a bunch of men crippled—by doing nothing. You could've pulled in the reins on Tappin."

"I regret very much that those men were injured. But why should I create dissension within the council merely to stop Tappin? After all, any squabble between Stevens and the A&P can only benefit my people."

"Like it or not," Ryan pointed out, "the railroad's here to stay. All you've done is make yourself—and the Cherokees— some more enemies in Washington. You ought to start mending your fences instead."

Ross raised a questioning eyebrow. "Why are you so concerned with the Cherokees' welfare?"

Ryan didn't answer the question directly. "Stevens won't quit till he whips the A&P. He aims to make the Katy the dominant line in the Nations, and he will. You'd better learn to live with it."

"Would you suggest I run up the white flag today or wait awhile?"

"What I'd suggest," Ryan urged, "is that you face the facts, accept reality. Otherwise you'll just make it tougher on your people."

Ross regarded him thoughtfully for a moment, then shook his head. "You still haven't explained your sudden concern for the Cherokees."

"Nothing sudden about it. I'm just tired of killing people, that's all. I want it to stop."

Ryan stood, ending the conversation. When he walked from the room, Ross looked rather confounded. He thought the younger man's outburst was highly revealing. It seemed to him on the order of a confession or a plea for absolution. Or perhaps both.

The realization triggered something deeper and more personal. He sensed he'd misjudged John Ryan.

* * *

Elizabeth was waiting in the hallway. After being informed of Ryan's arrival, she had hurried downstairs. The door to the study was ajar, and while she hadn't meant to eavesdrop, she couldn't help herself. Some quick-felt hope had compelled her to listen.

Her sudden appearance startled Ryan. He seemed embarrassed, uncertain as to how much she'd overheard. Falling in beside him, she quickly dispelled any doubt. She smiled as they walked toward the vestibule.

"I heard everything," she said happily. "And I don't apologize for eavesdropping. I'm so very proud of you, John."

"For what?"

"For your . . ." She hesitated, choosing her words. "For your change of heart. You'll never regret breaking with the railroad."

"Hold on!" Ryan said, halting in midstride. "You jumped to the wrong conclusion. I'm still on the Katy payroll."

"But I thought—"

"All I said was, I'm tired of the killing. I want it stopped, but quitting my job wouldn't accomplish anything. I can do more to end it by staying right where I am."

"Can you?" Her voice dropped. "Or will it just go on until someone kills you?"

Ryan looked down, studied the floor. "What do you want of me, Elizabeth?"

"Too much, it seems," she said coolly. "So I'll just repay you for the advice you gave Father."

"You don't have to repay anything."

She smiled wanly. "Perhaps it will help end the killing. In any case, you should beware of David Tappin. He doesn't like talk of compromise."

"I knew that a long time ago."

"And he will never accept reality—or the railroad."

"If you're trying to tell me he's vindictive, I already got the message. He showed that with the A&P."

"There's more," she went on quickly. "I believe he's trying

to force my father's resignation. He has visions of himself as chief of the Cherokee Nation."

Ryan looked surprised. "How does your father feel about that?"

"He thinks I'm foolish," she admitted. "He won't listen or discuss it."

"Well, if it means anything, I believe you. Tappin strikes me as being too shifty for his own good."

"John"—she touched his arm—"won't you reconsider . . . about the railroad?"

"Sorry, but I'm no quitter. I couldn't walk away when the fight's half done."

They parted on that note. When he went through the door, her breath caught in her throat. She folded her arms around her waist, clasping herself as if she were cold. There was a look of anguish in her eyes.

She felt a strange sense of loss.

CHAPTER TWENTY-FIVE

The Verdigris River bridge once more took shape. Working marathon hours, Otis Gunn and his men swarmed over the demolished two-hundred-foot span. The resurrected structure was a visible testament to their efforts.

Support timbers were in place and work had begun on the superstructure as early as mid-October. Gunn estimated the center span could be opened to traffic toward the end of the month. Four miles south of Gibson Station, work was progressing as well on the Arkansas River bridge. The projected completion date was early December.

Robert Stevens fretted at the delays. Always the visionary, his mind leaped ahead of ongoing construction. He pored over maps of the Choctaw and Chickasaw Nations, planning depot stops and rail yards, estimating freight traffic. Yet, however preoccupied, his eyes would involuntarily skip down the map to the Red River. And Texas.

Negotiations were under way for the first terminus in the Lone Star State. Stevens had written off the Colbert's Ferry idea, principally because it would involve the Chickasaw Nation in his affairs. After his problems with the Cherokees, he was no longer fascinated with the notion of a town site in

Indian Territory. Instead, his attention had turned downriver to the Texas shoreline. He focused on the town of Sherman.

An existing community, it offered certain advantages. Foremost was the possibility of a bond issue, which represented payment by the town for the privilege of being selected a railroad terminus. But the town fathers of Sherman, who impressed Stevens as a bunch of skinflints, were resisting the proposal. While they wanted the railroad, they felt a bond issue was a legalized form of extortion. Their obduracy led him to yet another idea.

Stevens conceived a grand vision. A few miles north of Sherman was a stretch of prairie occupied by small ranchers and hardscrabble farmers. The land was literally dirt cheap and could be purchased secretly through land agents. All of which raised the possibility of an enormous financial coup. It was within his grasp to *create* an entire town.

Unknown to anyone at Gibson Station, Stevens had sent a confidential emissary to Texas. Henry Denison was a trusted aide, charged with overseeing the Katy's interests in Kansas. His mission in Texas was to contract for the purchase of several hundred acres north of Sherman. One section that immediately bordered the Red River was particularly suitable. The terrain was relatively flat and adequately watered, perfect for a town site.

Everything depended now on Henry Denison's progress. If he was able to put together a block of land, the surveyors would be sent south to plan a town site. As an added inducement, Stevens had promised him that the new town would be named Denison. Once the contracts were signed, a land company would be organized to sell town lots. The arrival of the railroad would instantly transform raw farmland into a veritable pot of gold.

Stevens was absorbed by the idea. While the project was a year away from completion, he already imagined it as a full-blown reality. Part of the lure was the fortune he himself would pocket through the land company. But the greater enticement was to put his mark on the map, create a town from whole cloth. There was the added attraction of watching the

Sherman skinflints go apoplectic over having lost the railroad. He thought of it as icing on the cake.

Still, for all his stargazing, Stevens was in a wretched mood. The present was depressingly bleak, however bright the future looked. Completion of the Arkansas River bridge was six weeks away, and track laying through the Creek Nation was stalled until the broad stream could be spanned. To compound the delay, twenty-three men from the Irish Brigade were still confined to the hospital car. Some of them would be hobbling on crutches for months to come and drawing full pay the entire time.

The drain on the Katy treasury was enormous and maddening. But expenses weren't restricted to the track-laying operation being bogged down or to so many of the Irish Brigade on the invalid list. Within the last two weeks independent freighters hauling up the Texas Road had begun avoiding Gibson Station. The long cavalcades of wagons were swinging north upon reaching the Fort Gibson cutoff and trailing on to Vinita. There the goods were shipped eastward on the A&P line.

The sheer audacity of this situation left Stevens in a fierce rage. Andrew Peirce, only four days after the moonlit battle, had reoccupied the original site. He correctly reasoned that the Katy, with so many injured men, would shy away from another confrontation. On the strength of his deal with Boudinot, he'd also obtained a federal court injunction barring the Katy from further interference. In short order, a track crossing was put through and the depot, as well as the warehouse, was rebuilt. To rub salt in the wound, the new station was named Vinita.

Stevens' hands were tied. He had staked everything on a show of force by routing the A&P construction crew, and he'd lost. All the planning, the savage battle and the injured men, not to mention the cost of the operation, had come to nothing. He'd been betrayed by Boudinot and undermined still again by the Cherokees. But the deeper humiliation had little to do with the Indians' treachery or the fact that a battle had been fought to no advantage. What stung him most was that he'd been outmaneuvered by his rival, Andrew Peirce.

There was a practical aspect to be considered apart from injured pride. Several freighters had been questioned as to their reason for bypassing Gibson Station. Their response was chilling in its implications. Agents for the A&P were offering large rebates to anyone who would take their wagons all the way to Vinita from northern Texas. The A&P made it profitable for teamsters to haul the longer distance. Fully nine out of ten wagons coming up the Texas Road were now shipping with the A&P.

Andrew Peirce's intent was patently obvious. He meant nothing less than the financial ruin of Stevens and the Katy line. Whether it was revenge or merely underhanded business practice, the blow was timed perfectly. With the onset of winter and the trailing season at an end, revenue from the Texas cattle trade had fallen off sharply. Army contracts, however profitable, would never generate sufficient income to keep the Katy solvent. The loss of business from independent freighters represented a critical blow.

Problems seemed to beget problems. Over the past week guerrilla warfare had broken out along the Katy line. Sections of track were ripped from the roadbed at isolated spots throughout the Cherokee Nation. The ties were then piled into mounds and set afire. Rail traffic out of Gibson Station ground to a halt until work gangs could repair the damage. While the Cherokees were the logical suspects, no one had yet been caught in the act. There was no way to patrol a hundred miles of track, and the saboteurs had struck only at night. Putting a halt to the raids seemed almost impossible at this point.

Stevens' dour mood was understandable. Loss of sleep left him cranky and irritable, and the prospect of financial ruin put a steely edge on his anger. The morning's news from north Texas, relayed by letter from Henry Denison, was the proverbial last straw. He sent for John Ryan.

Stevens wasted no time on preliminaries. He went straight to the point, his voice hot with rage. "I've just had word that

Peirce has upped the stakes. As of today, it's a cutthroat game!"

"What's he done now?"

"The dirty bastard!" Stevens ranted. "His agents in Texas are offering an even trickier deal. Anyone who ships freight with us from Gibson Station and transfers to the A&P at Vinita will get a fatter rebate than before!"

"It's clever," Ryan acknowledged. "We make chickenfeed running back and forth between Vinita, and he winds up with the business."

"Precisely!" Stevens said acidly. "In effect, he's turned Vinita into a strangler's knot. We're cut off from routing through traffic to St. Louis."

"What's the difference? Unless we put a stop to the sabotage, we're snookered anyway. We'll never get a train out of the Cherokee Nation."

"That's another thing!" Stevens bridled. "I'm told that the A&P agents in Texas have been doing a bit of bragging. They said Peirce is working hand in glove with some unnamed Cherokee to stir up the tribe. Would you care to guess who the Cherokee is?"

"Probably Boudinot," Ryan said. "And he's likely operating under Tappin's protection. That would account for why we haven't caught anybody. Who's going to spill the beans on another Cherokee?"

Stevens grimaced. "We're talking about conspiracy! A criminal act of the worse sort, and I want it stopped."

"You can't send *me* back to Tahlequah. I've just about played out my string with Ross."

A wintry smile lighted Stevens' eyes. "Forget Ross and Boudinot and everyone else. I want you to pay a call on Andrew Peirce."

Ryan stared at him. "You're not talking about any rough stuff, are you?"

"On the contrary," Stevens reassured him. "I merely want you to deliver a message."

"What sort of message?"

"Tell him two can play the same game. I demand—

demand!—that he cease all of his underhanded schemes. Otherwise it's tit for tat from now on."

"You're saying you would sabotage his tracks, maybe blow his bridges—is that it?"

"Exactly!"

Ryan studied him a moment, finally nodded. "I'll deliver your message. But don't count on me if push comes to shove. I'm not a hit-and-run night rider—not for you or anyone else."

"Don't worry," Stevens said, smiling. "I can always import outside help. All I want from you is one thing—make a believer out of Peirce."

"I'll do my damnedest, Colonel."

Later, reflecting on it, Stevens decided he'd taken the right step. Andrew Peirce was a buccaneer and a scoundrel, the type of man who responded only to force. So it was fitting, Stevens told himself, to send a man who was something of a natural force.

He thought Ryan's "damnedest" would do very nicely.

The sky was like dull granite. Heavy clouds rolled in from the north and a sharp wind rattled branches on the trees. A flock of crows took wing from the woods, cawing raucously as they wheeled away.

Ryan scanned the overcast sky. It was too early for snow, and he'd forgotten to bring along a rain slicker. Later yesterday, after talking with Stevens, he had saddled the roan and ridden out of Gibson Station. The night had been spent on the trail, and now, in the early afternoon, he was within a few miles of the A&P camp. He followed the tracks northward, holding the roan to a walk.

Earlier when he'd passed a section of rebuilt track, it occurred to him that he wasn't surprised by the sabotage. For several months now, he'd been expecting some form of reprisal from the Cherokees. Nor was he surprised that Elias Boudinot had been made the straw man, the apparent leader of the night riders. The true leaders of a conspiracy were seldom willing to reveal themselves publicly. Major David Tappin was no exception; he would, at all costs, try to avoid the limelight of a conspiracy. Tribal politics dictated that he at least appear above reproach.

There was, as well, the matter of William Ross. While Ryan doubted that Ross was directly involved in the conspiracy, he recalled Elizabeth's concern for her father. Her comment about Tappin and his ambition to take over as tribal chief seemed all the more relevant. The sabotage, though directed at the Katy, might easily have a hidden purpose. Open rebellion by the Cherokees could be turned inward, brought to the floor of the tribal council and used as a means of forcing Ross to resign his office. And thereby open the door for David Tappin.

The prospect troubled Ryan. He admired Ross, believed him to be an honorable man. So it was in the interest of everyone involved to expose the conspiracy. Yet curiously enough, he felt no great urge to catch the night riders. They were merely dupes, sacrificial pawns in a larger game, even less important than Boudinot. There was, moreover, a personal reason for not attempting to trap them. To avoid capture, they would almost certainly fight. And he simply didn't want to kill any more Cherokees. Or anyone else, for that matter. White or red, he was weary of killing men.

The thought gave Ryan a moment of sardonic reflection. In the Cherokee Nation, he was already something of a legend. They called him the Indian Killer, and spoke it with the harsh inflection of a curse. The burden of the name weighed heavily on him as he rode into the A & P camp. He reminded himself that he was there to deliver a message and nothing more. He wouldn't be goaded into a fight or another killing.

The area around the depot was crawling with men. To Ryan's great relief, none of them seemed to recognize him. He was nonetheless on edge, for these were the very men who had taken part in the midnight battle. West of the new track crossing, he saw a construction train, and farther away, the track-laying gangs. He spotted a private railway car shunted on to a siding. Ryan noted wryly that Peirce's private car was almost identical to Stevens'. He reined his horse toward the siding.

On the rear platform of the car, he knocked loudly. A voice ordered him to enter and he stepped through the door. The interior layout was more businesslike than Stevens' car. A section had been partitioned off and furnished as an office. Seated at a wide mahogany desk was a man who appeared to be in his early fifties. He was heavily built, with a sweeping mustache and a square, thick-jowled face. Behind wire-rimmed spectacles his eyes were gray and chill, stern as a church deacon's. He motioned Ryan forward.

"What is it?"

"Are you Andrew Peirce?"

"I am," Peirce said impatiently.

"I've got a message for you, Mr. Peirce—from Robert Stevens."

Peirce looked surprised, then suddenly irritated. "Who the hell are you?"

"The name's Ryan." Halting at the desk, Ryan held his gaze. "I work for the Colonel."

"John Ryan?" Peirce asked. "Stevens' hired gun?"

"I'm not here to swap insults, Mr. Peirce. Let's just stick to business."

"Well, Ryan, you have some nerve coming here. Every man in this camp would give his eyeteeth for a crack at you."

A smile appeared at the corner of Ryan's mouth. "I reckon they've already had that and more. I don't especially care for a rematch."

"No doubt," Peirce said with a short, emphatic nod. "Although my boys tell me you and Tom Scullin gave a good account of yourselves."

"We got about as much as we gave."

Peirce took off his glasses, wiped them with a handkerchief. "So Bob Stevens sent you with a message? Knowing him, I'd wager it's some half-assed threat."

"No, sir," Ryan said evenly. "It's more on the order of a declaration of war."

"What's that?" Peirce looked as though his ears were plugged. "What did you say?"

"I'll give it to you in Stevens' own words. He said two can

play at the same game. If you don't back off, he plans to let you have tit for tat."

"What does that mean exactly?"

"Word's out," Ryan said, "that you've riled up the Cherokees. Our tracks are being torn up faster than we can rebuild them. The Colonel wants you to have a talk with Boudinot—or Tappin—and put a stop to it."

Peirce shook his head in mock wonder. "Are you accusing me of sabotaging the Katy?"

Ryan ignored the question. "There's more," he said. "Stevens wants you to lift the freight rebates, starting today. If you don't, then the fat's in the fire."

"Tell him to go straight to hell! I'll run my business any way I see fit."

"Sorry to hear you say that, Mr. Peirce. Whatever else he is, the Colonel's a man of his word. He'll make you pay a dear price."

"Will he?" Peirce demanded. "And what form would this tit for tat take?"

"Hit and run," Ryan answered in a low voice. "Your tracks would be torn up and burned. Your bridges would be blown and your rolling stock derailed. Stevens would go whole hog and then some."

Peirce's eyes were angry, commanding. "If he wants war, then by God he can have it! I'll destroy him, run him out of the Nations!"

Ryan regarded him with great calmness. "Yeah, you could do that. But while you were about it, he'd take you down with him. When the dust settled, you'd both be out of business."

Peirce sat quietly for a moment with his eyes narrowed thoughtfully. After a moment he looked around. "How would you like a job, Mr. Ryan?"

"Thanks all the same," Ryan said. "I've got a job."

"A pity," Peirce observed. "I could use a man with quick wits. I'd be willing to double your salary."

"No sale, Mr. Peirce. What should I tell the Colonel?"

Peirce glowered back at him with an owlish frown. "Tell your boss he's the sorriest excuse for a railroader that I've ever met. And then tell him"—he paused, waved his hand disdainfully—"he's got himself a deal."

Ryan nodded, moving to the door without another word. Outside the car he went down the steps and walked directly to his horse. After climbing into the saddle, he turned the roan away from Vinita. As he rode off, he wondered what sort of reception Peirce would get in Tahlequah.

Major David Tappin had his own ax to grind. And in some ways it had nothing to do with the railroad.

CHAPTER TWENTY-SIX

On November 7 the Verdigris River bridge was once more opened to traffic. The first construction train, loaded with bridge timbers, crossed the river late that morning. Crowded onto one of the flatcars were Scullin and a contingent of the Irish Brigade.

Stevens observed the operation from a window inside his private car. The weather was dismal, with low-hanging clouds and whirling snow flurries. While the interior of the car was toasty warm, it did nothing to improve his mood. He munched an unlit cigar, watching the train disappear across the bridge. The sight gave him only fleeting comfort.

For every problem resolved there seemed to be a dozen more awaiting his attention. With the bridge open and four miles of track completed to the Arkansas River, it was now possible to move vast amounts of supplies forward. He'd considered doing just that and then ferrying the materials to the south shore of the Arkansas. It would have required a herculean effort by the Irish Brigade, loading and offloading every shipment at least four times. But the alternative was to wait another month while the Arkansas River bridge was being completed.

Frustrated by delay, Stevens had ordered the plan implemented. Scullin could once again start laying track, and thirty days gained would put end-of-track deep in the Creek Nation. Yet, as though fated, the plan began to unravel. A week of cold, drizzling rain turned the canebrakes south of the Arkansas into a waterlogged swamp. On the heels of the rain, there was freezing sleet and then several days of intermittent snowfall. The plan was scotched, awaiting a hard freeze to make the canebrakes passable. Scullin and the Irish Brigade were assigned instead to resume work with the bridge builders.

So far as Stevens could see there was only one bright spot in the whole affair. Ryan's talk with Andrew Peirce had produced immediate and highly profitable results. All freight rebates were rescinded, thereby removing any incentive to ship with the A&P through Vinita. Wagon trains from northern Texas again began arriving at Gibson Station, their freight consigned for shipment with the Katy. The sudden jump in revenue averted what might have been a financial debacle. The railway line was restored to solvency just in the nick of time.

Of no less consequence was the abrupt disappearance of the night riders. The message delivered by Ryan apparently had a profound effect. While the details were unknown, it could be surmised that Peirce had in some way blackmailed Major David Tappin. Sabotage of the Katy tracks had ceased virtually overnight, and there had been no further encounters with the Cherokees. What that portended for the future was a matter of conjecture. But for the moment the Katy was enjoying a time of peace and prosperity.

Stevens took mordant satisfaction in the victory. He reveled in the fact that he'd had the last laugh on Andrew Peirce. Though he hadn't destroyed the A&P, he had upset Peirce's time schedule beyond repair. The Katy would be the first to cross the Red River and roll onward into the Southwest. For that, Stevens owed a large vote of thanks to John Ryan. Few men could have brought Peirce to see the light so quickly and with such clarity. The outcome spoke reams about Ryan's persuasive talents.

What form that persuasion had taken was still something

of a mystery. To Stevens' questions, Ryan had replied in only the vaguest terms. Thereafter, Stevens became increasingly concerned, for he noticed an unaccountable change in Ryan's attitude. A quiet man by nature, Ryan had now become withdrawn and almost taciturn. He spoke only when he was spoken to, and even with Scullin, who was his closest friend, he seemed strangely distant. His manner was somehow neutral, as though he'd lost interest in what went on around him.

Stevens lit his cigar and stared out the window. His reverie was suddenly broken as he saw Ryan emerge from the bunk car. Wearing a woolly mackinaw, Ryan walked off toward the stock pens, carrying his shotgun. Stevens watched until the solitary figure disappeared into the snow flurries. He knew Ryan would saddle the roan gelding and ride off on a morning scout of the bridge site. What he didn't know was why Ryan had withdrawn into a shell.

Not knowing troubled him. He valued Ryan, and while they'd had their differences, they had always managed to work together. He puffed on his cigar, vaguely uneasy.

Ryan propped his shotgun against a fence post. The gelding trotted over, whinnying in recognition, and stood waiting. One of the mules in the next pen over brayed and that set off a chorus from the other mules. With track laying at a halt, none of them had been out of their pens in almost two months.

Ryan started toward the harness shed to collect his saddle. He suddenly stopped, watching as a number of horsemen materialized like ghostly apparitions out of the snow flurries. A cold sense of foreboding swept over him as he recognized the lead rider, Major David Tappin. Behind, ranked two by two, rode six Light Horse Police. He moved swiftly to the fence and picked up his shotgun. Hefting it, he hooked a thumb over the near-side hammer.

Tappin reined to a halt. He sat there a moment, the Light Horse drawn up behind him, their mounts snorting frosty puffs of air. His expression was one of veiled mockery, amused contempt. At length he lifted his chin, indicating the shotgun.

"Are you expecting trouble, Mr. Ryan?"

"Never know," Ryan said woodenly. "There's lots of it around these days."

"Oh?" Tappin replied. "I understood your problems were all solved."

Ryan looked him directly in the eye. "Things have been pretty quiet the last couple of weeks. You and Peirce must've had a heart-to-heart talk."

Tappin studied him with a kind of clinical detachment. "I assume you're referring to Andrew Peirce, president of the A&P. To the best of my knowledge, we've never met."

"How about that!" Ryan said with a touch of disbelief. "And here I thought you two were bosom buddies."

"I repeat"—Tappin paused to underscore the words—"we've never met."

"I suppose a go-between works just as well. Course, Boudinot must get tired of hotfootin' it back and forth between Vinita and Tahlequah. Or do you meet him out on a dark road somewhere?"

"Who I meet, and where, are none of your concern, Mr. Ryan."

"Another time maybe," Ryan said, letting it drop. "What brings you to Gibson Station, Major?"

"Brad Collins."

"What about him?"

"I believe you have a payroll shipment coming through tomorrow afternoon. I understand it's usually aboard the express car, locked in a strongbox—and all cash."

Ryan frowned. "How'd you know that?"

"I hear things," Tappin answered genially. "Collins got drunk and bragged to the wrong people. He and his gang plan to rob the payroll train."

"That a fact?" Ryan said without expression. "Why would you ride all the way down here to save the Katy's payroll?"

"Just following orders," Tappin said with an odd smile. "When I informed Chief Ross, he asked me to alert you personally. He feels that the Cherokee Nation cannot condone robbery—even by a half-breed outcast."

Ryan considered a moment. "Any idea where the holdup might take place?"

"Pryor's Creek," Tappin said. "Collins intends to block the bridge."

"And you figured I might want to prepare a reception for him?"

"No," Tappin said firmly. "Your payroll means nothing to me one way or the other. I'm here at Chief Ross' request."

"You'll be sure to thank him for me, won't you?"

Tappin ignored the wry tone. "As a gesture of good faith, he's also offering assistance. I was ordered to bring along a squad of Light Horse and place them at your command."

Ryan hesitated, doubly vigilant now. "Why would the Light Horse serve under me? I killed a couple of their friends at the courthouse."

"These men," Tappin said, gesturing to the stolid-faced horsemen, "will obey without question. Their orders are to place themselves at your disposal."

"I have my own guards."

"Hardly enough," Tappin noted. "Collins has that many or more in his gang. Besides, if you refuse, it will be a direct affront to Chief Ross. As I said, these men represent a token of his good faith."

"Tell you what; I'll leave it up to Colonel Stevens. You and your men just wait here."

Ryan moved around the riders, eyeing them as he went past. The Light Horse sat like bronzed statues, staring straight ahead. He walked toward the rail yard.

"I don't like it!" Stevens grunted, shaking his head. "Why should Ross want to save our bacon?"

Ryan stood with the shotgun in the crook of his arm. His mackinaw was wet with melting snow and a puddle had formed around his boots. He nodded imperceptibly, his mouth set in a narrow line.

"It's Tappin I'm worried about. I don't trust him as far as I could spit."

"Do you believe Ross actually sent him here?"

"Yeah," Ryan said slowly. "Tappin wouldn't have come otherwise. His story's too easy to check out."

Stevens' eyes squinted in concentration. "So that brings us back to Ross. What's he after?"

"Maybe it's on the up-and-up. I'd like to think Ross would side with us over Collins."

"You'd like to," Stevens asked, "but the question is, do you?"

Ryan rubbed his jaw, considering. "I've always figured Ross for an honorable man. So I'd have to say he's given us the straight goods."

"Then we've no choice, do we? We either accept his help or risk offending him. And who knows where that would lead?"

"All right," Ryan said. "I'll tell Tappin we're agreeable."

"Just make damn sure you take our men along! We can't trust that payroll to a bunch of redskins."

"Don't worry, Colonel. It's as good as done."

Outside, the wind had dropped off and heavy snowflakes were falling in a thick, white curtain. Ryan began formulating a plan as he walked back to the stock pens.

A freight train pulled out of Gibson Station early next morning. Aboard the caboose were Ryan and five railway guards, as well as the squad of Light Horse. Tappin had returned to Tahlequah the previous afternoon.

Shortly before noon the northbound freight stopped at Boudinot's original town site. Asa Johnson, the station master, exhibited only mild curiosity as Ryan and his peculiar alliance trooped into the depot. For the next two hours, with hardly a word spoken, they warmed themselves around a pot-bellied stove. Johnson played the attentive host and kept the coffeepot perking.

The southbound train arrived only a few minutes behind schedule. Coupled to the rear of the engine and tender were the express car and two passenger coaches. Earlier, from Gibson Station, Ryan had wired ahead to Kansas, ordering that no passengers be allowed to board the train. He now split his force of eleven men into separate teams. The railway guards were placed inside the first passenger coach, and the Light Horse were seated in the rear coach to be less visible. His position was with the regular express messenger, locked in the express car.

Ryan's orders to the men were precise and clear. All of them understood that there was to be no gunplay unless the outlaws opened fire first. Even then, any of the robbers who could be captured rather than killed were to be taken prisoner. He particularly wanted Brad Collins taken alive, and he'd repeatedly stressed that point. Only in the last extreme was the gang leader to be fired on. His purpose, which he kept to himself, had to do with the Verdigris River bridge and other acts of sabotage. He wanted the opportunity to question Collins.

Pryor's Creek was roughly twenty miles south of the depot. An hour or so later, as the train rounded a slight bend, the engineer suddenly throttled down and set the brake. While it had stopped snowing, the roadbed and the surrounding countryside were blanketed with white. A short distance downtrack the bridge had been sealed off with a barricade of fallen trees. The engine lost speed rapidly and jarred the men in the cars behind. Only a few yards short of the bridge, the train rolled to a halt.

On the east side of the tracks, several men emerged on foot from a thick stand of woods. They were spaced far apart, their guns drawn, and appeared to be well organized. One man hopped onto the steps of the engine, covering the engineer and the fireman. Another hurried toward the end of the train, blocking any exit from the last passenger coach. Still another halted at the steps between the passenger coaches, and a fourth took a similar position between the lead coach and the express car. Brad Collins and the sixth gang member walked directly to the express car, stopping in front of the door. Collins hammered on it with the butt of his pistol.

"Open up in there! If you don't, we're gonna start killin' your friends. The engineer goes first!"

The door slammed open. Ryan stood to one side, the shotgun pointed downward, both hammers cocked. The express messenger was opposite him, also partially concealed, his pistol extended through the open door. Collins and his partner appeared stunned, frozen in a moment of indecision. Ryan wagged the muzzle of his shotgun.

"Drop your guns or you're dead."

Collins obeyed, his eyes glued to the scattergun. The other man hastily followed suit, tossing his revolver into the snow. Without being told, they both raised their hands overhead. Ryan motioned them back a step, then took a quick peek out the door. He saw the remaining gang members moving cautiously toward the express car, their guns leveled. He looked back at Collins.

"Tell your boys to call it quits. I've got men back—"

At the rear of the train, the Light Horse Police poured out of the last passenger coach. As though on command, they shouldered their carbines and delivered a withering volley into the robbers. The four gang members at the rear were cut down from behind, shot in the back. Collins and the man at his side were knocked sprawling under the impact of the heavy slugs. They went down, arms and legs flailing, flattened alongside the snowy roadbed. The only robber to escape was the man on the steps of the locomotive. A bullet whizzed past his head, and he leaped, rolling down the embankment. He darted into the woods before the Light Horse could unleash another volley.

Ryan jumped through the open door. He landed on his feet and turned, planting himself solidly. Facing the rear of the train, he shouldered the shotgun and took dead aim at the Light Horse. Bunched together, they hesitated uncertainly and slowly lowered their carbines. At that instant the railway guards tumbled from the lead coach, looking from Ryan to the Light Horse. Ryan rapped out a command.

"Disarm the bastards! Keep 'em covered!"

Whirling around, Ryan hurried down the embankment. Collins lay on his side, the snow underneath him stained a bright cherry red. When Ryan knelt down, rolling him over, the outlaw appeared dead. His eyes were closed and the upper part of his coat was matted with blood. Then he wheezed, coughing raggedly, and his eyes fluttered open. A trickle of blood leaked out of his mouth as he focused on Ryan.

"Funny, ain't it?" he said shallowly. "Shot down by the goddamn Light Horse."

"Tough luck, Collins," Ryan said, bending closer. "I told them not to fire unless you started it."

"How'd they get here?"

"Major Tappin sent them along. He warned me about the holdup."

"Warned you!" Collins feebly grabbed the front of his mackinaw. "Tappin told you I was gonna rob the train?"

Ryan nodded, watching him closely. "How else would I have found out?"

Collins gasped, fighting for breath. "Son of a bitch double-crossed me . . . murdered me. . . ."

"Why would he do that, Collins?"

"I dunno," Collins whispered, barely audible. "I wouldn't never have talked. Not about the bridge or tearin' up tracks or nothin' . . . he wanted . . . done. . . ."

A reddish froth bubbled over his lips and his voice trailed off. His mouth opened in a low death rattle, then he trembled and lay still. His eyes rolled back in his head.

Ryan stared down at the outlaw a moment. As if a veil had been lifted, everything was suddenly clear. Only one man could link Tappin to the bridge collapse and the track sabotage. But to put the Light Horse on Collins' trail or kill him outright would have been too obvious. The better plan was to arrange a bogus loan of the Light Horse, with orders to shoot on sight. And credit the railroad with Brad Collins' death!

Hefting the shotgun, Ryan climbed to his feet. He considered questioning the Light Horse, then discarded the idea. Threats wouldn't work and no amount of interrogation would make them betray Tappin. With a sense of resignation, he ordered the railway guards to turn them loose. It was a thirty-mile walk to Tahlequah, and snow all the way. The thought gave him some satisfaction, but it ended nothing. Ryan made himself a solemn promise.

David Tappin would be brought to accounting—for murder.

CHAPTER TWENTY-SEVEN

The train pulled into Gibson Station late that afternoon. Ryan hopped off the rear passenger coach as the engineer decreased speed in the rail car. He walked toward Stevens' private car.

All the way from Pryor's Creek, he had maintained a thoughtful silence. The railway guards who had loaded the outlaws' bodies onto the express car were equally pensive. Seated by himself, he'd stared out the window, considering his next move. The decision he had finally made seemed the only one possible under the circumstances. He felt comfortable with himself for the first time in a long while.

Stevens' manservant answered his knock. Inside the car Ryan found Stevens and Sally Palmer seated in lounge chairs. The girl, who was sipping a rye and water, looked at him inquisitively. Her expression was neutral, as though his safe return prompted only mild curiosity. Stevens bounded out of his chair with a laugh, hurrying forward. His eyes were ablaze with excitement.

"I knew it!" he said, grinning. "You pulled it off, didn't you?"

"The payroll's safe," Ryan informed him. "And there are six dead men in the express car. One of them is Brad Collins."

"What'd I tell you?" Stevens whooped, glancing back at the girl. "Didn't I tell you Ryan wouldn't let me down?"

"That's what you told me," she said indifferently.

"Only one trouble," Ryan interjected. "It was the Light Horse that got him, not me."

"What?" Stevens said, looking baffled. "The Light Horse got Collins?"

Ryan quickly recounted the day's events. He ended with the gang leader's dying words about Tappin's involvement in the conspiracy. When he finished, there was a moment of stunned silence.

"I'll be damned," Stevens finally muttered. "It was an execution! Tappin rigged the whole thing just to get Collins!"

Ryan nodded. "Collins was the only witness against him. Nobody else could tie him to the bridge collapse."

"And the murder of six of our men—six *white* men!"

"Not much doubt about it. He couldn't risk a federal murder warrant or a trial in Fort Smith. He knew he'd wind up getting hung."

"So he suckered us into helping him! A payroll robbery makes Collins' death look legitimate."

"Except for one thing," Ryan noted. "He never figured on Collins living long enough to talk."

"Wait a minute," Stevens said anxiously. "Will that hold up in court?"

"It should," Ryan allowed. "I think it'd be treated the same as a deathbed confession. Especially where it concerns murder."

"Then we've got him! And don't forget, it's premeditated murder. He *ordered* the trestles on that bridge to be cut through."

"We don't have him until we get him to Fort Smith. But I'll see to that myself, first thing tomorrow."

"Why not send for federal marshals?"

"It's personal." Ryan's voice was hard and determined. "I aim to settle Tappin's account myself."

Stevens agreed. "I understand completely. You handle it however you see fit."

"One other thing."

"Yes?"

"As of today, I'm off the payroll. I quit."

"You . . ." Stevens faltered, gave him a dumbfounded stare. "You're resigning?"

"That's about the size of it."

"But you can't! We're only halfway through the Nations. I still need your help!"

"Not anymore," Ryan said. "Tappin was behind all your trouble, start to finish. I'll tend to him tomorrow."

"Even so, you're leaving me in the lurch. Why not delay awhile and think it over?"

"Nothing to think over. Besides, you'll replace me easy enough. You pay too good for the job to go begging."

Stevens fixed him with a skeptical look. "There's more to it, isn't there? You're just using Tappin as an excuse."

"Why push it any farther? I've already quit."

"No!" Stevens said sharply. "I want to hear your reason. I insist on it!"

"All right," Ryan said without expression. "I don't like you and I don't much care for the way you do business. Guess I finally got a bellyful."

Stevens waved his hand as though dusting away the insult. "Why do we have to like each other? What's that got to do with your job?"

Ryan's mouth lifted in a tight grin. "You're one of a kind, Colonel. It's been an education knowing you."

"Now, hold on!" Stevens said as he turned away. "At least give me a chance—"

Ryan went through the door without looking back. As he started down the steps, Sally Palmer rushed out onto the rear platform. Her china-blue eyes were dancing, and her face was wreathed in a big smile. She stuck out her hand.

"Before you go, I just wanted to shake your hand."

"Yeah?" Ryan said, taking her hand. "Why's that?"

"You told him off good, and he was overdue. I suppose it makes up a little for the way you've treated me."

"Nothing personal," Ryan assured her. "Another time, another place, we might've got together."

"I tend to doubt it. But I'll make believe you're telling me the truth."

"Look, if things are so bad, why not pack a bag? I'll see to it you get on the next train out."

She laughed, shook her head. "I'd just end up in another parlor house. And believe it or not, Stevens beats that!"

"Maybe so." Ryan smiled. "Take care of yourself, Sally."

A short while later Ryan found Tom Scullin. The big Irishman was overseeing loading of a train for the Arkansas River bridge site. He whooped when he saw Ryan.

"By the Jesus! You're back and all in one piece!"

"Just passing through, Tom."

"Passin' through?" Scullin repeated. "You talk like a man on his way to somewheres."

"I guess I am, at that. I just quit the railroad."

"You *what*?"

Ryan explained the reasons behind his decision. He went on to elaborate regarding sabotage of the Verdigris River bridge and David Tappin's involvement. Cursing savagely, Scullin's features mottled with rage. The murdered men were members of the Irish Brigade, and he swore revenge. Ryan firmly declined his offer of assistance.

"Leave it to me, Tom. It's a job for one man, and it's the kind of work I know best. I'll see to it that Tappin gets his neck stretched."

"God's blood!" Scullin said, frowning. "How do you hope to pull it off by yourself?"

"I don't," Ryan said calmly. "William Ross will deliver him into my hands."

"You're mad!"

Scullin's arguments were wasted. He saw that Ryan simply would not be dissuaded. He wished the younger man Godspeed and good hunting. They shook hands with the warmth of two strong men who had shared a dangerous time and emerged friends.

An hour later Ryan rode out of town on the roan gelding. His direction was northeast.

The sky was dark as indigo. Ryan tied his horse behind the stables and paused only long enough to loosen the cinch. Then, skirting the corral, he walked toward the house.

A chill wind knifed out of the northwest. The snow had crusted over and his footsteps sounded crunchy as he circled the house. On the front driveway he spotted a shaft of light from a side room. Cautiously, he made his way to the tall windows outside the study. He saw Ross seated at the desk, bathed in the glow of lamplight.

The Cherokee leader was alone, hunched over a sheaf of papers. Visibly startled, he jumped when Ryan rapped on the window. Then, peering closer, he rose and moved across the room. His features were set in a scowl as he raised the window and stepped aside. Ryan boosted himself over the sill and onto the floor.

"Your gall amazes me," Ross said, closing the window. "Unannounced and uninvited, in the dead of night."

"Sorry about the hour," Ryan replied. "But it won't wait till morning. I have to talk to you now."

"About what?"

"David Tappin."

Once more Ryan recounted the details of the aborted train robbery. He stressed Brad Collins' last words, which implicated Tappin in the murder of six railroad workers. Then, after mentioning that he'd quit the Katy, he went to the reason for his late night visit.

"I intend to arrest Tappin," he said in a low voice. "I'll need your help to do it without bloodshed."

Ross appeared at a loss for words. He walked to his desk and stood there a moment. Then without turning he finally spoke.

"I have a confession to make," he said. "I suspected that

Tappin was behind the assassination attempts and all the rest. But there was no proof and I chose to take the easy way out. It seemed politically expedient."

"What's past is past," Ryan said quietly. "All I'm interested in now is getting Tappin to Fort Smith. He's got a date with the hangman."

Ross turned from the desk. He studied Ryan with a thoughtful frown. "You're no longer a marshal," he said. "In fact, you're no longer a special agent for the railroad. You have no authority to make an arrest."

Ryan's eyes narrowed. "What's your point?"

"You could never arrest Tappin without a fight. In the end you would have to kill him."

"Are you saying you won't help?"

"No," Ross said crisply. "I'm offering you an alternative."

"Such as?"

"Bring Tappin to trial for murder in a Cherokee court."

"I don't follow you."

"Brad Collins," Ross said in a musing tone, "was both an outlaw and an outcast. But he and his gang were nonetheless members of the Cherokee tribe. And Tappin ordered them shot down in cold blood."

Ryan regarded him with an odd, steadfast look. "You're joking! Charge Tappin with Collins' murder? It'll never stick."

"On the contrary," Ross assured him earnestly. "I have the authority to make it stick. I'll see him tried, convicted, and executed."

"Without witnesses?"

"We have your testimony as to Collins' dying words. That establishes a motive."

"It's not enough for conviction."

Ross pursed his lips, nodded solemnly. "Could you identify the Light Horse who shot Collins and the other gang members?"

"What if I could?" Ryan persisted. "They're not about to testify that they acted on Tappin's orders."

"Oh, I think they will. In exchange for immunity, they'll

gladly betray Tappin. In fact, I can guarantee you their testimony."

"Maybe so," Ryan said with no inward conviction. "But you can't guarantee that a Cherokee jury will deliver a verdict of guilty. Not against the head of the Light Horse Police for killing outlaws."

"Then you've lost nothing," Ross countered. "You can always prosecute Tappin on the federal charge. Or kill him yourself."

There was a long moment of deliberation. Then, finally, Ryan conceded the point. "All right, we'll try it your way."

"Good," Ross said equably. "Now while I attend to things here, I suggest you return to Fort Smith. Otherwise Tappin will most certainly make an attempt on your life."

"How soon can you bring him to trial?"

Ross smiled. "Far sooner than in a white man's court. Don't worry, I'll send for you in plenty of time."

"Well . . ." Ryan hesitated, staring at the older man. "Before I leave, I'd like to see Elizabeth. Any objection?"

"None whatever. I'll wake her and ask her to come down. Just wait here."

Ross walked from the room. Ryan took off his hat and mackinaw and slumped into one of the armchairs. He suddenly felt worn out.

Elizabeth joined him several minutes later. Her hair was pinned atop her head and she wore a cambric housecoat over her nightgown. There was an awkward moment before they got themselves seated opposite one another. Then Ryan began talking.

Her father had briefly explained the situation. She was dismayed, though hardly shocked, by the charge lodged against Tappin. Her reaction to Ryan's break with the railroad was a mix of hope and appreciation. But now, attentive to his every word, she listened without comment or interruption. She let him talk himself out.

"So that's it," he said at length. "I've quit the railroad for good."

"I know it wasn't easy, John. I'm proud of you and very happy. Happier than you could ever imagine."

"Then maybe you'll understand what I've been leading up to. I want you to come with me."

Surprise washed over her face. "Come with you?"

"I know it's a little sudden. We've never exactly talked about it, but I . . ." He paused, groping for words. "Well, I just figured you felt the same way."

Her voice was hushed. "Are you talking about marriage?"

Ryan nodded soberly. "We could find a preacher in Fort Smith."

"I couldn't," she murmured. "I'll never fit into the white world. Even if they accepted me, I could never accept them."

Ryan slowly shook his head. "Doesn't that make you as prejudiced as them?"

"Yes," she said softly. "What they've done to our people— what they are still doing—breeds prejudice. I'm ashamed of it and wish it were different, but it's not."

"So what's the answer?"

She looked at him and tried to smile. "You could stay here."

"Never work," Ryan said darkly. "I've killed too many Cherokees. Their kin would be honor bound to come after me."

"And there would be more killing."

"Neither one of us wants that—do we?"

"No," she whispered, desperation in her voice.

Ryan took a deep breath and let it out heavily. "How about farther west? Maybe somewhere in California or Oregon. It's a long ways from the Nations."

"I . . ." Her eyes were shining moistly. "Will you give me some time? Let me think about it . . . please?"

"I reckon I owe you that."

"Thank you, John."

"Maybe . . ." Ryan began, then stopped with a sudden grin. "Well, maybe you could give me an answer when I come back for Tappin's trial. Think so?"

"I'll try."

Ryan stood, extending his hands, and took a step forward. Her mouth quivered and she fought to control the tears. She rose from her chair and rushed into his arms. He embraced her and she buried her face against his chest, holding him with fierce possession. Her voice was husky, almost inaudible.

"Don't say anything. Just hold me."

CHAPTER TWENTY-EIGHT

Justice in the Cherokee Nation moved swiftly. Major David Tappin was arrested and brought to trial within a week. He pleaded not guilty to five counts of murder.

There were grave repercussions throughout the Cherokee Nation. Supporters of David Tappin, including several influential members of the Union Party, were enraged. The murder charges were labeled a plot of the railroad and Robert Stevens, designed to neutralize the Katy's most resolute opponent. A movement arose to bring the matter to the floor of the tribal council. Some men spoke of armed rebellion.

The Southern Party wisely made no attempt to capitalize on the situation. Shunned because of their alignment with the railroad, the party leaders cautioned their followers to take a nonpartisan stance. Elias Boudinot, fearing new reprisals, went on a long trip to Washington and points east. Stand Watie surrounded himself with loyal guards, and seldom went outside after dark. No one sympathized publicly with the railroad.

Robert Stevens took equally prudent measures. He hired a former Texas Ranger as the Katy's new special agent. Additional railway guards were also hired. Every train crossing the Cherokee Nation bristled with armed men. Work on the Arkansas River bridge went forward without incident with completion set for early December. No great resistance was expected from either the Choctaws or the Chickasaws. Stevens' target date for crossing the Red River was revised to late 1872.

William Ross moved decisively to quell his opposition. His first step was to appoint a Union Party loyalist as head of the Light Horse Police. Assured that order would be maintained, he then called all his political markers with members of the tribal council. Pressure was applied on the followers of David Tappin, and any thought of a fight on the council floor quickly went by the boards. Those who had spoken of armed rebellion retreated to a position of tactful silence. A sense of calm and political coexistence once more settled over the Cherokee Nation.

On November 16 David Tappin was brought to trial. A jury was impaneled by late morning and the prosecution began its case after the noon recess. One by one the six Light Horse Police who had taken part in the aborted train holdup were called to the stand. They testified that Tappin had ordered them to kill Brad Collins and his gang. Further, Tappin had instructed them that no prisoners were to be taken, even though some might attempt to surrender. Collins and his men, as ordered, had been shot down while their hands were in the air.

The prosecutor was granted wide latitude by the judge. Over defense objections, he was allowed to pose questions not directly related to the case. The six Light Horse were asked whether they believed William Ross had any foreknowledge of Tappin's orders. To a man, they related how Tappin had insinuated that Chief Ross had been gulled into authorizing the mission. They further testified that Tappin had spoken openly about his plan to hoodwink the railroad. The onus for the killings was to be laid at the doorstep of John Ryan and the Katy.

Spectators and jurors alike were aware that politics had entered the courtroom. The central issue was to establish the guilt or innocence of David Tappin, but a secondary purpose of the testimony was to remove any stigma from William Ross. The principal chief of the Cherokee Nation was shown to be a victim of his misguided trust. It was Major Tappin, deceiving both his tribal superior and the railroad, who had orchestrated the murder of Brad Collins. The responsibility, and the blame, stopped there.

John Ryan took the witness stand last. He'd ridden into town that morning after being summoned by messenger from Fort Smith. A squad of Light Horse, sworn to protect him with their lives, surrounded him the moment he'd dismounted in front of the courthouse. His testimony represented the pivotal point of the prosecution's case. Under oath, he recounted the attempted holdup, the killings, and Brad Collins' dying words. Tappin's motive, which was to silence Collins about the Verdigris River bridge, was established beyond doubt. The prosecutor allowed Ryan to put on record that six railway workers had died in the bridge collapse.

Counsel for the defense unleashed a vitriolic personal attack on Ryan on cross-examination. He secured an admission that Ryan and Major Tappin were bitter enemies. He next established that Ryan had killed no less than nine Cherokees while employed by the railroad. He tried to create the illusion that Ryan and his railway guards had killed the Collins gang. His contention was that the railroad sought to throw the blame on Tappin and thereby rid itself of the Katy's most outspoken opponent in the Cherokee Nation. The jurors looked unpersuaded by the argument.

The prosecution rested its case shortly before three o'clock. After a brief recess, defense counsel called Major David Tappin to the stand. In his own defense Tappin rebutted the testimony of the six Light Horse, as well as that of John Ryan. He termed the trial a travesty, the work of perjuring tribesmen and *tibo* railroaders. He swore his innocence, depicting himself as a Cherokee patriot and a man of honor. The prosecutor on cross-examination was unable to rattle Tappin. Looking composed and confident, the defendant parried every question with sardonic brilliance.

After closing arguments, the judge instructed the jury. By Cherokee law, he told them, the defendant was required to prove nothing. The burden of proof fell on the prosecution, and even the slightest doubt was sufficient to forestall conviction. When the jurors withdrew for deliberations, an uneasy tension settled over the courtroom. Some of the spectators stepped out for a smoke, only to be called back inside before ten minutes had elapsed. The jury filed back into the box with an air of grave solemnity. Their verdict, read aloud by the foreman, was unanimous: guilty on all counts.

The judge pronounced sentence immediately. Ordered to rise, Tappin was informed that Cherokee law exacted the death penalty for a capital crime. The date of execution was set for November 18, at the hour of dawn. The judge hammered his gavel and adjourned the proceedings. It was 4:32 on the courtroom clock.

The appellate process in the Cherokee Nation was no less efficient. Early the following morning, the Supreme Court heard an eloquent appeal, delivered by David Tappin's lawyer. Pleading insufficient proof as well as mitigating circumstances, defense counsel requested that the sentence be reversed. The court promptly upheld the conviction and declined to stay the execution. The appellate hearing took only slightly more than an hour.

Dawn tore a gray line across the horizon on the morning of November 18. It was bitter cold, with a metallic sky and gusty winds. Light flurries carpeted the ground with a fresh layer of snow.

The wagons halted in a wooded clearing outside Tahlequah. David Tappin rode in the lead wagon, his hands manacled and shackles locked around his ankles. Escorting him were four grim-faced Light Horse armed with Spencer carbines. In the second wagon, similarly armed, was a squad of six Light Horse. Their new commander, Joseph Starr, rode beside the wagon, mounted on a dun gelding.

A short distance to the rear was the carriage of William Ross. Acting as outriders, a squad of Light Horse rode with their carbines laid across the saddle. The carriage drew to a stop behind the wagons and the mounted Light Horse fanned out along the road. The carriage door opened and William Ross, wearing a somber greatcoat, stepped down. Ryan followed directly behind, bundled in the woolly mackinaw. The two men waited at the edge of the clearing.

Tappin was assisted from the lead wagon by his escort. The leg shackles were taken off and he was marched to the far end of the clearing. The treeline formed an irregular oval, with densely wooded terrain on three sides. One of the Light Horse removed Tappin's hat and his outer coat, which had been draped over his shoulders. Underneath he wore a dark suit, with a matching vest and a four-in-hand tie. He looked, as always, impeccably groomed.

Execution in the Cherokee Nation was performed by firing squad. With Tappin in place, the six Light Horse in the second wagon moved forward. They were accompanied by Joseph Starr, who formed them in line some twenty paces from the condemned man. Starr then walked purposefully to Tappin, who studiously ignored him. From his pocket Starr took out a piece of white cloth cut in the shape of a circle and exactly three inches in diameter. He pinned the white circle onto Tappin's suit jacket, directly over the heart.

No one had spoken a word during the preparations, but now, taking a step backward, Starr pulled a sheet of paper from his pocket. He unfolded it and began to read the death warrant in a loud, clear voice. The crisp air punctuated every word with a puff of frost. Tappin betrayed no emotion as he heard himself sentenced to execution. He stood there, seemingly impervious to the cold, his manacled hands drawn tightly together. He appeared vaguely bored by the proceedings.

Starr finished reading and returned the paper to his pocket. He looked at Tappin. "Do you wish to say anything?"

"Yes," Tappin answered in a resolute voice. "I am a *Tsalagi* and I will die well. Let no one say otherwise when I am dead."

"Anything else?"

Tappin seemed to consider a moment. Then, as though it

wasn't worth the effort, he shook his head. Starr pulled a large black kerchief from his coat pocket. He started forward.

"No blindfold," Tappin said flatly. "I prefer to see the men who kill me."

Starr nodded, replacing the kerchief in his pocket. He turned and walked away, followed by Tappin's four-man escort. Upon reaching the firing squad, he halted and took a position off to one side. The escort continued on to the edge of the clearing.

David Tappin stood alone. His features were immobile under the dappled light of oncoming dawn. Squaring his shoulders, he stared past the firing squad. His gaze settled on William Ross, and an ashen smile touched the corner of his mouth. After a moment his eyes shifted almost involuntarily to Ryan. His expression altered into a cold look of hate.

"Ready!"

At Starr's command the firing squad shouldered their carbines. Tappin's eyes snapped around as though compelled to watch. He stared straight into the muzzles.

"Aim!"

The firing squad seemed frozen in place, staring impassively across their sights. Everyone but the condemned man held his breath.

"Fire!"

All six carbines cracked in unison. The white cloth circle imploded, vanishing in a ragged starburst of blood. Tappin wilted under the impact of the slugs, literally blown off his feet. He hit the ground on his back and one leg jerked in an afterspasm of death. His eyes were open and stared at nothing.

A powdery silt of snow, shaken off the trees by the muzzle blast, dusted the clearing. The firing squad slowly lowered their rifles and there was a long moment of silence. Finally, as the others watched quietly, Joseph Starr walked to the fallen man. He went down on one knee, inspecting the body closely. Satisfied, he climbed to his feet and turned, nodding to William Ross. His voice was firm and clear.

"Sentence has been carried out according to warrant. David Tappin is dead."

Ross gave no sign of acknowledgment. He wheeled sharply about and walked to the carriage. Ryan was only a pace behind, following him through the door. The driver lightly popped the reins and the matched set of grays took off down the road. The mounted Light Horse, formed in a column of twos, brought up the rear.

Some while passed before Ross seemed to recover himself. When he spoke, his tone was curiously muted. "A nasty business and well finished. At least he died with dignity."

Ryan nodded. "Tappin was never short on grit."

"Indeed he wasn't." Ross hesitated, then turned to Ryan. "Tell me, what are your plans now?"

"I reckon that depends on Elizabeth."

For appearance's sake, Ryan had spent the last two nights with Dr. Frank Porter. It seemed the wiser choice, since he was a witness in the case and Ross was technically an officer of the state. His plan was to call on Elizabeth sometime later in the day.

"May I speak frankly?" Ross asked.

"Don't see why not."

"Elizabeth and I discussed your idea about moving West."

Ryan waited, his expression stoic.

"Her place is here," Ross went on. "As she told you, she could never be happy in the white world. But more importantly, she could never be happy away from her people. Before anything else, she is a Cherokee."

"Yeah, I know," Ryan said, looking down at his hands. "I guess I was just kidding myself."

Ross studied him intently for a moment. "Do you think the Cherokees can win the fight to retain independence?"

"No," Ryan said without hesitation.

"Why not?"

"Because you're up against the United States government. Add that to crooked politicians and men like Stevens and it's a lost cause. You'll win a few battles, but you won't win the war."

"How long do you think we could stave them off?"

"All depends," Ryan said. "You could take a lesson from

Boudinot, though. Whatever battles you win will be won in Washington—not here in the Territory."

"Fork-tongued diplomacy," Ross said with a smile. "Is that the idea?"

"Sometimes you've got no choice but to play by the other fellow's rules."

"Suppose it would postpone the inevitable for another twenty years, perhaps a generation. Would you say the end justifies the means?"

"If I were you," Ryan said honestly, "I'd go at it no holds barred. The longer the fight lasts, the longer you keep your independence."

"I couldn't agree more. In fact, after our experience with the railroad, I've decided to revise our tactics completely. Washington will soon be overrun with red delegations."

Ryan laughed out loud. "That ought to be a sight to see."

"Would you care to join me in the fight?"

"Join you!" Ryan said, visibly startled.

Ross gave him a wise look. "You've had experience with bureaucrats and crooked politicians and men like Robert Stevens. I also have faith in your sympathy with the Cherokee cause. I'd say you're well qualified for the job."

"Wouldn't work," Ryan observed. "Too many Cherokees want a piece of my hide. It'd just start another round of killing."

"I think not," Ross said confidently. "You'll recall that I have a certain influence within the Cherokee Nation. No one would seriously consider antagonizing my son-in-law."

Ryan stared at him. With an easy laugh, Ross patted his arm. "Put your worries aside, John. Once you've joined us, the past will soon be forgotten. Cherokees love no man quite so much as the one who rallies to their cause."

"Level with me," Ryan said pointedly. "Elizabeth put you up to this, didn't she?"

"Well, after all, John, she is her father's daughter."

William Ross chuckled with robust good humor. His words were all the affirmation Ryan needed. Father and daughter had extended the greatest gift of all. It was what he himself wanted most—a new life and a fresh start. A chance to dwell among the Cherokees.

A short while later the carriage rolled to a stop before the house. As Ryan stepped out of the coach, the front door opened. Elizabeth hurried across the veranda, then halted at the top of the steps. Her eyes went past him and something unspoken passed between father and daughter. Her face suddenly radiated joy and she rushed to meet Ryan. Her voice was warm and inviting.

"Welcome home, John."

Ryan gathered her into his arms. Some smoldering instinct told him that he was where he belonged, where he would stay. The killing, all his days of wandering were in the past.

His death work was done.